THE WINTER OF THE LIONS

Jan Costin Wagner was born in 1972 in Langen, Hesse near Frankfurt. After studying German language, literature and history at Frankfurt University, he went on to work as a journalist and freelance writer. He divides his time between Germany and Finland (the home country of his wife). His previous crime novels featuring Detective Kimmo Joentaa are *Ice Moon* (2006) and *Silence* (2010). *Silence* won the 2008 German Crime Prize.

ALSO BY JAN COSTIN WAGNER

Ice Moon
Silence

JAN COSTIN WAGNER

The Winter of
the Lions

TRANSLATED FROM THE GERMAN BY
Anthea Bell

VINTAGE BOOKS
London

Published by Vintage 2012

2 4 6 8 10 9 7 5 3 1

First published with the title *Im Winter der Löwen* in 2009 by
Eichborn Verlag, Frankfurt am Main

First published in Great Britain in 2011 by
Harvill Secker

Vintage
Random House, 20 Vauxhall Bridge Road,
London SW1V 2SA

www.vintage-books.co.uk

Addresses for companies within The Random House Group Limited
can be found at: www.randomhouse.co.uk/offices.htm

The Random House Group Limited Reg. No. 954009

A CIP catalogue record for this book
is available from the British Library

ISBN 9780099546436

The translation of this work was supported by a grant from the
Goethe-Institut that is funded by the Ministry of Foreign Affairs

The Random House Group Limited supports The Forest
Stewardship Council (FSC®), the leading international forest
certification organisation. Our books carrying the FSC label are
printed on FSC® certified paper. FSC is the only forest certification
scheme endorsed by the leading environmental organisations,
including Greenpeace. Our paper procurement policy can be found
at www.randomhouse.co.uk/environment

Printed in Great Britain by Clays Ltd, St Ives plc

24–26 December

I

Kimmo Joentaa had been planning to spend the last hours of Christmas Eve on his own, but it didn't turn out like that.

He had applied early to be on duty on 24 December, as in previous years, and he spent the day in the quiet police building, which might have been deserted.

Sundström was on a skiing holiday, Grönholm was in the Caribbean – a long-cherished dream – and Tuomas Heinonen went home early in the afternoon to decorate the Christmas tree and put on a Santa Claus costume for his family. He could be reached there if anything suddenly came up, but nothing did.

Joentaa dealt with some paperwork that could have waited. The radio was playing Christmas music: violin, piano and the high, clear voices of a children's choir. After that a philosopher who was also a theologian explained that Jesus Christ had in fact been born in summer. Joentaa stopped work for a moment and tried to concentrate on the voice on the radio, but the programme had already gone back to music, some kind of Christmas rap. He frowned and turned back to the sheet of paper in front of him.

Early in the evening he strolled through the large hall to the cafeteria, which was in darkness. The only light came from the Christmas tree decorated in red and gold standing next to the drinks machine.

It was snowing outside the window. Joentaa sat down at one of the tables. There was a plate of biscuits on it.

Star-shaped biscuits. Joentaa took one, tasted maple syrup on his tongue, breathed in the aroma of pine needles, and saw a woman standing in the entrance area near the reception desk. He thought there was something odd about her. She stood there motionless. Joentaa waited for a while, but the woman didn't move, and did not seem to be surprised to find no one at reception. None of the uniformed police officers who hurried past now and then thought of asking what she wanted, but that didn't appear to bother her either.

The woman was watching the snow falling on the other side of the glass. She was small and slim – in her mid-twenties, he thought. Her hair was long and blonde, and she was chewing gum. She remained as motionless as ever when Joentaa went towards her, even when he was right in front of her and trying to meet her eyes.

'Excuse me?' he said.

The young woman turned away from the windows. Her cheeks were flushed and swollen.

'Can I . . . are you all right?' asked Joentaa.

'Rape,' said the woman.

'You mean . . .'

'I've been raped. I want to report it to the police, you idiot.'

'Sorry. Can I . . . let's go to my office for a start.'

'Ari Pekka Sorajärvi,' said the woman

'Let's . . .'

'That's the name of the man I want to report.'

'Come along,' said Joentaa, trying to lead the way, but the woman did not move.

Her voice was soft as she said, 'I'd like to go home soon. Can't you take it all down here?'

'Sorry, no. Some colleagues of mine ought really to be doing this anyway. I could take your statement and then pass it on, but I have to get it on the computer in any case.'

She seemed to hesitate briefly, then followed him over to the lift.

Dim neon lighting illuminated the third floor. A bleat of laughter came from one of the offices.

'It's creepy up here,' she said.

'Some of the neon tubes have gone. It's usually brighter,' said Joentaa.

'I see,' said the woman, and seemed to smile, although Joentaa wasn't sure.

'Have you been to the hospital?' he asked.

'The hospital?'

'Yes,' said Joentaa.

'It's not that bad,' she said.

'I . . . I could drive you there later,' said Joentaa. 'It's possible . . . well, traces might still be found, and they could be important if the case comes to trial.'

'Just type this shit into the computer and then I'm going home.'

'Sorry.'

'You don't have to keep saying sorry for anything and everything.'

Joentaa nodded, and led her into his office. The computer monitor was flickering. The screen saver showed the red church at Lenganiemi. Sanna was buried in the graveyard behind it.

The world outside the windows was dark and white. The woman looked at him expectantly.

'Sorry. Do sit down,' said Joentaa.

'Could you *please* stop saying sorry for everything?'

Joentaa tried to concentrate on the screen and the keyboard. He searched about for a while and finally found the program with the requisite form. Name, address, date of birth.

'What's your name?' he began.

'What?'

'Your name. I need it for the . . .'

'What does my name matter? I've been raped by Ari Pekka Sorajärvi and I want to report it.'

'But . . .'

The woman uttered a long, high-pitched scream. Joentaa looked at her. She sat there apparently motionless and relaxed, and apart from her slightly opened mouth there was nothing to suggest that she was the person emitting this scream. A shrill, numb kind of scream.

The scream went on and on, and a colleague hurried into the room. 'Everything all right here?' he asked.

'Yes, no problem,' said Kimmo Joentaa.

'Okay,' said his colleague. He hesitated for a moment, then wished Joentaa good luck and closed the door.

Joentaa looked at the woman sitting opposite him and smiling. He could still hear her scream ringing in his ears.

'Henrikinkatu 28,' said the woman in a matter-of-fact voice.

'That's . . .'

'That's Ari Pekka Sorajärvi's address.'

'Is he . . .'

'Ari Pekka Sorajärvi.'

'Yes, is he or was he your boyfriend?'

'My what?'

'Are you . . . er, living with or married to Ari Pekka Sorajärvi?'

The woman stared at him. 'No, I'm not,' she said at last.

'Then how . . .'

'Ari Pekka Sorajärvi is a client,' she said.

Joentaa did not reply.

'A punter. Sex for money. Ever heard of it?'

'So he is . . .'

'My best client, if you really want to know. Always wanting a bit more than the others, but he paid a proper price for it.'

'I understand,' said Joentaa.

'Well, that's nice,' she said.

'But . . . how do you know his name? Isn't it usual for people to stay anonymous in, well . . . in such circles . . .'

The woman laughed. Laughed at him. Laughed so loud that his worried colleague would be back in the doorway again any moment now.

'You're so inhibited,' she said, with a new tone in her voice and a different vocabulary. 'You have to learn to recognise and express your own sexuality. You'd better begin with a film. A porn film. They can be a real help, believe me. Or maybe that's not your problem, and you have to work on a drastic reduction in your consumption of porn films instead.' She stopped, focused on him, her eyes slightly narrowed, and seemed to be thinking. 'Anyway, it's one or the other. A case of either–or,' she concluded.

Several seconds passed.

'There could be something in that,' said Kimmo Joentaa.

Now the woman was smiling suddenly, and for the first time it was a friendly smile. Joentaa returned it.

They sat smiling at each other, or maybe past each other. Joentaa didn't know which.

'And in case you're surprised that I know Ari Pekka Sorajärvi's name and address,' she said, throwing something down on the snow-white table between them, 'it's because I nabbed his driving licence just now while he was seeing to his broken nose.'

2

It's only a picture. A picture that can't be covered up. Cover the picture with a white cloth. A cloth of impenetrable whiteness.

She knows it won't work any more. Belief in whiteness covering everything up used to be important to her, but now she's lost her faith in it.

She lays a white cloth over her thoughts, and watches it fall into its component parts in a soundless process of dissolution, revealing the view of another cloth, a blue one.

The blue cloth is lifted. A man is lying under the blue cloth. The man has one leg. The leg is a stump. Half of it is missing. The other leg isn't there at all.

The man lies on the stretcher in an unnaturally cramped position, his skin has a dark tinge. Beside the man is the blue cloth, above him a laughing face. And another. And another.

An arm reaches for the man's head and straightens it. Now she can see the face. The look of the closed eyes.

Somewhere outside her field of vision people are laughing. They are there with her, beside her, over her, under her, but she can't see them. She only hears their laughter. She tries to laugh with them.

She feels herself laughing, looks into the face of the man with only half a leg, and is relieved that he doesn't seem to hear her. In the moment when her laughter dies away something else also comes to an end, she doesn't know what it is, all she senses is the end.

The people around her go on laughing, and it sounds as if they will never stop.

She closes her eyes and opens them again.

The screen is flickering.

She winds back to the place where it ends, and in her mind she goes back to the day when it began.

3

Ari Pekka Sorajärvi was spared a charge of rape. When Kimmo Joentaa made another attempt to explain the formal course of events, the woman stood up, not in any hurry, more as if she were lost in thought, and said goodbye. She walked out, slowly but with firm footsteps, and closed the door almost without a sound.

Joentaa sat where he was for a while, looking at the empty form flickering on the screen. Name, address, date of birth.

Then he got to his feet, walked down the dimly lit corridor and through the driving snow to his car.

He drove to Lenganiemi. As the ferry made the crossing, he stood by the rail in the icy wind. He felt a vague sense of relief because the ferryman was sitting morosely in his little cabin as usual, in spite of the chain of fairy lights sticking to the window.

He went down the apparently endless woodland path until suddenly the church towered up to the sky, as if out of nowhere. The sound of the sea was a soft roar, and shadowy figures passed by as he entered the graveyard. Joentaa heard them talking to each other in muted tones. Heads bent, concentrating on the graves of their loved ones lying in the dark, but everyone knew where to look. Two of the shadows murmured a greeting, and Joentaa returned it as their paths crossed.

For a while he stood beside Sanna's grave without thinking of anything in particular. Then he took the candle out of his rucksack, lit it, and carefully placed it on the centre of the grave. He stared at the light until it began to blur before his eyes; then he tore himself away and left. Singing and the monotonous, long-drawn-out chords of the organ came from the church.

The ferryman's expression remained just the same on the return crossing; then Kimmo Joentaa drove home.

4

In the evening she writes Christmas cards. She has printed out a photo that she likes. It shows Ilmari and Veikko in front of a wintry scene in Stockholm. They spent Christmas there with Ilmari's sister last year. She has printed out the photo twelve times. On the back she writes, twelve times: *All good wishes for the festive season.*

Then she opens the door and goes out into the stairwell. She goes from door to door, putting a card through each letterbox.

She goes back into her apartment, lights the candles on the tree and looks at the still picture on the TV screen. A man smiling. Not an unpleasant or alarming smile, a happy, likeable smile. She doesn't understand that smile. After she has seen it, she sees a series of pictures that are in sequence but don't make sense, and while the pictures are running life stands still.

She hears a sound and looks away from the screen. There is a white envelope on the floor under the door. A neighbour replying to her Christmas greeting. She goes to the door, picks up the envelope and opens it. The card shows an angel. Marlies and Tuomo, the young couple on the first

floor. They write: *Happy Christmas and New Year to you too.*
Warm regards. She stands in the corridor smiling, and thinks
about words. How they can change, yet do the same thing.
Two names missing from the salutation, two words extra at
the end of the sentence. Warm regards. Her eyes rest on the
words.

Later she goes back into the living room. She crushes the
angel in her hand and looks at the face on the screen, the smile
that she must get rid of before she can feel anything.

5

Pasi and Liisa Laaksonen, his neighbours, waved to Kimmo
Joentaa and called 'Happy Christmas' as he got out of
the car. Each was holding one of their granddaughter Marja's
hands, and she was laughing because Pasi and Liisa were
swinging her up in the air.

Kimmo Joentaa returned their greeting and hurried indoors.
He stood in the corridor for a while in silence, waiting for
the snow to melt and run down the back of his neck. Then
he took off his jacket, cap and scarf, and went from room to
room switching on all the lights.

Later he stood in the living room, looking at the frozen
lake beyond the window and thinking of Kari Niemi, head
of the scene-of-crime unit, who had asked if he would like
to spend Christmas with him and his family. He had been
very glad of the invitation, but declined it. Maybe next year.
He had said the same when his mother Anita asked if he
would like to spend the festive season with her in Kitee. He
had also refused the annual invitation from Sanna's parents

Merja and Jussi Silvonen, saying that unfortunately he had his hands full over Christmas and would hardly get time to stop and take breath.

He would visit Merja and Jussi tomorrow. They would be quiet, and after a while they would all talk about Sanna in their different ways. Exchanging memories that hovered in the air above them for a while. Weightless. Elusive. They would not talk about the weeks after her cancer diagnosis, the last days in hospital. There would be the clink of cups, and Merja offering a plate of home-made biscuits. In an empty house.

Tomorrow. And tomorrow he'd ring his mother too.

He went into the kitchen, feeling pleasantly silly as he took the unopened vodka bottle out of the fridge and sat down at the kitchen table. He thought of Sanna, who had seldom drunk, but when she did drink, she did it thoroughly. A quality he had liked, and after her death he was the same himself. On the rare occasions when he drank, he too did it thoroughly.

This was one of those times. Maybe. He wasn't sure. He toyed with the thought of drinking a glass of milk and going straight to bed.

He was still thinking of various tempting alternatives when the doorbell rang.

Pasi, he thought. Pasi Laaksonen come to ask if he wouldn't like to spend Christmas Day next door, with them and their children and grandchildren.

Or Anita. His mother had got on the train and come to visit him although he had firmly asked her not to.

He opened the door and looked at the face of the woman who had broken Ari Pekka Sorajärvi's nose and whose name he didn't know. She looked like a snowman, since she was wearing a snow-white coat and a snow-white cap, and both were covered with snow.

The woman said nothing. There seemed to be a quiet smile on her lips, but he could be wrong about that.

'Oh . . . hello,' he said.

'Hello,' she said, walking past him and into the corridor.

'I . . . how did you . . .'

'Kimmo Joentaa. Says so on the nameplate outside your office door. And on an envelope lying on your desk. There's only one Kimmo Joentaa in Turku. Unusual name. Sanna and Kimmo Joentaa, it says in the phone book. Is your wife here?'

'N . . . no.'

She nodded, as if she had expected that answer, and went towards the living room.

'What . . . what did you want?' asked Joentaa.

She turned and looked at him for a while.

'I don't know,' she said. 'Nothing, probably. Do you have anything to drink?'

'Er, of course. Milk . . . milk or vodka?'

The woman seemed unimpressed by this selection. 'Both,' she said, going purposefully into the living room.

'Er . . .' said Joentaa. He went into the kitchen and filled one glass with milk and another with vodka.

The woman was sitting on the living-room sofa looking at the lake outside the window. 'Nice view,' she said.

Joentaa put the glasses down. 'Can I help you? If it's about the report you wanted to . . .'

The woman laughed. Laughed at him again. The last person who had been able to laugh at him so heartily and regularly was Sanna.

'No,' said the woman. 'No, it's not about the report. I really can't remember the man's name anyway.'

'Ari Pekka Sorajärvi,' said Joentaa mechanically, and the woman laughed again. Even louder, a laugh ending in a squeal. She couldn't calm down.

'Sorry,' said Joentaa, and the woman laughed and laughed

as if he were the funniest comic act she had ever seen. Her slim body was convulsed by fits of laughter.

Kimmo Joentaa went into the kitchen, drank four large shots of vodka in swift succession, and felt rather better as he went back to the laughing woman sitting on his living-room sofa. He sat down in the old armchair beside the sofa.

'There's something I'd like to ask you, it's important,' he said, and against all the dictates of logic he had an idea he was babbling already. 'Did that . . . did that Sorajärvi hurt you?'

The woman laughed again, but only briefly this time. 'You talk just like senior citizens must have talked in the nineteenth century.'

'Sorry.'

'Oh, damn it all, can't you ever stop saying sorry?'

'What I mean is . . . I think you ought to report the man to the police, which is what you were planning to do, after all. And I could understand you better then. I simply don't understand you yet.'

'Ari Pekka Sorajärvi was a little rougher with me than agreed,' she said. 'In return I broke his nose. Get the idea?'

Joentaa thought about that for a moment. 'Okay,' he said, and the woman began laughing again.

'As you say, okay.'

'Sorry, all I meant was maybe I understand the situation a little better now.'

'If you say sorry again for no reason I'll be breaking another nose today.'

'I can't help you unless I understand what happened,' said Joentaa.

The woman looked at him for a long time. 'Who says I want you to help me?'

'I thought . . .'

'You're crazy, you just don't know it,' she said.

'I think I . . .'

'There's something the matter with you,' she said.

Joentaa waited.

'Something very much indeed the matter with you,' said the woman.

Joentaa still waited.

'There's something the matter with you, and I'd really like to find out what it is,' she said.

Then she stood up and put her arms round him. The old armchair creaked. He felt her hair against his cheek, her tongue in his mouth, and a great cry filled his brain.

6

Kimmo Joentaa lay awake. The snow and the night were melting away beyond the windows. He sat up carefully so as not to wake the woman lying beside him.

He looked down at her for a few minutes.

Heard her breathing quietly and regularly.

Then he let his head drop back against the sofa cushion and felt the woman whose name he didn't know clutching his arm with her hand. She was moaning slightly, as if in pain. Probably dreaming. He wondered whether he ought to wake her and liberate her from the dream, but after a while she lay at rest, breathing regularly again, and Joentaa closed his eyes and thought, for the first time in a long while, of that last night in the hospital.

Thought of the last few hours that turned into the last few minutes, the last few seconds. Sanna too had slept. Sanna too had been breathing peacefully and regularly. Peacefully, regularly and barely perceptibly. Then her breathing had stopped.

He had been waiting for that. Had been waiting, together with Sanna, for that moment, because he had known it would be the most important moment in his life. A never-ending moment.

When he heard a knock at the door he thought at first that he had imagined it. When the knocking came again, a little louder and more insistent, he sat up and looked at the green glow of the numbers on the DVD recorder. Two in the morning. It couldn't be Pasi Laaksonen from next door. Nor his mother, because no trains from Kitee arrived in the middle of the night. Nor the woman who had broken Ari Pekka Sorajärvi's nose, because she was already lying beside him.

He heard the knocking again, a little softer this time, with some slight hesitation. He got up and put on his T-shirt and trousers. He picked up the sofa throw, which was lying half on the floor, and covered up the woman, who seemed to be fast asleep.

Then, legs feeling shaky, he went to the door. His back ached. He opened the door and felt the clear, cold air on his skin. There was no one outside, but under the apple tree with its covering of white snow stood a man, just about to get back into his car.

'Hello?' said Joentaa.

The man stopped and seemed to hesitate briefly. 'Kimmo. Sorry. I thought . . . I wasn't going to ring the bell, only knock, because I thought you might be asleep.'

The man came towards him. It was Santa Claus.

'Tuomas . . .' said Joentaa.

Tuomas Heinonen. He couldn't remember Tuomas Heinonen ever visiting him before. Tuomas Heinonen dressed up as Santa Claus.

'What . . . come on in,' said Joentaa.

'Yes. Thanks.'

Tuomas Heinonen stood in the corridor, stooping and frozen, and seemed to be at a loss for words.

'Would you like a hot drink? You look as if you're freezing,' said Joentaa, smiling, but Tuomas Heinonen probably wasn't listening to him.

'I've had a few problems at home. I . . . we had our present-giving and it went wrong, you might say. And then . . . then I thought of you. I'm glad you were still awake – or had you gone to sleep?'

'Come on, let's sit down and have something to drink first,' said Joentaa, going into the kitchen.

Tuomas Heinonen followed. He sat down, lost in thought, and looked at the vodka bottle and the milk container standing on the table.

'The trouble is it's all my fault. That's the worst of it,' said Heinonen.

'What's happened?' asked Joentaa.

Heinonen looked at him, forcing a painful smile, and hesitated. 'Maybe we're all washed up,' he said at last, leaning back as if that explained everything.

Joentaa sat down opposite him and waited.

'If you . . .' he began, but Heinonen interrupted him. He was talking at a frantic pace now. 'It's like this, I'd like to tell you about it but I don't know if I can. It's . . . it's, well, difficult.'

'You don't have to . . .'

'It's like this, Kimmo, the twins, they were just too much for me.'

Once again Heinonen slumped back as if that told the whole story.

'Twins?' said Joentaa.

'Yes, you know we have twins, don't you? Tarja and Vanessa.'

Joentaa nodded.

'Of course they're great . . . great little girls. Sorry, I'm sure this is all nonsense I'm talking. I'm so sorry . . .'

If you say sorry for no reason once again, thought Joentaa vaguely.

'It was too much for me, I could have done without it,' said Tuomas Heinonen. 'I could have done without all that, I never wanted kids. I love them, of course, but I didn't want to have them. Do you understand?'

'I'm not sure,' said Joentaa, seeing pictures in his mind's eye. Pictures of the twins' christening. Joentaa had been there, and had felt out of place, because he hadn't known anyone apart from a few colleagues. Heinonen carrying the two little girls under his arms like rugby balls, laughing as he ran with them.

'It's all too much for me. We don't have any time these days. Nothing happens any more, it's the kids all the time.'

Joentaa nodded.

'The problem is . . . well, it's like this,' said Heinonen. 'I . . . I looked around for some kind of, well, compensation.'

Joentaa waited.

'I . . . I've been gambling.'

'Gambling?'

'Gambling money away. A lot of money. Almost everything we'd saved up for a rainy day.'

Joentaa nodded, wondering what to say.

'Internet betting,' said Heinonen. 'On sporting events. Virtual poker. But the money is real enough, you could say. If you . . . I lost control of myself and it came out. Paulina discovered what was going on, I don't know how. But this evening she suddenly started on about it.'

Joentaa nodded.

Heinonen stared at the table, then at the sleeve of his Santa

Claus coat. 'Oh . . . sorry, I've only just noticed I still have this stupid costume on,' he said in surprise.

'Doesn't matter,' said Joentaa.

'Hm . . .' Heinonen began to chuckle. 'Kimmo, how do you do it? I mean, how do you manage it, keeping perfectly straight-faced in the most outlandish situations?'

'Well, it was obvious that you're feeling sad.'

'Yes,' said Tuomas Heinonen. He seemed to be thinking. 'What I'd like to ask you, Kimmo, sorry if I'm bothering you, but anyway I'm really sorry about turning up here like this . . .'

'You don't have to keep saying sorry.'

'But how . . . how have you managed over these last few years, since your wife's death . . . how have you managed living like this for years, I mean, on your own? I've often wondered. I'm sure it sounds silly, but I do kind of admire you for having this . . . this world of your own to live in, so peaceful, at least that's the way you . . .'

Joentaa wondered what Tuomas was getting at. He looked up into the eyes of the woman he didn't know. She was standing in the doorway, sleepy and naked.

'What are you two talking about all this time?' she asked.

Heinonen turned to look at her.

There was silence for a while, then Kimmo said, 'Tuomas, may I introduce you to . . . this is . . .'

'Names don't matter, but you can call me Larissa,' said the woman.

Larissa, thought Joentaa.

'That's what the others call me,' she added.

There was a long pause.

Heinonen stared at the woman in the doorway. The woman in the doorway did not seem to mind either the silence or the way Heinonen looked at her.

Larissa, thought Joentaa, suddenly feeling his heart lift.

'I . . . I think I'd better be . . .' Tuomas Heinonen began, then broke off. Kimmo Joentaa concentrated on the silence.

An easy, a different silence. A new silence.

Names don't matter, he thought.

'I really didn't want to barge in on you two . . . I mean I didn't know that . . . that you . . . well, Paulina will be waiting, and there's the twins . . .'

'Let's get some sleep,' said Joentaa.

7

Tuomas Heinonen slept on the living-room sofa, the woman whose name he didn't know slept beside him in his bed in the bedroom, and Kimmo Joentaa lay awake.

Again, he concentrated on the woman's quiet, regular breathing and the silence in the background. A clear day was beginning to dawn outside.

He still felt light. Tired and light and thirsty. He went about on tiptoe so as not to wake his guest. Tuomas Heinonen was sprawled on the sofa. Judging by the look of him, he was fast asleep. The bottle and the milk carton stood on the kitchen table.

Joentaa drank a glass of water and watched the morning turn bluer and brighter and whiter and sunnier, until it filled the rectangle of the window like a perfect picture postcard. He thought of the silence, and at almost the same time heard the telephone ringing and a heavy thud. 'Shit . . . what's that, then?' muttered Heinonen, who was lying on the floor.

'You all right?' asked Joentaa.

'I fell out of bed . . . I mean off the sofa,' said Heinonen, as Joentaa searched about for the phone. He couldn't find it. Heinonen scrambled up and asked vaguely if he could help.

'It must be here somewhere,' said Joentaa.

'These cordless things . . . I can never find ours either, and then there's a twin in each arm and I'd need a third hand to find the phone,' said Heinonen sleepily.

The phone stopped ringing, and a few seconds later the ring tone of Joentaa's mobile sounded out in the corridor. He went and got it out of his coat pocket.

'Joentaa.'

'Kimmo, Paavo here. Christmas is over. I came back on duty early. The crime scene is in the forest. Go out of town down Eerikinkatu right to the end of the road, then turn left, keep going up the rise for quite a while and then along the forest track until you get there.'

'Right, I'll . . .'

'Are you with me so far?'

'Yes, sure . . . have Laukkanen or his colleagues been informed yet?'

'Laukkanen is there already. He's the victim.'

'Right, I'll just go and get . . .'

'Are you awake yet? I said, Laukkanen is the victim.'

'Laukkanen . . .'

'Our forensic pathologist Laukkanen is lying out there in the forest. He's wearing cross-country skis and he's dead,' said Paavo Sundström.

Joentaa said nothing.

Silence is easy, he thought.

'What is it?' asked Heinonen behind him.

'Will you call Heinonen? I'll inform Petri Grönholm. As far as I know he should have been back from the Caribbean yesterday,' said Sundström.

'Yes, I'll . . .'

'Kimmo, get moving, please!' said Sundström, cutting the connection.

'What's up?' asked Heinonen again.

'Laukkanen . . .' said Joentaa.

'Yes?'

'Paavo Sundström says he's dead,' said Joentaa.

'Oh?' Heinonen looked at him like a question mark personified.

'Paavo's there already. He said Laukkanen was the victim.'

'But that's crazy,' said Heinonen.

'Let's get out there,' said Joentaa.

'He's taking the piss. These practical jokes are getting to be a pain,' said Heinonen.

'Let's get out there,' said Joentaa again.

Heinonen nodded. 'Of course. But there's something wrong about this. I mean, it's crazy,' he said, reaching for his clothes, which he had left draped over the armchair. 'Oh . . . sorry, I'm afraid you'll have to lend me something. I had that Santa Claus outfit on.'

'Just a moment.' Joentaa went into the bedroom and put on a pair of trousers and a pullover. The woman had wrapped herself up in the duvet and was fast asleep. He looked at her for a while. Then he took a shirt and a pair of trousers for Tuomas Heinonen out of the wardrobe, carefully closed the bedroom door, and went back into the living room.

Heinonen had the clothes on within seconds. 'Shall we go?' he asked.

'Wait a moment.'

Joentaa found a piece of paper and a pen, and stood there, wondering what to say.

'Er . . . Kimmo?' said Heinonen.

'Sorry,' said Joentaa, and he wrote: *Dear Larissa, I have to go out on a case. Hope you slept well. Would be nice if you were still here when I get home. Kimmo.*

He put the note and the spare front-door key to the house on the living-room table, where she would be bound to see them. The winter day was yellow and blue, and gave him a prickling feeling behind his eyes.

Heinonen called his wife as they drove off, and Kimmo Joentaa thought of coming home to an empty house in the evening. And then he thought that he didn't know her address, or her date of birth. All he knew was that her name was not Larissa.

8

The snow crunched underfoot. Heinonen muttered something incomprehensible, and Joentaa thought this wasn't real. A picture, a staged scene outside the context of reality.

The dead man lay on his back, one of his skis sticking vertically up in the air. His pale blue sports jacket was drenched in blood. The scene-of-crime officers, in their white overalls, merged into the snow.

Kari Niemi, head of the forensic unit, was giving instructions in his calm way. The cross-country ski trail lay behind and in front of the body on the ground, disappearing into the forest on the right and going all the way to the horizon on the left. The winter sun hung over the horizon. Paavo Sundström came to meet them, saying, 'That was quick.'

Heinonen said something or other, and Joentaa walked past them both and round the dead man. A pointed woollen cap, the same light blue as the sports jacket and the sky, lay beside the man's head, which was turned to one side and away from them. Joentaa crouched down and looked at Patrik Laukkanen's face.

'Two boys and a woman found him. He must have been taken by surprise. Presumably attacked from behind, seems to have been stabbed with a knife. At least, that's what Salomon thinks,' said Sundström.

Joentaa looked up and saw Salomon Hietalahti sitting on a bench a little way off. Hietalahti had worked more closely with Laukkanen than anyone else at the Forensic Institute. Joentaa himself hadn't known Laukkanen well, but he did know that he and Hietalahti had worked very harmoniously together. Perhaps they had even been friends.

He stood up and went over to the bench, which offered a picturesque view of the snow-covered city. 'Salomon,' he said.

'Hello, Kimmo,' said Hietalahti abstractedly.

Joentaa sat down on the bench beside him.

'Maybe you shouldn't . . . maybe you shouldn't be working on this case,' said Joentaa.

'Maybe not,' said Hietalahti.

On the periphery of his vision, Joentaa saw Heinonen and Sundström deep in energetic conversation. Petri Grönholm was near the police barrier that had been put up. Beside him were the two little boys who had found Patrik Laukkanen, and who were now following what went on wide-eyed and with mixed feelings. They looked horrified and at the same time excited. Down below, in the city, church bells were ringing.

'Did you know he'd only recently become a father? Patrik, I mean,' asked Hietalahti.

'No.'

'Old to be a father for the first time. In his early fifties. He never said much about himself, but then this happened. He thought he might be too old, he might die before his son was grown up . . . that bothered him a good deal.'

Joentaa nodded, and sought for words.

'She doesn't know yet. Leena . . .' said Salomon. 'I mean, Leena doesn't know that Patrik . . . that he's dead. Will you see to it? Tell her?'

'I don't know . . . look, I'll discuss it with Paavo Sundström.'

'It might be a good idea to do it soon.'

'Yes, sure. You're right.'

'They've been a couple for quite a long time. At least thirteen years, all the time we've been working together, and back then, when I was just beginning here, Patrik was already with Leena. I sometimes went round to their place for a meal . . . not all that often, but it was always very nice. Patrik told me Leena was incredibly happy about the baby . . . he never said so straight out, but I think they . . . they'd been trying for some time before it worked.'

Joentaa nodded.

'They live quite close to here. Two or three kilometres away,' said Hietalahti.

In the distance, Sundström was gesticulating. Joentaa watched the show for a while before he realised that Sundström's gesticulations were for him. He got up and went over to Sundström.

'What is it?' he called before he got there.

'We ought to let his wife know,' Sundström called back.

'Girlfriend,' said Heinonen, when Joentaa had joined them.

'Hm?'

'Girlfriend. Laukkanen wasn't married. I'm fairly sure he isn't married to Leena,' said Heinonen.

'Makes no difference, we have to inform the woman Laukkanen was living with . . . Hang on a moment. Number 17 Yriönkatu. Do you two know her?'

Joentaa and Heinonen nodded.

'So?' asked Sundström.

'You know her too. She was at the Christmas party two weeks ago,' said Heinonen.

'She was?' said Sundström.

'She's a good deal younger than Patrik. Late thirties, I'd guess,' said Heinonen. 'Sandy hair.'

'Ah,' said Sundström. 'Yes . . . yes, I remember. I was afraid Laukkanen would make advances while he was pissed, I felt ashamed for him.'

'Well . . .' said Heinonen.

'Or . . . or maybe I was just envious because it did look as if Laukkanen was getting somewhere with his silly advances.'

'Well . . .' said Heinonen again.

Joentaa looked at the dead man in the snow, and remembered talking to Patrik Laukkanen only a couple of days ago.

In a down-to-earth tone, about death.

They had both been bending over the body of a young woman presumed dead from an overdose of strong sleeping tablets.

'Leena, did you say? Damn good-looking woman,' said Sundström.

Laukkanen. He had always seemed to be bustling about, his restlessness in curious contrast with the silence of the mortuaries where he worked.

'Kimmo?' said Sundström.

'Hm?'

'Shall we go?'

'Yes, of course,' said Joentaa.

He felt a little dizzy as he followed Sundström to the car. He was thinking of Laukkanen, and how Laukkanen's assessments had always been clear-sighted and often very helpful. Perhaps that was what was wrong in this picture. Laukkanen lifeless in the snow. Laukkanen restless and efficient in the silence of the green-painted mortuaries. Laukkanen who had given an impression of having more control over death than anyone else.

9

She parks the car and takes the rucksack off the passenger seat. She walks through slush on a radiantly blue day and smiles at Aapeli, who thanks her for the Christmas card.

'My children forgot me, but you don't,' says Aapeli.

She smiles.

'A lovely photo of Ilmari and Veikko. Where . . . where did you take it?'

'In Stockholm, by the river,' she says, smiling.

Aapeli nods. 'Well, see you soon,' he says.

'See you soon,' she replies.

'And all the best. All good wishes,' says Aapeli.

'The same to you,' she says.

She watches Aapeli taking each step carefully as he walks towards the white trees.

Pushing the door to the stairwell open, she goes down to the laundry room. She takes the clothes out of the rucksack and looks at the stains for a while. She knows what has happened, but she can't remember it.

She puts the clothes in the washing machine, adds detergent, and feeds a coin into the slot. For a while she watches the water as it mingles with the detergent and begins to foam.

She takes the knife out of the rucksack, goes over to the sink, turns the tap on and holds the knife under the flowing water until it looks like new.

Then she goes upstairs. While she is unlocking the door to her apartment she feels hungry for the first time in a long while.

IO

They don't have far to drive. Patrik Laukkanen had been found murdered very close to his house. A clinker-built wooden house surrounded by a large garden. It looked as if it had only recently been painted, a soft pastel shade of orange reminiscent of apricots. This was the first time Joentaa had been there.

'Here we are,' said Sundström.

Joentaa nodded.

Sundström sat where he was, and Joentaa thought of what Salomon had said.

'They have a child. A small baby,' he said.

'Oh, no, that too,' said Sundström. He slumped back in his seat. Then he catapulted himself forward and opened the car door. 'Right, let's get this over with,' he said, climbing out. Joentaa followed him. He thought he saw the silhouette of a woman behind the window next to the front door. The nameplate on the letterbox said *Laukkanen/Jauhiainen*. Sundström rang the bell. Joentaa heard footsteps on the other side of the door, and felt a stabbing pain inside him. Leena Jauhiainen opened the door.

'Oh, Kimmo . . . and . . .'

'Sundström. Paavo Sundström. We met briefly at the Christmas party.'

'Of course. I remember. Patrik isn't here. Since the snow started he's been going out cross-country skiing every morning. I hope . . . I hope he doesn't have to go in to work today, does he?'

'Leena . . .'

'Yes?' she said. A baby was crying in the background. 'Is . . . is everything all right?'

'May we come in?'

'Of course. Go into the living room, I must just see to Kalle for a moment.' She went into another room, and Joentaa followed Sundström into the house. A large, lavishly decorated Christmas tree stood in the living room. Leena came back with the baby, who was not crying so noisily now, in her arms.

They stood looking at each other for a little while.

'Has . . . has anything happened? You're kind of frightening me,' she said.

'Patrik is dead,' said Sundström. 'He was . . . was attacked while he was skiing and killed.'

Leena did not reply, and Joentaa froze.

'I . . . I'm very sorry,' said Sundström, and Leena shook her head.

The baby smiled.

I I

She stands at the foot of the slope for a while, looking at the long building. In the strong winter sunlight its yellow paint is the colour of lemon ice cream. The children are tobogganing. Their laughter, many voices all at once, drifts down to her, and she feels that the sound must carry all over the city.

Slowly, she goes up the hill, past the children racing triumphantly down the slope. She has been looking for Rauna, but Rauna doesn't seem to be among the children tobogganing.

She goes down the long corridors. There are Christmas stars made of paper and cardboard on the walls, along with Christmas trees, dark green triangles on little trunks. She finds Rauna in the day room, sitting at a table with Hilma. The two of them are doing jigsaw puzzles. Hilma is humming to herself, rocking her chair back and forth, while Rauna concentrates on putting the pieces of the jigsaw carefully in place.

She stands in the doorway, watching them for a little while. 'Aren't you two going out to toboggan?' she asks.

'That's what I said too, but Rauna wants to finish that silly puzzle,' says Hilma.

Rauna smiles and beckons her over. She moves away from the door and goes up to the table.

'Nearly finished,' says Rauna, looking in turn from the pieces of the jigsaw to the lid of the box showing the complete picture. A Noah's Ark. Lions, elephants, giraffes, monkeys, and a bearded man already waiting at the helm to put out into the water. Hilma jumps up and presses her face to the windowpane beyond which the children are tobogganing. Rauna fits the last piece into the jigsaw and examines the picture for a while before clapping her hands. 'Done it!' she cries.

'So now let's go on the toboggans!' cries Hilma, running off.

'Will you watch?' asks Rauna.

She nods.

Rauna jumps up and follows Hilma, and she looks down again at the picture that Rauna's hands have put together. Piece by piece until the parts make up a whole. She gently caresses it. Then she slowly goes out of doors. Hilma and Rauna are standing in line to get one of the toboggans. Hilma is given a brown wooden toboggan, Rauna gets a red plastic one.

'First down is the winner!' cries Hilma, launching herself down the slope. She has a start on Rauna, who hesitates for a moment and then sits down carefully and pushes herself off. Down at the bottom Hilma shouts that she has won the race. Rauna nods, turns, looks uphill and seems to be in search of something.

'Here I am, Rauna!' she calls. 'Up here. I saw you slide down!'

She waves, and Rauna waves back.

12

It was snowing that evening, and there were no lights on in the house.

Kimmo Joentaa left his car under the apple tree and walked through the cold air. Once inside, he stood motionless in the corridor, straining his ears for any sounds suggesting the presence of a human being. No address, no date of birth. He didn't know her name; he'd never find her again.

He went into the kitchen and switched the light on. The milk carton and vodka bottle were standing on the table. On the draining board beside the sink stood a bowl and the packet of oat flakes, with a spoon beside them.

Obviously the woman had eaten a bowl of cereal after getting up. Before closing the door after her and leaving.

Joentaa sat down at the table and thought about Patrik Laukkanen and the way they had been discussing death in calm, down-to-earth tones a couple of days ago. About Leena, holding a baby in her arms while Sundström tried to explain the incomprehensible facts to her. About Sundström, who marked out everyone's special areas of responsibility in his striving for efficiency. About Heinonen who, when Kimmo drove him home that evening, had said quietly, abstractedly, 'I won't be going out there again,' and Kimmo hadn't grasped his meaning. The big matches in England were on tomorrow, Heinonen had said, and Kimmo still didn't understand.

'That's when the English Football League has its Boxing Day games. I've got quite a lot riding on Manchester United versus Arsenal.'

Kimmo had just stared at Heinonen.

'You see what I mean?' Heinonen had asked, and Joentaa had nodded vaguely.

Heinonen had said goodnight, and Kimmo had seen Paulina opening the door and Heinonen bending down to pick up the twins in his arms.

Joentaa stood up and went into the living room. Children were playing ice hockey on the lake outside the picture window. There was a pale moon in the sky above them, and Tuomas Heinonen's Santa Claus outfit still lay on the sofa.

He thought he heard knocking behind his back. He waited. Yes, there it was again. Someone knocking at his door. Probably Pasi Laaksonen, asking if he'd like to go round and eat with them that evening. He hurried to the door, and was slightly out of breath when he opened it.

'Watch out,' she said, and Joentaa stood back as the blonde woman precariously staggered past him with a tree. A spruce about a metre high. She made straight for the living room and put it down at the far side of the room beside the picture window.

'This is where I'd like it best,' she said, and Joentaa nodded.

'What do you think?' she asked.

'Yes, definitely. Looks good,' he said.

'Got anything to decorate it with?' she asked.

'To . . .?'

'Well, you know, like red baubles, for instance.'

'Yes, yes . . . I'm afraid I'll have to search for them.'

'Then get searching,' she said.

Joentaa nodded, and went downstairs to the cellar. He knew where to look. He knew all about the chaos in his laundry room. The red baubles she wanted were in a cardboard box along with several wooden angels and an assortment of Magi.

He took the whole box upstairs with him. Larissa was beside the tree checking to see if it was straight.

'Here . . . baubles and so forth,' said Joentaa, handing her the cardboard box.

'Looks good, don't you think?' she asked.

Joentaa nodded, and watched her carefully arranging the Christmas decorations on the spruce tree. Then they stood side by side in silence.

Out on the lake the children were arguing. Their voices came through the glass. There seemed to be a disagreement about the state of play.

Joentaa stared at the tree, and felt a smile spreading over his face.

13

He woke up in the night because a heavy weight was pressing down on his body, and when he opened his eyes he saw that Larissa had gone to sleep on top of him.

He cautiously sat up and pushed her over to the side. Covered her up and hugged her. Kept his arms round her until, half asleep, she began to laugh and asked if he wanted to squeeze her to death.

'Definitely not,' he said, loosening his grip.

She nodded, and quickly dropped off to sleep again.

He looked at the swirling snowflakes outside the window and thought of Leena Jauhiainen, who had quietly collapsed at midday. She had been sitting on the sofa for several minutes, holding the baby and asking questions that Paavo Sundström had answered. She had seemed very calm all that time, but then she carefully put the child down beside her and slipped off the sofa to the floor in floods of tears. Joentaa had sat down between her and the baby, holding her shoulder with one hand and the baby's hand with the other. The baby had been lying still on the sofa, eyes wide open. Sundström had rung the doctor on emergency call, who came quickly and prescribed her tranquillisers.

He got up and went into the kitchen, made himself some herbal tea and sat down at the table with the steaming cup. He wondered whether Leena Jauhiainen was asleep now. Probably she was, thanks to the drugs. Only two days ago he and Patrik Laukkanen had been talking about exactly such drugs. A woman dead of an overdose of sleeping tablets, and now Leena was taking them because Patrik was dead, and tomorrow was Boxing Day. A big day in the English Football League, so Tuomas had said. Joentaa wondered exactly what Tuomas meant when he said he had quite a lot riding on Manchester United versus Arsenal.

'Everything all right?' asked Larissa.

She was standing in the doorway, wrapped in the quilt, and Kimmo Joentaa felt a surge of relief and happiness because she was there, and he wondered why.

'Everything's fine,' he said.

She sat down at the table opposite him.

'Would you like a cup of tea too?' he asked.

She nodded.

'Peppermint okay?'

'Lovely.'

They sat opposite each other, and he began talking about Laukkanen. And Leena. She just nodded, and did not seem greatly impressed.

'Not that expert pathologist on TV, was he?' she asked.

'What do you mean?'

'That forensic pathologist who was on *Hämäläinen*.'

'I don't understand a word you're saying.'

'Hämäläinen's chat show, there were these two characters on it a little while ago. One of them was a forensic pathologist, the other was a make-up artist or a puppet-maker or whatever you call the people who make those puppets for TV, dead bodies for films.'

'Yes . . .?' said Joentaa, still at sea.

'It was about those puppets, and how they're made to look very like the real thing, and the forensic guy said dead bodies can give the investigating officers important clues to their murderers, and he illustrated it with the puppets.'

'Oh,' said Joentaa.

'You're the policeman around here, you ought to know what I'm talking about.'

'Yes . . . in principle,' said Joentaa, and now he vaguely remembered that Heinonen and Grönholm had been talking about it. How forensic medicine was going to be discussed on Hämäläinen's chat show. For some reason or other they'd thought it hilariously amusing. Had they mentioned Patrik Laukkanen? He had followed the conversation only with half an ear, wondering what the hilarity was all about.

'I hated that bit of the show,' said Larissa.

Joentaa nodded.

'I don't remember just why, but something about the show really upset me,' she said.

Joentaa decided to ask Heinonen and Grönholm about the Hämäläinen chat show when he got the chance, although it presumably had nothing to do with the murder investigation.

14

When Kimmo Joentaa woke in the morning Larissa was up already. He heard the water rushing in the shower. After a while she came in and said she was going back to work today. He lay in bed sleepily thinking of what she had just said.

'You mean . . .' he said, as she looked for her clothes.

'Back to work. Doing my job,' she said. 'The clients start getting their act together again on the last day of the holiday.'

Joentaa nodded.

'Would it be okay if I drop by this evening?' she asked.

Joentaa looked at her for a while, and nodded again. He was trying to work something out in his mind as she dressed. Something he wanted to ask her.

'See you later,' she said, and went out.

He sat up straight and motionless in bed as the front door closed.

He drove to Turku. He was late getting there. The darkness was slowly retreating before another picture postcard day. Sunlight fell through the branches of the trees, and the newly fallen snow looked like candyfloss. The road was broad and empty.

He turned left into the narrow street leading to the police station, and passed the low, long building that housed the

Forensic Institute, just after the Accident and Emergency hospital. As he slowed down he thought he could see the silhouette of Salomon Hietalahti through one of the windows. Salomon was talking to a woman forensic officer. Today Patrik Laukkanen, who had been head of this institute only a couple of days ago, was one of the cases his colleagues had to deal with. He wondered who would carry out the autopsy, and his mind dwelt vaguely on what Larissa, or whatever her name was, had told him about the *Hämäläinen* chat show. He drove on.

When he got into the office Tuomas Heinonen and Petri Grönholm were already sitting at their computers. If they had been surprised to arrive before him this morning for once, they didn't let it show.

Sundström came out of the next room. 'You're late, Kimmo,' he said. 'If I didn't know you better I'd say there was a new woman in your life.'

'Hello,' said Joentaa.

Heinonen and Grönholm murmured morning greetings. Kimmo thought of Tuomas Heinonen sitting in his house like a human question mark on the night when Larissa appeared in the doorway. He looked at him, and caught a glance that was difficult to interpret. He thought he saw a small smile on his face. Even that night Kimmo had felt that Heinonen, curious as the whole thing might seem to him, was glad to see he had a 'new woman in his life', but perhaps in view of his own problems Heinonen hadn't had an eye for detail.

Joentaa returned the smile and thought of Boxing Day and the English Football League; then he thought of Patrik Laukkanen again, and Salomon Hietalahti who would probably carry out the autopsy. He sat down at his desk and started the computer. He tried to meet Heinonen's eyes again, but Heinonen's head was lowered and he was staring at his monitor.

'Meeting in the conference room at 14.30 hours,' said Sundström. 'The other officers who'll be drawn into this investigation will be there as well. By then, anyway, I'd like to have something substantial about Laukkanen's private circumstances available. Okay?'

Everyone nodded.

'Kimmo, I'd like you to go out and see Leena Jauhiainen again. I called her; she seems to be a little better. She's drawn up a list of all Patrik's important contacts, so we already have that.'

Joentaa nodded. Private contacts. Professional contacts. What had he liked? What had scared him? Where had he succeeded, where had he had problems? Whom did he admire, whom did he hate? Things that hadn't mattered at all when Laukkanen had still been alive.

Sundström handed round printouts of the list to everyone. A neatly drawn up document, names, contact dates. Joentaa imagined Leena sitting at the computer writing it. While the baby slept and her life had come off its hinges.

'I've divided them up between you. By midday I want everyone to be able to contribute something about the contacts he's covering,' said Sundström.

'Right,' said Petri Grönholm.

'It wouldn't be a bad notion to get some idea of any motive for murder very quickly,' finished Sundström.

Joentaa thought again of the conversation he had had with Larissa in the middle of the night. 'Was it really Patrik on Hämäläinen's chat show a little while ago?'

Sundström didn't seem to know what he was talking about.

'Yes,' said Grönholm. 'It was rather good.'

Heinonen nodded. 'Is that important?'

'Probably not. It's just that I was . . . someone asked me about it, and didn't know for sure if it had been Patrik or someone else from Forensics.'

'Is anyone going to tell me what this is all about?' asked Sundström.

'Patrik Laukkanen was on the *Hämäläinen* chat show. He did very well, got laugh after laugh,' said Heinonen.

'I must have missed it,' said Sundström.

'He really was good. Surprisingly witty, quick off the mark with the repartee,' said Grönholm.

'Aha,' said Sundström.

'It probably isn't important,' said Joentaa.

He drove to the outskirts of Turku and the attractive residential area on the Klosterberg where Patrik Laukkanen had lived in the pastel orange house. He sat opposite Leena Jauhiainen, who was holding the baby in her arms and told him that the tablets had helped. 'First I felt tired, then it was like being weightless. Amazing what those little white pills can do,' she said.

Joentaa nodded.

'I hope the effects will last for a while. I must go very easy on the tablets while I'm still breastfeeding.'

They sat in silence for some time. Then he began asking questions. Leena seemed to be concentrating and at the same time somewhere far away as she answered them, and Joentaa got to know a new side of Patrik Laukkanen. The Laukkanen who had loved classical music and was an enthusiastic dancer – 1989 classical dance champion of Finland.

'We met out dancing. At one of the competitions. I thought at first he . . . well, swung the other way. It's not unusual in that line. Luckily I was wrong.'

Joentaa nodded.

'Oh, how wrong I was!' she said, with a little smile. The baby started crying, and Leena began feeding him. Kimmo Joentaa thought of the Laukkanen he had known, the efficient Laukkanen who talked fast and to the point, and seemed to have no time to do anything but look death in the face. But then, during autopsies, there was an aura of calm composure about him that had almost frightened Joentaa.

When he left the baby had gone to sleep, and Leena stood in the doorway to see him off. The world beyond the wind-screen was sunny and white, and from the first the meeting in the conference room was dominated by Sundström's prin-ciple of the utmost possible efficiency and clarity, which was in stark contrast to the fact that there weren't even the begin-nings of a lead to any explanation of Patrik Laukkanen's death. Twelve CID officers were present along with eight uniformed police officers, conscripted for the early phase of the case.

When Joentaa, in the course of his report, mentioned that Patrik Laukkanen had been a good dancer, most of the others present laughed. And when, in the hope of putting a stop to the laughter, he pointed out that Laukkanen had been good enough to win the Finnish championship, it became hilarious mirth, but then it died away abruptly when everyone realised that they were laughing at a colleague who wasn't alive any more.

Around 15.30 Sundström suggested a break, and Heinonen, who was sitting next to Joentaa, rushed out of the room as if he had been just waiting for that moment.

'Everything okay?' asked Joentaa when Heinonen came back.

'Yes, yes. They're two hours behind us, but it'll soon be kick-off.'

Joentaa looked enquiringly at him.

'The matches. Boxing Day. Kick-off any time now,' said Heinonen, looking at his watch again. Joentaa followed the direction of his gaze: 13.37 hours. Heinonen had put his watch back to British local time.

'Wish me luck,' he whispered as they went back into the conference room. His gaze was abstracted, as if focused on some distant point, like Leena Jauhiainen's that morning in the orange house.

'Who did you bet on?' asked Joentaa.

Heinonen was leafing aimlessly through his papers, and didn't seem to have heard him.

'Tuomas . . .'

'What? Sorry.'

'Who did you bet on? Can't wish you luck without knowing who I'm crossing my fingers for.'

'Manchester United. To win away,' said Heinonen.

Joentaa nodded, and Heinonen stared at him. 'Wish me luck,' he said again, and Joentaa felt an urge to ask Heinonen the question that was really on his mind – how much had he bet on the match?

Sundström cleared his throat and asked Kari Niemi to sum up the results from the scene of the crime so far. For the first time that day a mood of confidence and a certain readiness for action could be felt, as Niemi told them that the number of clues found at the scene was surprisingly large.

'We found just about everything you might expect to find. Fibres from the murderer's clothes on the clothing of the . . . on what Patrik was wearing. The kids who found him contaminated the scene of the crime, but all the same what we've been able to assess so far allows us to say that Patrik was attacked not, as we first assumed, from behind but from in front. Anterior wounds. And it looks as if he didn't try to avoid the killer until the last moment.'

Kari Niemi looked down at his notes, and in the tense silence Paavo Sundström asked, 'Are you sure?'

'A reconstruction like that is always speculative, but our assumption agrees with Salomon Hietalahti's first analysis after examination of the angle of the stab wounds. And in spite of the contamination it's certain that the struggle between murderer and victim was confined to a very small area. There's no indication that Patrik made any attempt to change direction. Which would suggest that the murderer didn't set off any early flight impulse in him.'

Sundström nodded for a while. 'Thanks, that's interesting,' he said at last.

'So that's as far as we've gone at present,' said Niemi. 'The problem is that we can't evaluate the clues we have until it's possible to compare them with the clothes and items carried by a suspect. That means they're not much use to us at present. And as I said, the two kids trampled all over the scene of the crime and came . . . came quite close to Patrik's body before the woman who called us joined them a few minutes later. So we have to separate the tracks left by the children from those that can be said to relate to the crime in order to get a fuller picture.'

'Yes,' said Sundström. 'But thanks all the same. It's a start.'

A little later the meeting broke up, and Sundström issued instructions for the rest of the day. From his office, Joentaa called Salomon Hietalahti, whose voice sounded very far away as he talked about parameters, the direction of the wound channels, and the resistance offered to the stabbing instrument by the victim's clothing, skin and bone structure.

'You see we can never judge these things precisely. But one impression has been confirmed: it seems to have been done in a . . . a frenzied rage,' he said.

Joentaa waited for Hietalahti to expand further on this, but he did not. 'What do you mean?' he asked.

'It looks as if he was struck down by an assailant in a state of frenzy. The stab wounds are random, distributed over almost the whole of his torso. Some are superficial, some go deep. It's like the attack hadn't been thought out in advance, it was more like sudden fury . . . do you understand?'

'Yes. Thanks, that could be helpful,' said Joentaa.

'Do you think so?'

'Yes . . . yes, I do,' said Joentaa.

'It doesn't get *me* any further, because I can't imagine anyone who . . . well, I just can't imagine it. And I really did know Patrik well,' said Hietalahti.

Joentaa had no idea what to say to that. He ended the call, and thought about Patrik Laukkanen and how on earth he could have been the object of such furious frenzy as Salomon had described. Patrik hadn't tried to get away. The person facing him had not set off any flight instinct.

He looked across his desk at Tuomas Heinonen, who was concentrating on the screen of his computer and muttering curses from time to time.

'Tuomas?'

'Yes, sorry . . . I was only taking a quick look.'

Joentaa nodded.

'They've just kicked off. No goals yet,' said Heinonen.

15

'I glide over the snow, it's like being on rails,' she says.

She smiles apologetically, because she knows that doesn't answer his question. He seems to be waiting for her to add something more precise.

'I went to see Rauna this afternoon,' she says.

He nods.

'It was nice,' she says.

'It's a good thing if you can give each other strength,' he says. 'But a time may come when Rauna begins to connect you personally with the incident. And then you might not be able to help her any more. It might become more of a burden on her. Do you understand what I'm saying?'

'Rauna was glad to see me,' she says.

'I know. I'm just trying to point out that it will take her a long time to work her way through the incident and go through the various stages.'

The incident, she thinks. How matter-of-fact he sounds when he says it. She likes him. He is clever, but clumsy at the same time. She likes that odd mixture, he sometimes reminds her of Ilmari. They don't look like each other, but they're about the same age, and Ilmari too was clever and clumsy. Would Ilmari have described the moment when the sky fell in as an incident?

'What good does that do us?' she asks.

He waits.

'What good does it do to talk about an incident?'

He waits a moment, then says, 'I think it's important to find a term that creates distance. You need distance before you can begin again.'

'Do you really think so?'

He nods.

'Because that's what you were taught?'

For a while he says nothing.

'What did you mean when you said you were gliding over the snow as if you were on rails?' he asks.

'It's what I'd most like to do. Glide over the snow on rails and put the world to rights,' she says.

He waits, but she doesn't know what else she could say to him.

'Do you understand?' she asks.

He nods.

When she goes out into the cold it is snowing, and Ilmari and Veikko still lie buried under the ruins of the sky.

16

When Joentaa got home the house was dark. He opened the door and stood on the threshold for a while.

'Larissa?' he said softly.

No reply. He went into the living room, dropped on to the sofa and looked at the little spruce tree beside the picture window for some time. He tried to concentrate on Patrik Laukkanen. On any possible motive for his murder. That was how Sundström had put it. An efficient investigation had been set in motion, there was a conclusive scenario, there were clues that could be assessed, but no sign of what, in most cases, emerges quite early as at least a possibility – there was no indication of the murderer's motives.

Joentaa stared at the television screen, at the silhouette of his own body reflected in it, and heard a faint crunching outside and felt a cold draught of air as the front door was opened. He sat there motionless, holding his breath. In the kitchen, the fridge was opened. He heard the clink of a glass, the rushing of water. After a while, someone drawing long breaths. Someone breathing there in his house. He waited.

'Hello, Kimmo,' said Larissa.

He turned, and saw her standing in the doorway. Her voice sounded different. Both strange and familiar.

'Hello,' said Kimmo.

'I'm rather tired,' she said. 'I think I'll go to bed soon.'

'Do that,' he said.

She took off her jacket, perched on the arm of the comfortable living-room chair and looked at him.

'Everything . . . everything all right?' he asked.

She nodded, stood up and undressed. She put her clothes in a neat pile on the sofa beside him.

'I'm glad . . .' said Joentaa.

She looked enquiringly at him.

'I'm glad you're here.'

She was looking at him, but he couldn't interpret her expression.

'Sleep well, Kimmo,' she said. She went into the bedroom and closed the door without looking back.

27 December

17

When Joentaa woke up he wasn't sure where he was. After a few seconds he got his bearings. He was sitting on the living-room sofa, and the digits on the DVD player said the time was 6.38. He ran his hands over his face and thought of Tuomas Heinonen. Heinonen had set off that afternoon to compile a list of people who knew Patrik Laukkanen. 'Wish me luck,' he'd said before leaving the office. He probably hadn't been referring to the questioning sessions ahead of him, and Kimmo hadn't seen him since.

He sat up and went over to the TV set, picked up the remote control and turned the TV on. While the picture was coming into focus he tried to remember what Tuomas had said. Manchester. To win away.

He went into teletext, and felt a tingling as he tapped the code for the sports pages. The second headline gave the results for the top match in the English league. Three-all. Arsenal had scored an equaliser in the fifth minute of extra time.

Joentaa sat down cross-legged in front of the TV and read the text, which waxed enthusiastic about one of the most spectacular games of the season. He thought of Heinonen's veiled, harried expression.

It was probably just as well. Tuomas had to lose if he was ever going to come to his senses. Joentaa didn't know much about the psychology of gambling, but enough to be aware that the effect of winning was to lure a gambler into real disaster. When he and Sanna had been in France a few years ago, he had found a roulette table in a discotheque, and it took him only a few hours first to treble their holiday cash and then to gamble it all away.

He remembered that devastating feeling. Sanna's enquiring, disappointed glances. The anger she had suppressed because she felt sorry for him, and she had enough of a sense of humour to appreciate the funny side of the story.

He suspected that only such setbacks would help Tuomas, and at the same time wondered what price he was paying. He'd have to ask Tuomas how much he was betting.

When his mobile rang he felt sure it would be Tuomas. As he dug around in his pocket, he was trying to think of ways to stop him gambling.

It was Sundström. 'Things are moving fast,' he said.

Joentaa waited.

'Harri Mäkelä,' said Sundström.

'Who?' asked Joentaa.

'Harri Mäkelä, puppet-maker,' said Sundström.

Then Sundström fell silent as if that said it all, and Kimmo Joentaa felt dizzy.

'Found murdered. Around midnight. In Helsinki, where he lives. Lived,' said Sundström.

'The guy who was on Hämäläinen's chat show with Patrik?' said Joentaa.

'He went to buy cigarettes. After a while his housemate or boyfriend or whatever started wondering where he was, and a little later still he got the idea of going out to look for him, and he didn't have to go far, because there was Mäkelä lying right outside the window. By the side of the road. Bled to death. Multiple stab wounds inflicted by a knife, that's the way it looks.'

Joentaa closed his eyes, and tried to concentrate on Sundström's voice. In a corner of his mind he was listening to Larissa talking about the chat show.

'Our colleagues in Helsinki think he didn't even make it to the cigarette vending machine. At least, he had no cigarettes on him, and he lay there as if he'd only just walked out of the house.'

'That means . . .'

'That means the murderer must have been waiting for him, and it means he's not inclined to waste time. We have a first scenario pointing to an unusual murder procedure. Most of the stab wounds were in the region of Mäkelä's throat and head.'

'What?' said Joentaa.

'It's possible, and would fit what clues they have, that Mäkelä went over to a car, bent down to the window and was stabbed by the driver. They expect to lift a tyre tread.'

'Good,' said Joentaa.

'Investigation on the basis of a tyre tread doesn't hold out many prospects,' said Sundström.

'All the same . . .'

'Our colleagues were quick off the mark in connecting Mäkelä with Laukkanen. They take notice of a fellow officer's murder right away, even if it happens in Turku, and it seems like everyone except me watches that TV show. I've already called Salomon Hietalahti. The two forensic departments are comparing results to see if it was the same murder weapon both times. In any case, the method was similar.'

Joentaa said nothing.

'Their head investigator is Marko Westerberg. Do you know him?' asked Sundström.

'Hm?' said Joentaa. He was picturing a man leaving home. An attacker waiting for him. Just for that one man. Waiting patiently, focused.

'Westerberg. I was asking if you know him,' said Sundström.

'No,' said Joentaa.

'I do, from way back. He's a bit lethargic, but very

meticulous. When he's talking you get the feeling he might drop off to sleep any minute.'

'Hm,' said Joentaa.

'We'll go to Helsinki. Setting out at eight. I'd like you to tell Tuomas and Petri first, ask them to carry on here in Turku, I'll draw up a plan of action.'

An attacker, quiet, patient and focused, Joentaa thought.

'We must find out what connects Patrik Laukkanen to this Mäkelä. Apart from their appearance on the same chat show,' said Sundström.

Quiet, patient, focused. And driven by fury.

'I want to see the transmission of the show as soon as possible,' said Joentaa. 'Larissa . . . a friend of mine, she told me about it, she saw it at the time.'

'Larissa?' asked Sundström.

'We must ask the TV station for a DVD of the show,' said Joentaa. 'Or no, maybe Patrik recorded it. If I appeared on a chat show I'm sure I'd record it, wouldn't you?'

'Perfectly possible,' said Sundström.

'I'll ask Leena. We have to see that transmission, it's urgent.'

'Yes . . .'

'I'd like to have watched it before going to Helsinki. I'll call Leena right away. Speak to you later.'

'Er . . . Kimmo . . .'

Joentaa ended the call and called the number he had stored under the name of Patrik Laukkanen. He let the phone ring until Leena Jauhiainen answered in her abstracted, quiet voice.

'Sorry, Leena, I know it's early,' he said.

'Hello, Kimmo. I wasn't asleep,' said Leena.

'I have a question to ask you,' began Joentaa.

'Is there . . . it sounds like something . . .' Leena didn't finish her sentence. Presumably she had been about to say 'something important has happened', but what was important after Patrik's death?

'Patrik was on a TV talk show a few months ago . . .'

'Yes,' she said.

'Do you know if he recorded the programme?'

'Yes, Kimmo, I do. He called me about ten times to make quite sure I pressed the right buttons on the DVD player. It was . . . it was a great thing for him, it gave him a lot of pleasure, and he was really good.'

'Do you have the DVD? Could you lend it to me?'

'Of course.'

'Wonderful. I . . . I'd really like to pick it up at once, if that's okay.'

'Of course. Kimmo . . . what's going on? Why is that recording important?'

'I don't know yet. But the other man who was on the *Hämäläinen* show with Patrik . . .'

'The puppet-maker? Mäkelä?'

'Yes . . . had he and Patrik been in touch before? Were they friends?'

'No. They met for the first time on the talk show. I don't know that Patrik had anything to do with him later. Is this Mäkelä . . .?'

'He's dead,' said Joentaa. 'There's some kind of connection with Patrik. There has to be.'

Leena did not reply.

'I'll be with you in half an hour,' said Joentaa.

'Fine,' said Leena.

'See you,' said Joentaa, ending the call.

He phoned Grönholm, whose voice seemed to surface from the depths of sleep, and Heinonen, who sounded hunted.

Then he stood outside the closed door of his bedroom for a while. Finally he pressed down the handle and opened it. Larissa lay curled up in the foetal position. She seemed to be fast asleep.

Joentaa closed the door and stood undecidedly in the

living room with a piece of paper and a pencil. After some time he gave himself a little shake and wrote: *Dear Larissa, I have to go out. Looking forward to seeing you this evening. I could make us lasagne if you like. See you later, Kimmo.* He stared at the note for a while, then put it down on the table. The lake beyond the window was still dark, but the sky was clear, and Joentaa felt that the next wintry day would soon be dawning.

18

She has been gliding over the snow, setting the world to rights. The road was broad and empty. The man seemed surprised, and lay quite still as she looked down at him.

19

Patrik Laukkanen was laughing. It struck Joentaa that he had never seen him look happier, and he tried to concentrate on the words being exchanged, but he found it difficult, because he kept staring at the laughing Laukkanen until the picture blurred before his eyes.

Harri Mäkelä explained how he made models of dead bodies out of shapeless lumps of modelling material, and the presenter Hämäläinen nodded, asking a question now and then, and Patrik Laukkanen laughed. Laughed and laughed, explained something, praised Mäkelä's models because the puppet-maker observed a certain anatomical feature accurately in constructing them. Then he laughed again, Mäkelä joined in, Hämäläinen grinned wryly, the audience laughed and a stand-up comic came on stage, a man with some nervous tics who immediately began to imitate famous voices.

Sundström muted the sound. The pictures flickered silently. They all sat there in silence, Sundström and Tuomas Heinonen on chairs in front of the TV set, Petri Grönholm perched on the edge of the long, narrow table that dominated the conference room. Joentaa was kneeling in front of the TV set. He had put the DVD in the player and hadn't moved since Hämäläinen, on screen, invited his guests Harri Mäkelä and Patrik Laukkanen to come up on stage and join the models lying on stretchers under blue cloths.

'Well . . .' said Sundström after a while.

The comic on the screen twitched and seemed to be concentrating. He appeared to address some serious subject now. Hämäläinen nodded from time to time and returned the man's grave look.

The comic is sad, thought Joentaa vaguely, and death is a joke.

'Does that get us any further?' asked Sundström, breaking the silence.

No one replied. Tuomas Heinonen was pale, staring at the pictures on the screen. Three all, thought Joentaa.

'Patrik was good,' said Grönholm. 'That's all that really struck me.'

Sundström nodded.

'He was really good,' said Grönholm. 'What he said was based on facts and interesting. And witty.'

Sundström nodded again.

'I always thought Patrik had no sense of humour,' said Grönholm.

'Yes, well,' said Sundström.

'And the puppet-maker was an arsehole,' said Heinonen. They all turned to look at him. 'Sorry,' said Heinonen. 'It's just that the way he showed off because he makes models of corpses for TV got on my nerves.'

The comic's face twitched, and Joentaa wondered whether that was part of his act or for real. Perhaps both. Perhaps he'd submerged himself in his role until reality and illusion merged. With the nervous tics of a stand-up comic, he told serious stories from his life.

Joentaa thought about corpses for TV and what Larissa had said.

Harri Mäkelä and Patrik Laukkanen were also still sitting in their places with the rest of the people on the screen. Mäkelä seemed to take little interest in the comic's perform-ance; he was looking at the floor, lost in thought, and changed his expression only when he thought the camera was on him. Patrik Laukkanen seemed to be listening attentively to the comic. The presenter, Hämäläinen, sat motionless and upright at his desk, his body turned to whichever guest he happened to be addressing, always with the same expression on his face, the one that seemed to say he would understand anything. Whatever might come of it.

Hämäläinen, thought Joentaa vaguely.

Reality and illusion.

'I'd like to watch that again,' said Joentaa.

'What?' asked Sundström.

'I don't mean right now. I'll take the DVD home if that's okay.'

'Fine,' said Sundström.

'And we have to think about Hämäläinen.'

'Hämäläinen?'

'Three people took part in that conversation on the chat show. Two of them are dead, and Hämäläinen is the third.'

Sundström said nothing for a while. 'I see what you're getting at. The problem is, I just can't think how to construct a motive for murder out of that conversation on the chat show. It simply won't wash. Unless we assume we have here a murderer who kills people because they appear on TV.'

'We'd have to protect a hell of a lot of people,' said Grönholm.

'It was a joke, Petri,' said Sundström. 'Irony.'

Irony, thought Joentaa.

'Of course we'll talk to Hämäläinen,' said Sundström. 'I've already fixed it with our colleagues in Helsinki for us to be present when they interview him. But personal protection . . . at the moment that strikes me as a rather far-fetched notion.'

Joentaa nodded.

'What matters is to get an idea of what this is really all about,' said Sundström.

On the screen, the comic was telling sad stories from his life.

The dead bodies lying on stretchers under blue cloths had never been alive.

And Patrik Laukkanen, who wasn't alive any more, raised a glass of water to his mouth.

20

Joentaa drove to Helsinki with Sundström. The roads were wide and empty, the winter sunlight gave way to grey clouds, and it began to snow.

They sat in Westerberg's office and compared notes on

what they knew. Kimmo Joentaa couldn't get that picture out of his head, the image of a laughing Laukkanen raising the glass of water to his mouth.

Sundström had not been exaggerating. Marko Westerberg did indeed seem to be very tired as he described the state of their investigation in Helsinki so far.

They went to the house where Harri Mäkelä had lived, and where he had died outside the front entrance. A sky-blue, unusually extensive clinker-built wooden house. Police officers in white overalls were securing any clues. Neighbours and curious onlookers stood on the other side of yellow police tape. A thin young man was sitting on a sofa in the living room. His head was bowed and his eyes closed.

'Mr Vaasara?' said Westerberg in his melancholy voice, dragging the words out slowly.

The man looked up.

'These are colleagues of ours from Turku. Paavo Sundström and Kimmo Joentaa.'

The man nodded.

'Nuutti Vaasara,' said Westerberg. 'He's . . . he lived here with Harri Mäkelä. And they . . . they worked together too.' Westerberg sounded particularly weary as he gave this information.

The young man nodded, Sundström and Joentaa nodded.

'I'd like to know more about the work,' said Joentaa.

The young man stared at him for a while, and Joentaa wasn't sure if he had understood. He was about to ask again when Vaasara said, 'The studio's at the back of the house.'

'May I take a look at it?' asked Joentaa.

'Of course,' said Vaasara, and got to his feet. He was tall, and his movements were fluid and well coordinated. Joentaa, Sundström and Westerberg followed Vaasara down a long corridor and entered a world that had nothing to do with the warm, elegantly furnished living area of the house. Vaasara had opened the door and let Joentaa into the large white room first. On a long, massive wooden table in the middle of the room stood containers, spray cans and buckets of paint. Joentaa went over to the table and out of the corner of his eye saw human figures leaning against the wall. With their heads drooping. A red and yellow clown stood out sharply against the white that dominated the room. A dead body lay in the clown's lap.

A stand-up comic telling sad stories from his life, he thought.

Joentaa stood motionless, and Vaasara said, 'This is our studio.'

Joentaa nodded, shook off his rigidity and went over to the table. He looked inside the containers.

'Silicon, latex,' said Vaasara. 'Silicon, latex, plastics, they're the basic materials for making the puppets.'

Joentaa nodded. Out of the corner of his eye he saw the puppets up against the wall and felt a pang in his chest. In his chest and behind his forehead. He sensed an idea making space for itself.

'I'm the assistant. Harri is the artist,' said Vaasara.

Joentaa nodded. Not with the best will in the world, Sundström had said. By now Sundström had gone over to the table himself and was asking Vaasara a question that Joentaa did not hear, because the idea was taking over more space. An idea that he couldn't quite grasp yet. Westerberg was standing gloomily in the doorway.

'Are you all right?' asked Sundström. The words reached him in waves.

'Sure,' said Joentaa.

The idea was Sanna. The moment when the nurse on night duty had put out the light. Bright yellow light, like the light in this room. The same white walls. He had seen

Sanna's face and couldn't take in what he was seeing. Couldn't take it in. Hadn't taken it in to this day. He went out of the room.

'Kimmo?' he heard Sundström saying.

The name came to him in waves, Kimmo, Kimmo, Kimmo.

Kimmo, he had replied, when Sanna had asked who he was, what his name was. When she didn't recognise him any more, when the world in which they had lived together was slipping away from her, to be replaced by a new world that he didn't understand. Could he see her riding a horse, Sanna had asked, and he had nodded, and Sanna had smiled for the last time.

He went down the corridor back to the living room, where it was warm. He sat down on the sofa where Vaasara had been sitting. His head was bowed, like Vaasara's when they had arrived.

'Are you really all right, Kimmo?' asked Sundström behind his back.

'In a minute,' said Joentaa. He closed his eyes and concentrated on breathing regularly.

'It – they're only models,' said Vaasara. 'Puppets.'

Sundström laughed briefly.

'Thanks. We'd never have thought of that for ourselves,' said Westerberg wearily, standing in the doorway.

21

The conference room was dark, and smaller than their own in Turku. Jobs to be done were shared out, areas of responsibility named. Officers assigned to keep the flow of information going between Turku and Helsinki. Two cities, one murder case. Sundström and Westerberg agreed to call each other twice a day, at fixed times, to exchange the most important results of their investigations.

A forensics expert told them that an initial analysis showed the probable nature of the murder weapon in both cases.

Probable nature, thought Joentaa.

'As you know, features around the edges of wounds and the direction of the thrust allow conclusions to be drawn about the nature of the instrument used, but it's not an exact science,' said the forensics expert.

'Probability will do us for now,' said Sundström.

'A small but sharp blade,' said the forensics man. 'Presumably an ordinary household knife, meaning it'll be one widely sold in large quantities.'

Sundström and Westerberg nodded.

Joentaa heard little of what was being said. He was thinking of Sanna, Sanna's face when life had come to a stop behind it. The routine sympathy of the nurse on night duty. The drive home. The landing stage and the lake in the darkness. The cold of the water against his legs as the pain finally made its way into him and spread.

One of the Helsinki investigators talked about Harri Mäkelä. His voice sounded hunted, and rose and fell at unnaturally regular intervals. Mäkelä had been the best, he said. He'd made life-sized dummies not only for Finnish productions but also for the American movie industry. He'd even made the model of an Oscar prizewinner who had to fight a robot that looked just like him in a film. Joentaa wondered what the basic idea of that film could have been. The officer said, 'He was much in the media. Recently wrote a book. Kind of a semi-celebrity, here in Helsinki anyway.'

Silence filled the room.

'Hm,' said Sundström.

'We don't know much more about him yet,' said the officer apologetically.

Then they went along the corridor and stepped out into the driving snow. They drove to the TV station from which Kai-Petteri Hämäläinen's chat show went out with such success. A large, tall building, surrounded by its own extensive park, dominated by glass. While they made for the building Joentaa looked at the little people visible through the glass, and wondered whether the executives who ran the station deliberately put their employees on show as if they were on a huge screen.

The doorman stood to attention when Westerberg showed his ID, the woman editor of the *Hämäläinen* chat show welcomed them on the twelfth floor. She was in a cheerful mood. Kai-Petteri Hämäläinen entered the room a little later. He wore a black jacket and blue jeans, clothes expressing the mixture of gravity and the popular approach that presumably accounted for some of his success. Joentaa examined the best-known TV face in Finland and wondered what it was about it that he found so irritating.

'Hello,' said Hämäläinen, and shook hands one by one with Sundström, Westerberg and Joentaa. He sat down, crossed his legs, and looked at them with a friendly, enquiring expression.

Hämäläinen is playing the part of Hämäläinen, thought Joentaa, and Hämäläinen's expression darkened as Westerberg explained the reason for their visit: Harri Mäkelä, found dead outside his house.

'That . . . that's terrible,' said Hämäläinen.

'There's worse to come,' said Sundström.

Hämäläinen looked at him and waited.

'Patrik Laukkanen.'

Hämäläinen frowned and seemed to be thinking. 'Isn't that the forensic pathologist who was on our show with Mäkelä?'

'That's right,' said Sundström.

Hämäläinen waited.

'Laukkanen was also found dead,' said Sundström.

'Oh, good heavens,' said the editor.

'That . . . that's terrible,' said Hämäläinen, and for the first time he really did seem to be shaken.

'The only link between the two that we've been able to establish so far is your show. The appearance of both of them on the programme,' said Sundström.

Hämäläinen was silent for a while. 'I see,' he said at last.

'So far as we know, Mäkelä and Laukkanen met for the first time on your show. Can you think of any other connection between them?'

Hämäläinen shook his head, and seemed to be lost in thought.

'Nothing at all that stuck in your memory?'

'It was a good show that day, a good conversation, we had good . . .' He stopped.

We had good ratings, Joentaa suspected.

'We had a good conversation, they were nice guys and they came over that way. Good guests,' said Hämäläinen.

Sundström nodded.

'There's one idea we've discussed within our team, an idea we would like to put to you,' said Westerberg with ceremony and very, very wearily.

'What is it?' asked Hämäläinen's editor when the silence began to seem endless. Kai-Petteri Hämäläinen was staring at the glass walls around them.

'Do you . . . will you have anyone around for protection?' asked Westerberg.

Hämäläinen didn't seem to understand what he meant.

'Do you have personal protection? Bodyguards?' Westerberg specified.

'No,' said Hämäläinen. 'No, I'm not a . . . I lead a perfectly normal life.'

Westerberg nodded, and Joentaa thought of an interview with Hämäläinen he had read a few weeks ago. It had focused again and again on that statement. A perfectly normal life, a star within the reach of ordinary people. As far as he remembered, Hämäläinen was the father of two daughters. Twins. Like Tuomas Heinonen.

'Why do you ask that?' said Hämäläinen's editor. 'Do you really think that Kai-Petteri . . .?'

'To be honest,' said Sundström, 'at the moment we're overwhelmed by what's happened. We get that sometimes. We don't know anything, and we don't understand it. We're only registering events.'

They all fell silent, until Hämäläinen suddenly stood up and said, in an unnaturally loud voice, 'Absolutely out of the question.'

'I beg your pardon?' said Sundström.

'Out of the question. I'm very sorry about these deaths, but I didn't know either your forensic pathologist or Harri Mäkelä personally. I met them just once, at the time of that interview. I can't contribute anything, and of course I don't need personal protection or anything like that. Excuse me, please.' He shook hands with Sundström, Westerberg and Joentaa, and walked out of the room.

'That was quick,' said Westerberg slowly.

The editor took them down the now brightly lit corridors of the big glass case that was the TV station to the lift and said again, before the automatic doors closed, how terrible it was. The doorman stood to attention, the large car park was a picturesque scene in the dark of an early evening swirling with snowflakes.

They drove in silence, and Kimmo Joentaa thought of Kai-Petteri Hämäläinen acting the part of himself. A part that he had to play all day long. A man who was real on screen and only a copy in real life.

The sad comic imitates voices, the presenter imitates himself.

Joentaa closed his eyes, tried to concentrate on some distant but central nugget of information, and suddenly had to laugh at his own crazy idea. He laughed and chuckled, and thought, vaguely, that he must call Larissa.

'Kimmo's laughing,' said Sundström, and Westerberg only nodded, presumably because he didn't understand the joke and was not at all interested in understanding it.

22

On the drive back to Turku he tried to reach Larissa, but she wasn't there.

Of course not. He wondered why he felt such a great need to talk to her.

He repeatedly got through to his own mailbox, with the manufacturer's standard pre-recorded announcement, a metallic female voice that brusquely asked callers to leave a message. He had deleted the real announcement, Sanna's announcement in Sanna's voice, three years ago on the night of her death. It had been an almost unconscious act, one that he could hardly remember.

At the fourth attempt he closed his eyes and began speaking. 'This is Kimmo, Hello. I . . . I'll be a little later home than expected because . . . because of Helsinki, I've been in Helsinki, on a case, and I'm on my way back but the road . . . it's snowing heavily, so it could take some time . . . See you soon.' He was going to add something more, but sensed Sundström's eyes resting on him and broke the connection.

'What was all that about?' asked Sundström.

'Hm?'

'That was . . .'

'What?' asked Joentaa.

'That sounded like a new woman in your life.'

23

Kai-Petteri Hämäläinen was looking at the previous evening's ratings, handed to him by Tuula. His eyes rested on the figures, and he tried to remember the guests, to give faces to those numbers.

His head was empty. He had blacked out. Surely he could remember the people he had talked to yesterday evening? There was a knock at the door. It was Tuula, to say that the girl had arrived. He looked at her enquiringly.

'The girl. The girlfriend of that gunman who ran amok.'

He nodded.

'Do you want to speak to her. Or . . .?'

'Of course,' he said.

He stayed sitting there motionless, while Tuula lingered in the doorway.

'In a moment. I'll be with you in a moment,' he said. He kept thinking of his guests. The day before yesterday's guests. Of course. The Tango King. The Tango King had collided with an elk on a country road and died. He had talked to his widow the day before yesterday. Hence the figures. A great many viewers switching on. Even more than usual. The Tango King's widow. And today he was going to talk to another widow, if that was the way to describe the girl. That was an editorial mistake. He couldn't be seen talking to widows two evenings running.

Tuula came back and said it was already on the news. He didn't understand her.

'Mäkelä. And the other man. The news desk wants to know if they can show a clip from your programme. Of course I said yes.'

Hämäläinen nodded.

'Fantastic!' said Tuula.

'Yes,' said Hämäläinen.

Tuula was turning to go, but he held her back.

'Listen . . .'

She waited in the doorway.

'What do you think happened . . . to Mäkelä and the forensic pathologist?'

Tuula seemed to be waiting for him to be more specific with his question.

'Does it . . . does it have anything to do with us?' he said.

'Us? How do you mean?'

'I don't know . . . well, they were both on the programme with me. I talked to them, and now . . .'

'Lords of life and death,' said Tuula.

'What?'

'I remember the wording . . . that was the trailer we made for the programme they appeared on. Lords of life and death.'

Hämäläinen said nothing.

'Are you going to come and talk to the girl? She needs a bit of soothing and encouragement,' said Tuula.

'In a minute,' said Hämäläinen.

'The recording starts in twenty minutes,' said Tuula.

24

G liding over the snow.
    Setting the world to rights.

Sleeping, dreaming. Waking.

In the evening she visits Rauna. The children are eating in the large, brightly lit dining room, and she sits to one side, watching them. Pellervo Halonen, head of the Home, sits down beside her smiling. He asks how she's doing.

'All right,' she says. 'I'm feeling better.'

Rauna is eating with a hearty appetite, and laughs at them, and Pellervo Halonen says, 'Rauna always likes it when you come. It's good to see that, every time.'

She nods.

'I really hope you'll be able to help Rauna some day when . . . when she fully realises what happened. When she has to confront . . . well, the whole of it.'

She thinks about what he has said for a little while.

'I hope so too,' she says at last.

Pellervo Halonen rises to his feet and walks away, and she watches him. He is unusually young, younger than most of his staff, and he always walks very upright, turning to meet life. She noticed that on her very first visit.

She had been afraid of seeing Rauna again that time. It was a mixture of fear and longing. She talked to the psychologist about it. He advised against it, and she went to see Rauna the very next day.

Pellervo Halonen's upright carriage as he accompanied her to Rauna's room. She remembers that. And Rauna's distant face at the moment when their eyes met. Rauna said nothing, and for a few moments she thought that Rauna didn't remember her. Then the fear in Rauna's eyes gave way to longing. Rauna ran to her and hugged her, and laughed. Pellervo Hallonen laughed. Even she herself laughed, for the first time in a very long while.

'I've had enough to eat. Shall we do a jigsaw?' asks Rauna.

She opens her eyes and sees Rauna smiling.

She nods. Rauna runs ahead with a hop, skip and a jump, and she follows her to the playroom. Rauna does the Noah's Ark puzzle. Deep in thought, she fits all the pieces in place until the picture is complete.

'Finished!' says Rauna, and she claps her hands and says Rauna is the best at doing jigsaw puzzles for miles around, and Rauna asks where the third lion is. 'The third lion. The third monkey. The third giraffe.'

She can't think of an answer to that, and says it's a good question.

'The third lion is coming later. And so are the others,' says Rauna.

She nods.

'On another ship,' says Rauna. 'In the winter.'

A carer is standing in the doorway. Visiting time is over. She reads Rauna a bedtime story, and at the end of the story Rauna, in her pink pyjamas, is wide awake.

'See you again soon!' calls Rauna, and the carer, smiling, offers her hand as she says goodbye.

25

The house, white in the darkness. The apple tree wrapped in snow. He parked his car and went the few steps to the front door. Opened it and stood there in the silence. The note was lying on the living-room table, with the pen beside it. He looked at the note, read what he had written that morning, and wondered whether Larissa had read it. Turning his gaze away, he looked at the closed bedroom door. He imagined Larissa lying on the bed on the other side of the door. She had fallen asleep and had not woken up. Couldn't find her way back to the surface. The image spread, and he strode over to the door and opened it abruptly. The room was empty, the bed was made. The bedclothes and cushions were as tidily arranged as in a hotel bedroom when you first move in.

Joentaa closed the door and stood there for a while, indecisively. The little Christmas tree was an outline in the dark. He hurried out into the cold and fetched the DVD from the car. The snow crunched under his feet. Then he was sitting in front of the flickering screen. Patrik Laukkanen laughed, and an unseen audience joined in. Leena Jauhiainen lay awake. The baby was asleep. Hämäläinen lifted a blue cloth and revealed the view of an injured face.

'A funeral the wrong way round.'

He turned.

'That was what disturbed me. I remember it now,' said Larissa. She let her snow-white jacket slip to the floor and came towards him.

'I didn't hear you coming,' he said.

She sat down beside him and looked at him. He avoided meeting her eyes, looked at the pictures flickering on the screen, and sensed that her gaze was resting on him.

'What do you mean?' he asked.

She did not reply.

'What did you mean about . . .'

'A funeral the wrong way round. People were laughing, not mourning, the dead were on show and not buried,' she said.

Joentaa looked at her grave, sad face.

Her gaze was resting on his eyes.

He nodded. Waited. Her hand shot out fast, he felt a sharp pain on his cheeks and felt himself falling. Then she was lying on top of him, with her lips to his throat. Her movements were calm and regular. He closed his eyes and let himself drift. She was saying something in a voice that didn't belong to her. The TV audience was laughing in the background. Suppose it was always like this? Falling. Falling for ever and ever. In the distance, he heard her laugh. There was soft, cool fabric against his face.

'Sorry about that,' she said.

'Hm?'

'You're bleeding. I scratched a little too hard.'

'Mm.'

'I'll clean it up. Do you have any disinfectant?'

'Hm . . .'

'Never mind. I'll go and shower. Take this.'

He took the towel she handed him.

'You must hold it against the cut. It's only a scratch, looks worse than it is.'

He nodded and watched her going to the bathroom. He lay on the floor beside the sofa. The rushing of the shower. Water. An unseen audience. He picked up the remote control and muted the sound. He could taste blood at the corners of his mouth.

'I'd like to ask you something,' he said when she came back.

'Are you all right?' she asked.

'Yes. Why?'

'You're lying on the floor and the towel you're holding to your face is turning red.'

'Oh, it's not so bad,' he said.

She sat down cross-legged beside him.

'I'd like to ask you something,' he said again.

'Go ahead,' she said.

'What was the most wonderful experience you ever had?'

She did not reply.

'Is that so hard to answer?' he asked.

'No,' she said.

'Well?'

'I'd be telling you a lie.'

'You would?'

'Yes.'

He sat up and tried to meet her eyes.

'Go ahead, then,' he said.

'What?'

'I'd like to hear your lies.'

She still said nothing.

'How old are you? What's your name?' he asked.

'Twenty-two. Larissa.'

'I'd like to . . .'

'We always take a bit off our age, but never more than three years at the most.'

Then she got to her feet.

'Don't come in until the scratch has stopped bleeding, please, there are clean sheets on the bed,' she said as she left the room. She opened the bedroom door and closed it almost without a sound.

26

Kai-Petteri Hämäläinen was watching Kai-Petteri Hämäläinen, and already he felt a little better.

'It's only just begun,' said Irene. She gave him a kiss on the cheek, sat down again on the sofa and watched her husband on television.

'Today that girl was on the show, wasn't she?' she asked.

'Yes, the girlfriend of the gunman who ran amok,' said Hämäläinen.

He went into the bathroom, washed his hands and splashed a little water on his face. Then he went back to the living room, sat down beside Irene and put an arm round her.

'How did it go?' asked Irene.

'Fine,' said Hämäläinen.

On the screen, the girl kept her head lowered as she concentrated on finding words to describe something beyond description.

Yes, it had really gone very well.

He had steadied himself again. He had sat on his chair, seen his face in the mirror, thinking about ideas that were difficult to grasp, and Tuula had come along and said, yet again, that there wasn't much time, the recording was beginning and the girl seemed silent and unsure of herself. He had nodded, stood up, and went to interview the girl. He had talked, the girl had listened. His voice had filled the studio, and the girl had nodded gravely, and then his powers had returned to him. When the recording began he was still feeling a little dizzy, but he couldn't quite remember what had really disturbed him.

Lords of life and death, he had thought, and the girl had talked about her boyfriend, a gentle, affectionate young man, a model student, who had killed three people and then turned the gun on himself. He had nodded, and at every answer the girl gave, he knew what to ask next. Together with the girl he had swum in a river of words. His words, her words. A steadily flowing current.

The girl had concentrated on what she was saying, had not felt unsure of herself. Tuula had been wrong there, and anyway Hämäläinen was inclined to doubt Tuula's judgement. How the hell could she have come up with the idea of getting him to interview, on two successive evenings, women who had lost their men? The Tango King's widow, the girlfriend of the gunman who had run amok.

He looked at the TV screen and felt Irene's hand tickling the nape of his neck. It gave him a tingling sensation. He closed his eyes and listened to the girl's voice coming from the TV set.

'I won't forget him,' she was saying. 'He's always with me.'

His own voice putting a question. Calm, controlled, warm and understanding, yet also sceptical and with a touch of admonition. Lords of life and death, Tuula had said. There was something about that remark that he couldn't get out of his head.

'The one thing I can't forgive him is that he never really talked to me,' said the girl. Then another voice, croaking slightly. The psychologist sitting in the audience whose job it had been to contribute a scientific comment from time to time. Then he heard his own voice asking a question. A question that now hovered in the air.

'If I'd known, I'd have kept him from doing it. I could have done that,' said the girl.

A moment of silence.

'I could have kept him from doing it,' said the girl again.

- 74 -

Irene's hand at the nape of his neck. Hämäläinen opened his eyes. He saw himself on the screen, nodding thoughtfully. Then there was long applause.

'Good,' said Irene. It sounded curiously toneless.

'What did you say?' he asked.

'Good. I mean you were good today,' said Irene. She caressed the back of his neck, and he felt tired.

'How are those two little imps of ours?' he asked.

'Fine,' said Irene.

'When did they get to sleep?'

'Late. Just before you came in.'

He nodded.

'Lotta has her first race with the school cross-country skiing team at the weekend. She was all excited, so then of course Minna didn't want to go to sleep either.'

He nodded.

'Terrible,' she said, and he said, 'Goodnight, stay with us,' but that was on the screen. The credits came up, and Irene said, yet again, 'Terrible.'

'What . . .'

'That girl. She seemed to be . . . concentrating so hard. You too, both of you.'

He nodded.

'I never felt you were concentrating so hard as in this particular show,' she said.

'Thank you,' he said.

'It's hardly two weeks ago, and people have already stopped talking about it. They hardly even remember how many people that boy shot.'

'Three,' said Hämäläinen. 'And five wounded. You're right, we weren't . . .' But he didn't finish his sentence. That interview wasn't so topical any longer, he had been going to say. It hadn't been easy; first they had tried inviting the gunman's parents or relations of his victims on to the show, and after fruitless efforts in those quarters they had finally got hold of the boy's girlfriend. Not so topical, but relevant to the subject all the same. The girl had made a good guest.

Irene massaged the nape of his neck and his back. The children were asleep.

'Let's hope the girl can leave it all behind her one day and carry on with her life,' said Irene.

28 December

27

S undström held a well-attended press conference in the morning. Tuomas Heinonen looked pale as he stared at his computer.

Petri Grönholm asked Joentaa a question that irritated him. 'Who's this Ari Pekka Sorajärvi, then?'

Joentaa looked at him blankly. Ari Pekka . . . names don't matter, he thought vaguely. Grönholm held up a card and said, 'Ari Pekka Sorajärvi. His driving licence was lying on the floor under your desk.'

'Oh,' said Joentaa.

'Is it important in some way?'

'No, but thanks,' said Joentaa, taking the card. A round face, a self-confident expression. Joentaa imagined what the man would look like with a plaster on his nose.

'No, nothing important,' he said again.

They went downstairs to the large hall where the press conference was being held. Heinonen did not react when Grönholm asked whether he was coming too. He never took his eyes off his computer screen. Grönholm raised an eyebrow, and Kimmo Joentaa wondered what sporting events took place first thing in the morning.

Nurmela the police chief was in charge of the press conference. The hall was packed. The death of Laukkanen had been something of a sensation in Turku, the death of Mäkelä was sensational all over Finland, for it was he who, as his colleague in Helsinki aptly put it, had always been a semi-celebrity.

And the connection with the appearance of both men on

Hämäläinen's chat show had already been established. A reporter from *Illansanomat*, a tabloid with a wide circulation, asked what that connection meant, and Sundström said, with his own brand of disarming honesty, that he had no idea. The journalist, taken aback, said no more, and Sundström added, 'We're only at the start of this investigation. We suspect that the two victims stayed in touch after their appearance on the TV programme, and that the motive for the murders derives from this contact between them, but we don't yet know what that motive was.'

Sundström answered the questions that followed calmly and factually. Joentaa thought of Heinonen. No one, he noticed in passing, asked the question that was beginning to take shape in his mind, although he hadn't been able to express it earlier. A funeral the wrong way round, Larissa had said. Something about it had disturbed her. Petri Grönholm and Tuomas Heinonen, on the other hand, had thought the TV interview informative and entertaining. It had left Sundström cold and entirely indifferent. Patrik Laukkanen had been happy, and Kai-Petteri Hämäläinen had called them good guests.

Sundström closed the press conference and left the platform. The journalists got to their feet and pushed past Joentaa on their way to the door. Some of them looked serious and already seemed to be concentrating on the columns they were going to write. Others were laughing quietly. The reporter from *Illansanomat* wondered aloud what the world was coming to if not even people who took corpses apart and people who made models of them had a right to life.

He went upstairs. Tuomas Heinonen was sitting at his computer. He looked as if he hadn't moved since Kimmo and Petri Grönholm had left the room.

'Tuomas?'

Heinonen looked away from his screen.

'Everything all right?' asked Joentaa.

'Yes . . . fine,' said Heinonen.

Joentaa stood indecisively in the doorway, then pushed himself away from it and went over to Heinonen's desk. On the screen, under the curving logo of an online gambling site, he saw a long list of results. Heinonen had a notebook on the desk beside him, its pages scribbled all over with crosses and numbers. Presumably combination bets, attempts to classify things that only Tuomas Heinonen understood.

'Can I have a word with you?' said Kimmo Joentaa.

Heinonen looked up and smiled faintly.

'About the gambling,' said Joentaa.

Heinonen nodded.

'It's like this: the Manchester versus Arsenal match ended in a draw, so you lost. So it's over.'

Heinonen nodded.

'I really do think you should stop it. At once,' said Joentaa.

'Of course I should,' said Heinonen.

'But you still go on.'

'Of course I do,' said Heinonen.

Joentaa was silent for a while. 'How high are the stakes?' he finally asked.

'High,' said Heinonen.

'You said Paulina knows . . .' he said.

Heinonen nodded.

'Then she'll be able to keep you from gambling your money and hers away,' said Joentaa.

'Yes,' said Heinonen. He had turned back to the screen, and was now examining the pairings and rates and results.

'Meaning that you . . .'

'Paulina makes sure I can't touch our joint account,' said Heinonen.

'That . . . that's good.'

'I suggested it myself. I gave her sole control of it,' said

Heinonen. 'Paulina was grateful for that, and we're getting on well again.'

Joentaa nodded. 'Well, that's . . .'

'My parents left me a three-room apartment. In Hämeenlinna. Quite far from here. I recently sold it. Half the money's already gone, the rest is hidden between two books in my study.'

Joentaa did not comment. He was trying to think in figures. Three rooms. Hämeenlinna. Half the money gone. Heinonen seemed to have read his thoughts.

'Want to hear the figures?' he asked.

Joentaa waited.

'73,457 euros.'

Joentaa nodded.

'That's the exact figure. I've been keeping accounts. Would you be interested to know that I won at first? The very first time. Wigan versus Chelsea, huge odds. Chelsea playing with a B team because it was only the FA Cup and there were any number of other important games. A combination of three with two favourites winning, factor 22, a thousand euros grew to 22,400. Do you understand that?'

Joentaa nodded, although he did not understand at all.

'It started really well,' said Heinonen.

Joentaa thought of Sanna, and her forced smile when he had gambled their holiday money away. The feeling of helplessness, failure, and then a sense of liberation because they had understood that it didn't matter. Because there were more important things in life.

Heinonen let his eyes move over the sequences of digits in his notebook.

'You have to stop,' said Joentaa.

'I know,' said Heinonen, without raising his head again.

28

Kai-Petteri Hämäläinen woke up with the feeling that he had slept a dreamless sleep. He went downstairs, and he could already hear the clear voices of Lotta and Minna. They were sitting at the table shovelling cornflakes into their mouths. Irene stood beside the table, smiling.

He showered, shaved, dressed and kissed Irene's cheek before he drove off to start the new day. The big glass box in the bright light of winter. He took the lift up to the twelfth floor. Tuula came to meet him along the broad, grey-and-blue corridor, with a wide smile, and called out that their interview had won out over the Tango King.

A collision with an elk, he thought. Bloody bad luck. Bloody stupid, dumb bad luck.

'Forty per cent,' said Tuula. 'That girl was the lucky find.'

He nodded.

'The best value since Niskanen,' said Tuula.

He nodded. Niskanen, the Finnish cross-country skier who had emerged from the snow-covered forest into the TV picture with a ski broken in two places under his arm. Bloody awful, dumb bad luck. A ski broken in two places during the world championships. Three days later Niskanen was found guilty of doping and had said, in a curiously toneless, indifferent voice that he had broken the ski himself in the forest, at a place where the TV camera showed a gap in the trees. So that he could retire from the race and avoid taking a doping test. However, analysis of a sample he had already given before the world championship event had proved Niskanen guilty all the same.

Almost every other person in Finland had watched the final appearance of the best Finnish cross-country skier on the *Hämäläinen* show. Hämäläinen couldn't remember now just what had been said during the interview, all he knew was that he had taken Niskanen's hesitant reluctance to talk as a provocation. The critics had been kind. They had chalked it up to his credit that he had not given Niskanen any chance to talk his way out of the hole he was in. He had been relentless and, as he thought, strictly impartial in his approach to the fallen hero. A little like a judge in a criminal case, Irene had said that evening, and he had felt that she was right, but did not say so, and let her remark hover in the air.

'You were good,' said Tuula.

He nodded.

'Better than you've been for a long time.'

'Thanks,' he said, and went into his office, a glass box within the glass box. Above him hung the wintry blue sky, down below little people scurried around on toy streets. He looked down at them for a while and thought of Niskanen. What was he doing these days? Did he still live in the beautiful house that the Finnish government had given him for outstanding sporting achievement? Or had the gift been taken back when Niskanen was found guilty of doping? He couldn't remember. He did know that there had been a public discussion of the question, and it had been a point of significance in his interview of Niskanen. If he recollected correctly, he had suggested that Niskanen ought to give the house back. He had asked a number of leading questions, and a good many rhetorical questions as well, and he also recollected the way the sweat had broken out on Niskanen's forehead. An assistant had to keep coming on to mop it off his face. He felt a vague impulse to find out what Niskanen was doing now. Where he was living. How he was living.

He moved away from the wall of glass and left the room. He walked along the corridors of the open-plan office to the lift. To left and right of him his colleagues on the TV station sat in front of humming computers. He went down. The cafeteria was still almost empty, as usual between first thing in the morning and midday. He got himself a large white coffee and sat down at one of the tables. A little way from him, two young women from the news desk were trying to outdo each other in giggling. Otherwise there wasn't much to be heard.

Outside lay the snow-covered park. He looked at the meticulously clean, pale surface of the table, and tipped a little more sugar into his cup. He drank. Niskanen. Was Niskanen still skiing? Through snowy forests.

Behind him the young news editors giggled and whispered, and after a while he wondered if they were laughing at him. Presumably not. Presumably it was the opposite, and they wanted to attract his attention. He turned to look at them and smiled. Their faces froze rigid with awe.

He finished his coffee and got to his feet. He walked away. He thought of the forensic pathologist, trying to remember his name, but the name simply wouldn't come back to him. The police officers had mentioned his name. Hadn't the pathologist said, when they were talking before the show, that he was soon to be a father? Yes, he was sure of that. The pathologist's eyes had been shining, and they had talked about children for a few minutes – and now the world was slowing down. It didn't stop, but it was getting slower and slower. He saw the lift in the distance, and the wintry park beyond the glass, and he felt pain stealing into his stomach, into his back.

Kalle, the forensic pathologist had said. His son would soon be born, and they were going to call him Kalle.

He felt that he was falling.

He was lying on the floor.

The pain moved slowly through his body, and above him hung a glass sky.

He was hovering.

Then he was looking into the faces of the two news editors. They were pretty. One of them in particular. Now and then such thoughts crossed his mind, and he immediately banished them again. He could banish them in a fraction of a second. He was the father of a family. A perfectly normal married man with kids. The women's faces were above him. He was lying down. He had no idea why.

The two news editors seemed intent on talking to him, but he gathered only the faintest idea of their words, he was wading through a swamp, one step at a time. The two young women seemed to be trying to speak to him. He nodded. He nodded to tell them not to worry, he would listen and understand them.

He moved away from them. He heard new voices, but he couldn't make out what they were saying. He wanted to listen. He wanted to listen and understand, it was what he did best, but it didn't work. Above him were the blue sky and the trees laden with snow.

He heard Tuula's voice. Tuula's penetrating voice as she let out a scream. Then her face was above him. Tuula's face and behind it the blue sky. Tuula said something he didn't understand. He nodded.

He thought of the forensic pathologist and how he couldn't remember his name, but he could remember the name of the man's son. Kalle.

He nodded, and closed his eyes and saw Niskanen.

Niskanen.

A living legend.

A fallen angel.

Behind his closed eyelids he saw Niskanen, skiing

vigorously through the snowy forest, head bowed, focusing entirely on the elegance of his movements, in a picturesque winter landscape.

29

'Ari Pekka Sorajärvi?' asked Joentaa.

'Who wants to know?' replied the man in the doorway.

'I do,' said Joentaa.

The man stared at him for a few seconds. Round face. Self-confident expression. Suit and tie. About to leave for the office. His nose carefully covered with a white plaster.

'And who might you be?' asked the man.

'Joentaa. Police, criminal investigation department.'

The man smiled, a little uncertainly, rather amused. Presumably Joentaa didn't match up to Ari Pekka Sorajärvi's idea of a police officer.

'Do you mean that seriously?' asked Sorajärvi.

'You think I'd come knocking at your door just for fun?'

'Well, then what do you want?'

'Here's your driving licence,' said Joentaa, handing it to him.

Sorajärvi was taken aback. 'Oh,' he said.

'Didn't you notice it was missing?' asked Joentaa.

'Er . . . no. To be honest, no, I didn't. Where did you . . .?'

'Larissa,' said Joentaa, and Sorajärvi gawped at him.

'Oh.'

'You're lucky she broke your nose, because if she hadn't then at this moment I would be smashing it to smithereens myself.'

Sorajärvi went on gawping, and Joentaa wondered what kind of nonsense he was talking.

'Goodbye,' he said, turning away. He sensed Sorajärvi's eyes on his back. He was still standing in the doorway of his handsome house when Joentaa started his car. Fir trees covered with Christmas decorations stood to left and right of the front door.

As Joentaa drove away he began to laugh, and he laughed so much he couldn't stop. His mobile rang. It was Sundström, sounding far away. He spoke softly and distractedly.

'Hämäläinen,' he said.

'Yes?' asked Joentaa.

'Stabbed. In the cafeteria of the TV station.'

Joentaa felt a rushing in his head, and the tears of laughter still on his cheeks.

'He's in intensive care. We're driving to Helsinki.'

'Yes,' said Joentaa.

'See you,' said Sundström, cutting the connection.

30

They drove in silence. The snowploughs had cleared the motorway, and the snow was piled high to right and left of the road. Nurmela, the Turku chief of police, called several times to find out about the latest developments. He asked if it was all true. He wanted to know why Hämäläinen hadn't been given police protection. How was it possible for such a thing . . .? Sundström's answers were monosyllabic; he seemed to be deep in thought. He said nothing until they arrived in Helsinki and drew up outside the hospital entrance.

'Oh, shit,' said Sundström. Then he shut his mouth again.

Outside the hospital, hundreds of people were standing behind a barrier. There were outside-broadcast vehicles from several TV and radio stations. The phone rang. Nurmela's frantic voice filled the interior of the car.

'We're there,' said Sundström.

'And?'

'All hell's broken loose,' said Sundström.

'Call me as soon as you have any news,' said Nurmela.

They got out and made their way through the crowd. Sundström held his badge aloft. A uniformed officer waved them past the barrier and escorted them to the entrance. After a few minutes Marko Westerberg arrived. He seemed even wearier and more apathetic than usual. In his case, presumably that was a sign of stress.

'He's going to pull through,' said Westerberg. 'The doctors say he was extraordinarily lucky.'

They followed Westerberg towards the lifts. The peace and quiet inside the hospital was in marked contrast to the excitement outside. They stood in the reception area almost alone apart from a few people in white coats scurrying past. A woman with her leg in plaster sat on a bench against a yellow wall leafing through a magazine. She had two crutches propped beside her.

'Is that lift coming soon?' asked Sundström.

Westerberg pressed the button again, and they stared at the red light announcing the lift's arrival. Its broad door opened. Two paramedics pushed a stretcher past them. An old man who looked like a skeleton lay on the stretcher. His eyes passed over Joentaa as they got into the lift.

They went up to the fourth floor. A uniformed officer stood outside the door bearing the words *Intensive Care* in narrow white lettering. He nodded to them, and entered a code into a display of numbers. The door opened automatically. Beyond it chaos seemed to reign, but only at first glance. Joentaa heard several conversations going on at the same time. The doctors and nurses wore blue-green coats, they moved swiftly and purposefully, and Joentaa thought of that last night in the hospital. The moment when Sanna's pulse had stopped. He listened to the conversations: enquiring voices mingled with firm voices conveying reassurance. They went along the broad white corridor of the Intensive Care ward, stood at one window for a while and saw Kai-Petteri Hämäläinen on the other side of it, lying on a bed. Several tubes were inserted into his body, and he seemed to be asleep.

'A matter of centimetres,' said a voice behind him. Joentaa turned, and looked at the face of a young man of about his own age. His hair was cut short, and under the blue-green medical coat he looked very thin.

'A matter of centimetres,' he repeated. His voice sounded calm and confident. Joentaa thought of Rintanen, the doctor who had treated Sanna in the last weeks of her life. His voice had sounded much the same.

'He'll live,' said the young doctor. 'He probably won't have to spend more than a few days here with us. After that, nursing care at home should do the trick.'

Westerberg nodded, and Paavo Sundström breathed in deeply and out again. In and out. 'Well, isn't that great?' he said. 'Oh, brilliant.'

The young doctor and Westerberg looked at him in some irritation, and Sundström repeated it. 'Great. Just brilliant. Oh, yes.' Then he took out his mobile, saying he had to make a call. He moved away, and Joentaa turned back to the window beyond which Hämäläinen lay in his spartan room on a freshly made bed.

'When can we talk to him?' he heard Westerberg ask.

'Soon, I should think. Soon. Maybe this evening.'

'It's very important for us. He can probably give us useful information.'

'I realise that,' said the doctor.

Joentaa looked at Hämäläinen, who seemed to be sleeping peacefully. He turned away and saw a wall to one side covered with vast numbers of brightly coloured cards. Thank-you cards from mothers and fathers whose babies had been delivered in this hospital. Joentaa wondered why they were here rather than in the maternity ward. He went closer to read the cards. The parents had often signed in the names of their children, sometimes even deliberately scrawling names to suggest that the babies themselves had written the cards. Joentaa looked at the pictures, at the exuberantly happy messages, the recurrent phrases. He thought vaguely of Larissa. Or whatever her name was. He had no idea if she took precautions. He wasn't interested in that. He had no idea who she was. He didn't want to know. He felt like ringing her. Hearing her voice. He imagined touching her.

He thought of that last night in the hospital. It was years ago, but it was always as if it had been only last night. Sanna had fallen asleep, he had been holding her hand. He thought of the last moment. Of the pain that had been pulsating under his skin ever since. He didn't feel it, he just knew that it was there.

He moved away from the wall and looked back at Hämäläinen lying the other side of the glass. Out of the corner of his eye he spotted a movement to his right. Then a woman came into his field of vision and over to the viewing window. She shook her head and compressed her lips. Their eyes met.

'I heard it on TV,' she said.

Joentaa nodded, and the woman turned back to the window.

She said nothing more for a while.

Then she said, barely audibly, 'Heard it on TV. Like so much else about him.'

31

They drove to the TV station. Several police cars were parked right outside the building. The forensics people in their white overalls harmonised with both the snow and the futuristic glass structure rising to the sky behind them.

Westerberg phoned. Sundström phoned. Westerberg shouted over the phone at one of his men and managed to make even tearing someone off a strip sound apathetic. Sundström spoke to Nurmela, who was phoning almost every minute. The investigating team in Helsinki had fixed a press conference for 14.00 hours. Sundström was trying to make it clear to Nurmela that he would not be sitting on the platform himself, he would leave it to his colleagues to mention the close cooperation between Helsinki and Turku.

They entered the glass tower. There was only a doorman sitting behind the glass, and he hardly looked at them as they passed him. The catastrophe had already happened; he didn't seem to be expecting a second one.

The reception area and the cafeteria next to it were empty. Cleared for the scene-of-crime unit. Interviews were being held in a conference room on the first floor. Westerberg led the way to it without interrupting his conversation with his colleague, and did not lower his mobile until the man himself was face to face with him, also putting his own mobile away.

'This just can't be possible,' said Westerberg. He was not shouting any longer, he was speaking in a soft, slow voice.

'What can't be possible?' asked Sundström.

'We have nothing. Nothing at all,' said Westerberg. 'No one has the faintest idea who stabbed Hämäläinen.'

They went on into the room, which was full of people. Police officers sat at tables in conversation with employees of the TV station. Joentaa recognised one of the doormen, the man who had let them in the day before.

'It's like this: in a way this building is a self-enclosed area,' said Westerberg. 'But only in a way.'

'You're talking in riddles,' said Sundström.

'Well, in principle the identity of everyone who comes in is registered, which ought to reduce the circle of people we have to look at.'

'To the few hundred people who work here, you mean?'

'Yes, but even that doesn't cover everything.'

'Ah,' said Sundström.

'Because there were two guided tours of the station building this morning, for the winners of a crossword puzzle competition,' said Westerberg.

'Crossword puzzle competition,' said Sundström.

'So if we begin by considering that an outsider could have done it, and if we then assume that he would hardly have had himself registered here, name and address and all, before going on to attack Hämäläinen, then we suspect that somehow or other he mingled with the group on one of the guided tours and got into the building that way, without our knowledge.'

Sundström nodded. 'And then he stabbed Hämäläinen in the entrance hall and simply walked out again.'

'No,' said Westerberg.

'Really? No?'

'No. Hämäläinen was stabbed in the cafeteria,' said Westerberg. 'To be precise, between the cafeteria and the entrance hall. There's no door between the two, they just merge with each other.'

Sundström looked at Westerberg and suddenly began to laugh. 'Marko, are you taking the piss?'

'No,' said Westerberg.

'You're surely not telling me that no one noticed this TV station's star presenter lying on the floor seriously injured, gasping for breath? That's . . . I mean, there must have been someone in that cafeteria. Behind the counter, for instance.'

'There wasn't anyone behind the counter just at that minute because the girl on duty had gone to the loo. Two women, editors in the newsroom, told us they were drinking coffee at the same time as Hämäläinen, but they only saw him walk away, they didn't see him being attacked.'

Sundström nodded for a while, muttering something by way of agreement. 'Well, well. I see. Yes.'

'I'm as furious about this as you are.'

'You must be joking. See me fall about laughing,' shouted Sundström. The conversations in the room around them died down, and Sundström actually did begin to laugh. 'You point your cameras at everything, and then you miss the best bit, that's the irony of it, it's amazing,' he said. 'Kimmo, take a look at this, see if you get the joke.'

'Calm down, Paavo, and then we can go on,' said Westerberg.

'Right, let's do just that. Where do you get all that laid-back lethargy? Is it yoga or Tai Chi or what?'

'Paavo, let's . . .'

'Look, the most famous man in Finland was stabbed here today, and two other men are dead already, including a man I knew and liked. Are you with me so far?'

Westerberg nodded.

'I'd like to speak to the doormen now, the ones who let in the groups for the guided tours,' said Sundström. 'And to the people who were in those groups. At once. And Kimmo, have another word with the two women who saw Hämäläinen in the cafeteria.'

Westerberg nodded. 'I'll see to it,' he said, and spoke to his colleague, who was still standing there with his mobile in his hand.

'You know, I just can't think of any more jokes,' said Sundström.

Westerberg beckoned Joentaa over. He was standing with two young women who looked horrified, and at the same time elated and excited. Mixed feelings. Like the two boys who had been standing in the forest in Turku on the other side of the police tape, looking at Patrik Laukkanen lying on the ground.

Joentaa shook hands with both the editors and introduced himself. They sat down at one of the tables, and Joentaa asked the question to which he already knew they would reply 'No'.

'You saw nothing at all? Not even a faint indication of someone attacking Kai-Petteri Hämäläinen?'

The two women shook their heads.

'We were still sitting at our table in the cafeteria when . . . Kai-Petteri left. We stayed there and . . .'

'We watched him leave. We were talking about him,' said the other woman.

'Then he was out of sight from where we were sitting, and we stayed there for a few more minutes. We didn't . . . we didn't hear anything. Nothing at all.'

'When we left we went the same way he had, and then we saw him lying on the floor.'

Joentaa nodded. Several minutes. Kai-Petteri Hämäläinen had been lying in the middle of that glass box for several minutes, fighting for his life, and no one had noticed.

'He was lying sort of . . . perfectly peacefully. He looked at us and just nodded.'

'We ran to the doormen, and they called the emergency doctor. And a little while later everyone in the building seemed to know. Suddenly they were all there.'

'Try to concentrate on the people you saw. Was anyone among them who doesn't belong here? Or maybe outside in the park, maybe you saw someone through the windows while everyone was waiting for the emergency doctor . . .'

They shook their heads. 'There wasn't anyone there,' said the younger of the two women. 'First there was no one there, then crowds of people. But no one I specially noticed.'

Her colleague nodded in agreement.

Joentaa thanked them. The two women got to their feet and stood there indecisively, looking around and apparently not sure what to do next. Like most of the people in the room. A curious reversal of circumstances, thought Joentaa. The investigators were asking cogent questions, while the employees of the TV station, who spent their time devising new formats and new ways of presenting life's disasters, had run out of answers.

He thought of Kai-Petteri Hämäläinen and the expression on his face, which was always the same. If he understood the two news editors correctly, it had still been the same even when he was lying on the floor with life-threatening injuries.

He glanced at Sundström, who was heatedly addressing a group of people. Joentaa recognised one of the doormen, and assumed that the rest of the group had been on the two guided tours of the building. Sundström's voice and the suppressed fury in it carried to him. He saw Hämäläinen's assistant standing at one side of the room. Tuula Palonen, if he remembered correctly. She was talking to a grey-haired man of medium height, or rather seemed to be listening as he explained something to her. Joentaa went over to her. 'Excuse me,' he said.

Tuula Palonen turned to him abruptly. 'Can't you see that . . . oh, we . . .'

'Kimmo Joentaa. I was in your editorial offices yesterday with two colleagues.'

'Of course. I'm sorry, we were just . . . this is Raafael Mertaranta, the station's controller.'

'Pleased to meet you,' said Mertaranta, and Joentaa nodded.

'We hear . . . we hear that Kai-Petteri is doing better. That's wonderful,' said Mertaranta.

'The doctors tell us his condition is stable.'

'I'd like to go to the hospital,' said Tuula Palonen. 'But your colleague' – she pointed to Westerberg who was sitting at one of the tables deep in conversation – 'your colleague said everyone who works for the station should be available here.'

Joentaa nodded. 'We've already been to the hospital. No one can speak to him yet anyway. He's still unconscious.'

Tuula Palonen sighed, barely audibly, and Raafael Mertaranta said, 'Do you know when he'll be able to present the show again?'

Joentaa was too baffled to come up with any answer.

'We'll have to find a substitute for now, of course,' said Mertaranta.

Joentaa sought for words. 'Yes,' he said at last.

'They're running a special about Kai on the news today,' said Tuula.

Mertaranta nodded.

'Maybe we can transmit a longer version of the special on our own programme,' said Tuula.

Mertaranta thought for a while, and then said. 'Good idea.'

There was a short silence, and Mertaranta cast Joentaa a glance that he couldn't interpret.

'Please don't misunderstand us, but we have to make sure the screen doesn't stay blank. And when Kai is doing better, of course we'll be very relieved, and . . .'

Joentaa nodded.

'. . . and I can tell you something . . .' said Mertaranta.

Joentaa waited, thinking of Larissa and that he wanted to call her and hear her voice.

'. . . that's what Kai-Petteri himself would want. You know what Kai-Petteri would most like to do once he has his strength back?'

Has his strength back, thought Joentaa, remembering the body lying motionless with tubes inserted into it, and Mertaranta said, 'What he'd most like to do is interview himself.'

32

Gliding over the snow as if on rails.

Setting the world to rights.

'That's what you said the last time we talked. I remember it,' says the distant voice. 'Is there a special reason why you think of it now? Do you have some particular picture in your mind's eye?'

A particular picture . . .

'It's always the same one,' she says.

The bus turns into the narrow street. She lives at the end of it, with the grey lake to the left, the white football pitch to the right.

The telephone feels light in her hand.

'I'm seeing someone in a moment. Would you like to bring our next appointment forward? According to my diary we're not due to meet again until next week,' he says.

The grey lake where Ilmari used to swim.

'I can find time this evening,' he says.

The white football pitch where Veikko used to play.

'This evening at 18.30 hours? I'll square the fee, we can manage that,' he says.

The man lying on the floor. The questioning look in his eyes as he stares into the void. She stands on the edge, waiting. She doesn't know what she's waiting for.

She thinks of the letter that came with this morning's post. She stared at the sender's name for a long time. A friendly letter, a warm invitation, and two train tickets enclosed. There and back. Who can describe it if she can't?

'We'll talk about the picture you have in your mind's eye this evening,' he says.

An empty hall. The man lies on the floor, looking up. She follows the direction of his eyes. She can see the sky above a glass ceiling. She stands at the edge waiting for the sky to fall in.

But it doesn't.

Nothing happens.

'I'm making a note of it now: 18.30 hours. Are you still there?'

A stranger listens to her, listens to her silence.

33

Early in the evening the doctor phoned and said Kai-Petteri Hämäläinen was conscious and able to answer questions. They drove to the hospital.

Hämäläinen was lying motionless on the bed, surrounded by tubes and other apparatus, and nodded to them as they came in. 'The gentlemen from the police,' he murmured, and seemed to smile. He sat a little way up and looked relieved. Free of the fear of death, Joentaa suspected, and Westerberg began asking questions. Hämäläinen's quiet, surprising answers fell slowly into the silence, deepening it.

'Nothing?' said Sundström. 'You saw nothing at all? You didn't notice anything?'

'A shadow,' said Hämäläinen.

'A shadow?'

'I remember leaving the cafeteria and making for the lifts. I . . . I was trying to remember the name of that forensic pathologist, and I could only remember his son's name.'

'His son's name?' said Westerberg.

'Yes, it was Kalle. The forensic pathologist told me he was going to have a little boy and they would call him Kalle. I remembered it, and after that I saw a shadow, and then . . .'

'Yes?' asked Sundström.

'. . . then everything seemed very slow. I felt I was hovering, and I felt a pain in my back – as if something had grazed me or stabbed me.'

They waited.

'A shadow. And then that pain. And then I was out of there, being carried. Then I woke up here.'

They waited, but Kai-Petteri Hämäläinen had told them all he knew.

'That's impossible,' said Sundström.

Westerberg turned to look at him.

'Impossible,' Sundström repeated.

Hämäläinen nodded, and Joentaa thought again that he seemed different.

'I wish I could help you,' he said.

'Did you see anything earlier?' asked Sundström. 'When you came down and into the cafeteria? Or even before that, when you came into the building?'

Hämäläinen thought for a while, then shook his head.

'Someone or other who caught your attention? Someone who didn't belong in the TV station. Did you feel you were being watched?'

'No,' said Hämäläinen. 'Nothing at all. Naturally, there were people around when I arrived, and no doubt when I went to the cafeteria, but I didn't notice anything.'

Silence again.

'Isn't there . . . hasn't anyone . . . do you have no idea who did it?' asked Hämäläinen.

'I'm afraid not, no,' said Westerberg.

'But someone must have seen something.'

'We suspect that your attacker came into the building with a group going on a guided tour through the various editorial departments,' said Westerberg.

'Of course it's possible that it was someone who works there,' added Sundström.

Hämäläinen lay motionless and said nothing for a while. Then he said, 'What's going on, anyway? Why was I . . .?'

Westerberg tried to find words, and Sundström said, 'We don't know.'

'But it must . . . it must be something to do with that interview. The interview I did with Mäkelä and the forensic pathologist.'

Sundström did not reply, Westerberg did not reply, and Joentaa thought that Hämäläinen was stating the obvious.

'But what did we do, dammit?' said Hämäläinen. 'There was nothing out of the ordinary.'

Silence again.

'It was a perfectly normal interview. I've done hundreds of them,' said Hämäläinen. 'There was nothing special about it. A forensic pathologist talking about his everyday life, a puppet-maker describing his working methods. That was all.'

'We don't know what the background is. It's all the more

important for you to remember every detail of today's incident. You must . . . forgive me, but you must have noticed something.'

'A shadow,' said Hämäläinen. 'As I said.'

'A shadow's not enough,' said Sundström.

'I know.'

Behind them the door was opened. The woman who had been standing beside Kimmo at the viewing window in the morning, looking at the unconscious Hämäläinen, appeared in the doorway.

'Irene,' said Hämäläinen.

Irene Hämäläinen moved hesitantly into the room.

'It's not so bad,' said Hämäläinen quietly, but with the confident note in his voice that was his trademark as a presenter. 'Looks worse than it is.'

The woman nodded.

'Does it look bad, by the way? I'm feeling pretty good,' said Hämäläinen.

The woman nodded to them and went up to the bed.

'Where are those imps of ours?' asked Hämäläinen.

'With Mariella. They're in good spirits,' she said. Her voice sounded cracked, but also strong.

'That's good,' said Hämäläinen.

'Well . . . we'll be on our way,' said Sundström, getting to his feet. Halfway to the door, he turned back. 'The doctors say you'll be here for a few more days. There are police officers on duty to keep this ward secure. Only your wife and the doctors treating you have access. And so do we, of course.'

Hämäläinen nodded.

'We'll discuss everything else next time,' said Sundström.

Hämäläinen nodded again and looked at his wife, and Joentaa thought once more that he seemed different.

Exhausted. Marked by his experience. Relieved. Liberated.

Irene Hämäläinen sat down on the chair where Sundström

had been sitting. Joentaa turned away and thought of Kai-Petteri Hämäläinen, the expression on his face that was always the same, the smile when he said goodbye and his guests left the stage, and he thought:

Liberated, but not from the fear of death.

Liberated from the oppressive sense of being immortal.

34

The motionless, flickering picture. Always the same. 18.30 hours. She has only a few minutes to wait. Then she is sitting opposite him, saying no when he asks her if anything in particular has happened.

'It's unusual for you to call. You've never called in between our sessions before,' he says.

She nods.

'Have you been to see Rauna?' he asks.

She nods.

'How's she doing?'

'All right,' she says.

He does not reply, but puts his head on one side and looks through the window into the darkness.

'You said something about a picture . . .'

'No,' she says.

'No?'

'No. You said something about a picture, and I said I see one, always the same picture.'

'You're right. That's how it was,' he says.

She nods.

'Would you like to talk about the picture?'

'No,' she says.

'What would you like to talk about?'

'About Little My.'

He says nothing, and she smiles. She has succeeded in surprising him. She can see that from looking at him, and she likes it.

'Right,' he says. 'Tell me about her.'

'Not about her, about me,' she says.

'About you, then. Tell me about yourself.'

'I was Little My on the day I met Ilmari. I was working in Moomin World on the beach in Naantali. It's a children's theme park. The Moomin family.'

'I know,' he says. 'I've been there.'

'Do you have . . . children?'

'A son.'

'You have a son?' she says. 'How . . . how old is he?'

'Seven.'

She looks at him for a long time, and after a while she realises that she is trying to see from his face whether he is telling the truth. She looks away.

'I didn't know you had children,' she says.

'Only him. My son, Sami.'

'Why did you never say so?'

'You're the only one of my women patients who knows,' he says. 'It's not usual for me to talk about myself during sessions. So you were working at Moomin World?'

'Yes . . . yes, I was being Little My. The red-haired little girl. In the vacation before I began my training I'd been in a theatrical company engaged for Moomin World. I was much too big for Little My, but because of my red hair I got the part.'

'Did you enjoy it?'

'Very much. It was hot in the costume, but in the evening I always jumped straight into the water, and that was . . .'

'Yes?'

'That was . . . wonderful.'

He does not reply.

'It was so good that I can hardly believe it really happened.'

'And that was when you met Ilmari?'

'Yes, he was there with one of his groups. As you know, he looked after children with learning difficulties. Autistic kids.'

'Yes.'

'The children were . . . unusual. I didn't know that before. I wanted to give them some fun, and they just didn't react.'

He nods.

'They weren't friendly, they weren't unfriendly, it was as if they weren't there at all.'

He nods.

'The children were the way I feel now,' she says.

'Describe what you feel more closely.'

'I don't want to. I want to talk about Ilmari.'

'Then tell me about Ilmari.'

'He was looking after the children. He came to Moomin World with them, and he was the only one in the group who laughed. At my jokes. Well, I was playing Little My, so I had to be funny. Then they left. They went on somewhere else, and I had to see to the other children. That evening I'd taken off my costume, and there was Ilmari suddenly standing beside me, saying Little My was bigger than he'd thought.'

He has put his head on one side again. Not far. He probably doesn't even know he does that.

'Next day he was there again. And the day after that. We swam together. That was always the best part of it for me. Washing the sweat off my body in the evening.'

His head tilts to the other side.

'Yes, that was how it began.'

'And some time you will have to talk about how it ended,' he says.

His head is bolt upright now.

'So that you can begin again,' he says.

'I wonder who's being Little My at the theme park now,' she says.

He looks past her, glancing at the time.

35

Sundström and Kimmo Joentaa stayed in Helsinki overnight. They sat opposite each other in the empty hotel lobby and talked on their mobiles. Sundström called Petri Grönholm. Joentaa called Tuomas Heinonen. They exchanged notes on the day's events and the results of the investigations, without coming any closer to an explanation.

Joentaa thought of Patrik Laukkanen lying lifeless in the snow. An image with no relation to reality. He closed his eyes and thought there could be no explanation. Presumably it was simple enough: there was no explanation for images that didn't relate to reality. Or the explanation existed only on the level of a new reality that had created the picture.

He opened his eyes and saw that Sundström was staring at him. 'Everything okay?' he asked.

Joentaa nodded. 'I just had a . . . a rather way-out idea,' he said.

'Ah,' said Sundström, and called another number.

Joentaa's thoughts were wandering again as Sundström's voice assumed a different note. He was talking to Nurmela. Acquainting him with the present state of the investigation in a strictly objective tone. From time to time he winked at Joentaa, probably to show that he was putting on such airs of importance and gravity only for the moment and would soon feel like cracking jokes again.

Joentaa thought of Larissa.

And the little tree in the dark.

Sundström ended his conversation with Nurmela and said, 'What a bloody stupid mess. People just don't notice what goes on around them these days. Not one of those idiots on the guided tours has been able to give us anything useful so far.'

Joentaa nodded.

'And the TV people looking after the groups were pretty half-hearted about taking their personal details. Simply registered the group *as* a group at reception, and that was it. Anyone could have joined it. If we're looking for an outsider, he could easily have come in with the groups for the tours, and presumably marched out again in the chaos when Hämäläinen was seen lying there on the floor.'

'You can hardly plan a thing like that in advance,' said Joentaa.

Sundström stared at him.

'Yes, it sounds good, but it couldn't be planned,' said Joentaa. 'It's pure chance that there's no one in that hall. The murderer is taking enormous risks. He attacks Patrik in the middle of the day, he attacks Harri Mäkelä out in the road. And Hämäläinen in a vast glass tower full of people.'

'I don't know what you're on about. It worked very well for him,' said Sundström.

'Like I said, it sounds conclusive, but it can't be the result of any deliberate planning,' said Joentaa. 'And something else surprises me too.'

'Which is?' asked Sundström.

'That Hämäläinen's still alive.'

Sundström nodded.

'The murderer obviously wasn't disturbed. So why didn't he . . . well, go ahead and finish the job?' said Joentaa.

Sundström's mobile rang. He took the call, immediately making a face. Probably Nurmela again. Sundström took pains to sound self-controlled, and reported on the planned course of inquiries for tomorrow. 'Yes,' he said after a while. 'Of course. As you are aware, I have been doing work of this nature for several years. Yes. That's what I said. I really could not care less what you think about it.'

Joentaa picked up his mobile and rang his home number. He got the manufacturer's standard message. Larissa wasn't there, or she was asleep, or she just wasn't answering the phone. He tried again. 'I'll be in touch tomorrow,' he said finally, and cut the connection.

Sundström too had ended his conversation. He was muttering curses to himself. Then he abruptly leaned back, suddenly looked relaxed, and said that he and Marko Westerberg had already settled where Hämäläinen should go.

Joentaa looked at him enquiringly.

'Hämäläinen has to get away from here. If something else happens to him we might as well all pack our bags and emigrate.'

Joentaa nodded.

'As soon as he's able to leave the hospital we're taking him to North Finland. Away from the scene here. His family can go with him. There are two officers on security duty at Hämäläinen's house already, making sure nothing happens to his wife and daughters.'

'Have you discussed this with him?' asked Joentaa.

'Discussed what with whom?'

'Hämäläinen. About spiriting him off to North Finland.'

'There's nothing to discuss,' said Sundström. 'Now, tell me about that idea of yours.'

'Hm?'

'Your outlandish idea. Would you care to pass it on?'

'Er . . .'

'You do remember, don't you? You were saying something about a way-out idea.'

'Yes. I don't know if I can put it into words.'

'God help us,' said Sundström.

'I was . . . I was thinking of Patrik. And how we found him. I thought right away there was something wrong. A picture that didn't fit with the reality.'

Sundström looked at him hard.

'Do you see what I mean?' asked Joentaa.

'I'm trying my best,' said Sundström.

'The key is that TV programme. The discussion between the three of them,' said Joentaa.

Sundström did not respond.

'I don't think we're going to find a rational motive, and that's why nothing we're doing at the moment gets us anywhere.'

Sundström looked past him and seemed to be focusing on a distant point.

'I have the DVD with me,' said Joentaa. 'In my rucksack. I could watch the interview again.'

'Do that,' said Sundström, standing up. 'See you tomorrow morning. Breakfast at seven. Press conference at eleven. Nurmela insists that I'm to sit on the platform this time. After that it's our date with the Institute of Criminal Technology, among other things about the tread of the tyres. But our colleague at the Institute doesn't hold out much hope of results there. With a little luck it may narrow the circle of suspects to a few thousand. Sleep well. And don't drink too much.' Sundström turned away. 'Or at least not so much that people will notice in the morning,' he murmured as he left.

'Sleep well,' said Joentaa, but Sundström was already out of earshot. Joentaa saw him get into the lift. The doors closed, and Joentaa sat in the silence and muted light of the lobby. Now and then members of the hotel staff hurried by. A young woman was standing at the reception desk bending over some papers. He thought of the DVD in his rucksack.

'Excuse me,' he called to the woman.

She looked up. 'Can I help you?'

'Do you have a DVD player available? Or a laptop would do.'

'Is the TV programme that bad?' she asked.

'Er . . . no. It's just that I have to watch a DVD.'

'Or we have PAY-TV, if you . . .'

'It's a particular DVD I need to watch,' Joentaa said. 'Now.'

The woman shook her head, and Joentaa stood up, went over to the reception desk and took his police ID out of his trouser pocket. 'I'm a police officer, and you would be doing me a great service,' he said.

The woman looked at his ID first with a wry smile, then frowning. 'Well, of course that's no problem,' she said. 'There's an Internet terminal next to the breakfast room, with CD drives. I'll have to unlock the door for you; we lock it all up overnight.'

'That would be kind,' said Joentaa.

The woman went ahead, opened the door, and Joentaa thanked her. The flat screens and computers were lined up in front of unsuitable high bar stools. Joentaa sat down at a computer a little way to one side of the others, turned it on and put the DVD in the drive. The theme music began, and a dynamic female voice announced the guests on the show that evening. For the first time Joentaa listened carefully to what she was saying about them, Patrik Laukkanen and Harri Mäkelä. The lords of death. Then the picture of Kai-Petteri

Hämäläinen came up, sitting at his desk. And to friendly applause Patrik Laukkanen came on stage. Laukkanen, talking about his work. Entertaining, witty, Heinonen and Grönholm had said, and they were right.

This was a different Laukkanen. A Laukkanen well aware of the importance of the moment and the public nature of his appearance. It was a barely perceptible change, although you couldn't miss it, and it was of no significance. Just an ordinary observation. Someone appearing in public changed, reverting to his usual self later.

Joentaa heard Laukkanen's voice, that imperceptibly changed voice. The pictures on the screen flickered, the voices merged, and Joentaa stopped the disk, went back to the beginning and ran it again and again.

Out of the corner of his eye he saw the young woman from reception coming to the doorway from time to time, apparently asking him something. He did not react. He didn't hear what she was saying. She disappeared and returned after a while. Then she disappeared again.

Laukkanen talked. Mäkelä talked. Hämäläinen steered the conversation. Cloths were raised and lowered again. The audience clapped. A comic came on stage. Joentaa went back to the beginning of the disk and watched the recording yet again. There was an idea in there that he couldn't pinpoint.

The woman from reception was standing beside him, talking to him. A cloth was raised, then lowered again.

'Stop,' said Joentaa.

The woman retreated.

Joentaa pressed the Pause key.

'I'd be grateful if you could . . .' the woman began.

'Stop,' said Joentaa, and he looked at the frozen picture flickering slightly on the screen.

36

Kai-Petteri Hämäläinen lay on his back. First the day and then the night seeped away around him.

The young doctor or the nurses came in to check up on his condition. They smiled gently and looked at him as if he were a child.

Irene sat beside his bed, holding his hand, was silent for a long time, said the twins sent him their regards.

'Sounds kind of formal,' he said.

'You know what I mean,' she said.

From time to time one of the smiling nurses topped up the tubes surrounding him with fluids, and he asked Irene if she remembered Niskanen.

'The cross-country distance skier?'

He nodded.

'Of course,' she said.

'Do you know what he's doing these days?'

'How do you mean?' asked Irene.

'I wondered what's become of him.'

Irene said no, and went home. To the twins and her sister Mariella, who was being kind enough to look after the girls.

Sitting at a table. Drinking coffee. Walking down a corridor. A shadow, a stabbing feeling. A numb, damp sensation in his lower body. Pain turning in on him.

Irene had kissed him quickly on the mouth before she went, and the doctor checked the various items of apparatus. 'Sleep well,' he said finally.

'You too,' said Hämäläinen.

A young nurse emptied the bedpan, an older nurse checked his dressings.

He was not to do anything but lie on his back, the doctor had told him earlier that day, if possible without shifting at all to right or left.

He had lain on his back without moving, and asked the doctor checking the apparatus whether he remembered Niskanen.

'The cross-country skier?' the doctor had asked.

'Yes,' he said.

'Yes, of course,' the doctor had replied.

'Do you know what he's doing these days?'

The doctor didn't know.

He wondered which of the recorded programmes they had run. At 22.00 hours. Or maybe not until 22.15, if the attack on him had been a major item on tonight's news. As he suspected, as he strongly suspected it had. Maybe they had ended with his interview with Niskanen. It was long enough ago to bear repeating.

In neighbouring rooms people were shouting. Loud enough for him to hear them. He saw nurses and doctors scurrying past his window. First in one direction, then in another. He heard discussions going on, but he couldn't concentrate on the words. The words hovered above him.

'There's a lot going on today,' said the younger nurse, topping up one of the tubes.

'Is it night yet?' he asked.

'More like early morning. Three o'clock.'

He asked her if she could remember Niskanen the cross-country skier.

'Yes,' she said. 'Everyone knows his name.'

'Do you know . . .' he began.

'Yes?'

'Oh, never mind,' he said.

37

Kimmo Joentaa took the DVD out of the drive, switched off the computer, left the receptionist there and went to his room. He dropped on to the smooth white bed and thought for a while.

He hesitated briefly, then called Enquiries, but he got nowhere with his question. He took the list containing the phone numbers of the central investigators out of his rucksack. There were three numbers by Westerberg's name: office, mobile and home. He tried the home number.

After a few seconds Westerberg picked up the phone, sounding considerably more alert than during the day. Joentaa explained what it was about.

'Vaasara. The puppet-maker's assistant?' asked Westerberg.

'Exactly. Do you have his number? He lived with Mäkelä, but there's no entry in the phone book under either name.'

'Hm,' said Westerberg. 'Just a moment.'

Joentaa heard a woman's voice in the distance, and a rustling, and Westerberg murmured something not meant for him. Then he was back on the line. 'Got it,' he said.

'Good.'

'Hm. Ready to write it down?'

Joentaa got out a pen and noted down the number that Westerberg dictated to him. 'Thank you,' he said.

'You're welcome. Listen, Kimmo, why . . .'

'See you tomorrow,' said Joentaa, and broke the connection. There was no time to formulate his idea for Westerberg when it still eluded Joentaa himself.

He rang the number on the piece of paper and waited. He let the phone ring for several minutes, until Vaasara picked it up.

'Yes . . . hello?'

'Kimmo Joentaa from the Turku CID. I came to see you with two of my colleagues.'

'Yes . . .'

'I have to ask you something, something that strikes me as important, that's why I'm ringing so late at night.'

'Yes . . .'

'It's about the puppets.'

'Yes . . .'

'About the process of making them. What does a puppet-maker use as a model?'

'As a model?'

'Yes.'

'I . . . excuse me, but I . . .'

'What serves you as the model? You make exact copies. So what are they modelled on?'

'Well . . .' said Vaasara.

'Well?'

'Various things. It also depends on the way you go about making a particular puppet.'

'Meaning?'

'A puppet-maker commissioned to provide copies of dead bodies is well trained in human anatomy, of course. He needs that training for making other . . . well, normal puppets. And for copying corpses we use various sources. For instance, we've often used police literature. There are textbooks for trainees at police colleges, showing different kinds of deaths in great detail . . .'

Joentaa nodded.

'We work with the Forensic Institute in Helsinki, and the Faculty of Medicine at the university . . . we attend autopsies, and besides his craft training Harri also had diplomas in chemistry and biology, he . . . he was brilliant.'

Joentaa nodded. 'I meant something else,' he said.

'What?' asked Vaasara.

'Is it possible that someone related to a dead person could recognise that person, the one he's mourning for, in one of your puppets?'

Vaasara said nothing.

'Do you understand?' asked Joentaa.

'I think so, yes.'

'Well?'

'That's not possible,' said Vaasara.

'Why not?'

'We don't copy real dead people,' said Vaasara.

'But you use photos as models. Photos from police text-books, for instance.'

'Of course,' said Vaasara.

'Well then?'

'We use photos, yes. Harri more than me. Harri had whole data banks of such photographs, the Internet is full of them. Drowned bodies. People killed in various different ways, shot, run over, mutilated. Corpses in progressive stages of decomposition.'

'Then we agree,' said Joentaa.

'No,' said Vaasara. 'We use photos and copies just as we use our knowledge of chemical and biological processes and above all, of course, our craft skills to make puppets. Not real people.'

'Meaning?'

'Meaning that the real model, if there is one, doesn't look like the puppet that is our end product.'

Joentaa closed his eyes and felt the vague, outlandish idea take ever more concrete shape the longer Vaasara tried to convince him of its impossibility. Vaasara did not sound upset or offended, he was answering the questions calmly, in a drowsily abstracted way, and did not seem to understand what Joentaa was telling him.

'The faces,' said Joentaa.

'Faces?' asked Vaasara.

'The puppets' faces. Who is used as a model?'

'Which faces did you say?'

'The faces of the puppets,' said Joentaa.

'Oh, the puppets don't have any faces. Usually they're just blank surfaces, because when we make puppets for films, their heads aren't shown.'

'Sometimes you see the heads.'

'Yes, true, you do. But as a rule then they're unrecognisable . . . just raw flesh, or scraps of skin, or bloated . . .'

'That's not quite accurate,' said Joentaa.

'Hm . . . well, sometimes there *are* real faces, but they're the faces of the actors. We even made one of a dead Hollywood star once. It was used as a running gag in some silly comedy.'

'No, what I mean is the puppets in that talk show with Hämäläinen . . . they have faces.'

'Hm . . . no, I don't think so,' said Vaasara.

'Yes, for instance the victim of that air crash. The puppet's face was even shown in close-up for a few seconds.'

'Air crash?'

'Didn't you see the programme?'

'No, I was in the States working on a project at the time.'

'Well, you see the face . . .'

'You say an air crash; I don't think there'd be much of anyone's face left after that.'

'You see the face. Of course it's . . . well, badly injured, and . . .'

'Like I said, a mass of flesh with bloody streaks all over it, bloated . . . certainly unrecognisable. Maybe that one was modelled on Harri himself.'

'What do you mean?'

'Sometimes Harri gave the puppets his own face when he was making them. For – well, for fun.'

Vaasara sounded sad as he said that, and Joentaa felt exhausted. 'The face I'm talking about wasn't Harri Mäkelä's face,' he said.

'I'm only saying that sometimes Harri . . .' Vaasara began.

'No. I don't think we're getting anywhere,' said Joentaa.

'Well . . .'

'Thank you very much.'

'Well . . .' said Vaasara.

Joentaa ended the call.

He put his mobile down on his bedside table and sat on the bed for some time.

He thought of the face he had seen.

The face of a dead man who had no face.

The face of a dead man who wasn't dead.

He thought of the blonde woman, the stranger in his house, and didn't understand why he missed her.

After a while he closed his eyes, and seconds later fell into a sleep as vague as the pain and dizziness in his head.

29 December

38

Kimmo Joentaa woke up shivering and with a sense of knowing what he wanted to do next. He went down to the breakfast room. Sundström was sitting, lost in thought, in front of a cup of coffee and a bowl of cornflakes.

'Good morning,' said Joentaa, sitting down beside him.

'Morning,' said Sundström.

'I'd like us to approach this investigation from a new angle,' said Joentaa.

Sundström looked up.

'I don't think there's any rational motive. I think it's a motive by association,' said Joentaa. 'Something to do with that TV programme.'

'Go on,' said Sundström.

'I think the murderer was . . . was traumatised by the programme, felt it was some kind of attack on his peace of mind. That would explain the fury that seems to be behind the whole thing.'

He looked for signs of mockery or scepticism in Sundström's eyes, but found none.

'I still don't know how it all hangs together, but it must have something to do with those puppets and the way they were discussed on the show.'

'Puppets, Kimmo, only puppets.'

'Yes, but not for one viewer. Let's suppose that one viewer saw something else. Perhaps someone close to him, and he had lost that person and was mourning.'

For a long time Sundström said nothing. After a while he

began to eat his cornflakes. Then he put his spoon down and said, 'Funny idea.'

'I know,' said Joentaa. 'But I think it's right.'

'You think.'

'I watched the DVD again last night. And after that I phoned Vaasara. Mäkelä's assistant.'

'And?'

'He thought it was an outlandish idea.'

'Ah.'

'All the same . . .'

'Kimmo, I watched the programme myself, I know those puppets were only dummies. Corpses in a film. Props. Made of plastic.'

'You don't understand what I'm getting at.'

'Not entirely.'

'I'd like to look at the data banks of photos that Mäkelä built up,' said Joentaa.

'Why?'

'Vaasara said he had collected a lot of photos for research.'

'Yes, yes, but why do you want to look at them?'

'I don't know.'

Sundström looked down at his cornflakes again. 'That's a typical Kimmo Joentaa reason – "I don't know".'

'You yourself say that the interview plays a key part. And the puppets are at the centre of the interview.'

'Yes, I'm with you so far, but I don't understand your theory.'

'Do you have a better one?'

'At the moment I don't have any theory at all.'

'Then in that case . . .'

'Which of course will send me off to talk to the press in tearing good spirits. I'll probably have to spend the whole morning preparing for that ridiculous conference.'

Kimmo got to his feet. 'See you later. I'm off.'

'Kimmo, wait a minute . . .'

Joentaa walked quickly through the breakfast room to the entrance hall. When he turned round once more, he saw Sundström shaking his head as he contemplated his cornflakes.

He walked on through the hall, thinking about Sundström, who had seemed curiously passive since the attack on Hämäläinen, and for the first time since Joentaa had been working with him appeared to find that a situation was getting him down. Presumably his unique brand of humour had gone AWOL, and he had to rediscover it before he could operate with his usual efficiency.

On reaching the way out of the hotel Joentaa stopped, and on impulse took his mobile out of his coat pocket. He called his own number, and after a few seconds heard a strange voice, but it didn't sound like the standard announcement on the answering machine, and indeed it did not consist of the usual wording.

'Er . . . hello?'

'Yes, what is it?'

'Who . . . who's that speaking?'

'I think I'm the one who should be asking you.'

'Larissa?'

'No.'

'My name is Joentaa, and the telephone you're holding at this minute belongs to me.'

'Oh, it's you.'

'That's right. And I'd like to speak to Larissa.'

'She's not here.'

'Ah. And who are you?'

'Jennifer. A colleague of hers.'

'Is . . . is Larissa . . .'

'She's in the bathroom. I came to pick her up because she has such a long walk to the bus stop.'

'I see.'

'She was late yesterday. That's rather frowned upon.'

'Ah . . . well, it's good that you're picking her up.'

'Would you like her to call you back?'

'That would be nice.'

'Goodbye, then.'

'Er . . . just a moment . . .'

But Jennifer or whoever it was had cut the connection, and Kimmo Joentaa stood there for a while with his mobile in his hand. Then he put it away in his coat pocket and went out into the winter sunlight.

39

Pellervo Halonen, the head of the Home, waves, and Rauna turns in the child seat and waves back. 'Byeeee!' she calls, although Pellervo Halonen can't hear her.

On the way her neighbour Aapeli sits in the back of the car and tells Rauna stories. Rauna laughs almost the whole time. She is glad that Aapeli is with them. He was coming towards her this morning just as she was about to drive away. Aapeli said good morning and smiled, and she saw the sadness in his eyes and asked if he'd like to come too.

'Where to?'

'Moomin World. In Naantali.'

'The children's theme park?'

She nodded.

'Just the two of us?' Aapeli asked.

'And Rauna,' she replied. 'A friend, a little girl, we'll be fetching her.'

Aapeli stood there for a while in the swirling snowflakes thinking about it, then he nodded and went straight to the car with her instead of back indoors.

Now Aapeli is telling stories, and Rauna is laughing, and she glides over the snow as if on rails, and the world is set to rights.

Rauna asks how he knows all these stories, and Aapeli tells her they are the stories he can't tell his grandchildren because his children never come to visit.

'Why not?' asks Rauna.

'I think they don't have time,' says Aapeli.

'Why don't they have time?' asks Rauna.

'Because they have to work a lot, and they don't live near here.'

'Why don't they live near here?' asks Rauna

When they reach Naantali, the wooden houses are swathed in white, the restaurants are closed, and the sea is frozen. They go along the broad landing stage, and Aapeli says, 'Is Moomin World open in winter?'

She stops and looks at him.

'I was only thinking it's really much too cold for it now.'

They walk on to the end of the landing stage, and along the woodland path on the island until the large, fenced terrain of the park begins. The little ticket booths are unoccupied, the windows have blinds down over them.

'You're right, Aapeli,' she says.

'What a pity,' says Rauna.

'I ought to have remembered that it was always closed in winter,' she says.

Aapeli has gone a few steps ahead. 'Funnily enough the gates are wide open,' he calls back.

'So they are,' she says.

The ticket booths are closed, but the broad gates through which you enter the world of the Moomins are open.

'Let's just go on, then,' says Aapeli.

Rauna runs off, and she hesitates. She has always been afraid of doing something that's not allowed. Even if unintentionally.

'Come on,' calls Aapeli, and she thinks she has never seen him happier. Rauna takes Aapeli's hand, and she gives herself a little shake and follows the two of them.

They run around on a deserted island, and hear a recurrent knocking sound. At regular intervals. Men are calling to each other, saying something that she can't make out.

'They're doing renovation work here, that's why the entrance was open,' says Aapeli. They stop on the hill and see the blue wooden tower where the Moomins live. A man is standing on a ladder, banging at the red roof with a hammer. Another man is standing down below, giving instructions. The two men don't notice them at all as they pass.

'The bathing beach is further on,' she says. 'And if we keep left we'll come to Moominpappa's ship.'

'Super, I want to go there,' says Rauna.

'So do I,' says Aapeli.

The two of them go ahead, although they don't know the way, and she follows them, thinking of the summer when she worked here. It is not a memory but a sequence of elusive images.

She is Little My.

Ilmari is a stranger.

And Veikko isn't born yet.

The sensation of cold water on her skin in the sunny evenings.

'Left and up the steps,' she calls to Rauna and Aapeli.

She would have liked to bring Veikko here. Next summer. When Moomin World is open again.

'The lions go away on the ship,' calls Rauna. She is standing up on deck, turning the ship's wheel wildly in all directions.

'And that man with the beard isn't the captain, I'm the captain.'

'I'll be cabin boy,' says Aapeli.

She stands down below, craning her neck to see the two of them.

'Coming up?' calls Rauna.

Above her the grey sky. It drops away from the loose threads holding it. Ice floes crunch and break up on the water.

'Coming up with us?' calls Rauna.

Rauna's voice, and an image in her mind. Rauna's eyes. They fill her field of vision entirely. Rauna's eyes in the dark. 'Has the sky fallen down?' That's Rauna's voice, she feels her lips shaking and she would like to reach for her, touch her, but she can't move.

She opens her eyes and feels Rauna's cheek on her arm. 'Coming up with us?' she whispers.

'This is a great ship,' says Aapeli, her neighbour of many years whom she has really come to know only today.

'Anywhere you want to go,' she says.

'To the bathing beach,' says Rauna. 'Do you think we'll be able to walk on the water?'

40

Westerberg had already gone to the TV station, but a friendly colleague saw to getting all the photos on the hard disk of Harri Mäkelä's computer copied within minutes and placed at Joentaa's disposal.

Joentaa sat alone in a large, overheated room in front of a screen in a long row of obviously new computers, looking at a silently laughing Harri Mäkelä with an arm round a friend's shoulder. One of many private photos. Mäkelä was laughing in almost all of them, showing a self-confident, attractive smile.

It took him some time to understand the principle on which Mäkelä had arranged his photo archives. But then a simple pattern emerged. One set of the pictures that he was looking for had been assembled by Mäkelä in a folder called 'CorpsesForDummies'. Joentaa opened several of the files and brought up the pictures. His shivering fit came back.

As a rule the pictures had been taken at the scene of accidents. Accidents involving cycles, motorbikes, cars, helicopters, aircraft parts. Firefighting teams bending over the dead, paramedics spreading blankets over bodies.

Sometimes it took Joentaa several minutes to find the element in the picture that, as the puppet-maker saw it, qualified it for the 'CorpsesForDummies' folder. For instance, a severed human leg lying in undergrowth next to the wrecked fuselage of an aircraft. The photos seemed to have been taken by photographers from all over the world: some from Finland, but others from deserts and the tropics. Many appeared to have been taken in America, and there were hundreds of them.

The lords of death, thought Joentaa.

He let the pictures run, and wondered how they were going to help him understand the death of Mäkelä, the death of Patrik Laukkanen, and the attack on Hämäläinen.

A conversation about puppets was the peg that held all three together. And the pictures he was seeing had given Mäkelä ideas and an understanding of dead bodies, enabling him to make realistic models of the dead.

Realistic fiction. The longer he looked at the pictures, the more dubious the theories he was developing seemed. Of the hundreds of thousands of viewers who had watched the programme, most had surely had to come to terms with the death of someone close to them. Why should one of them take it personally when all the others had simply been entertained? Mäkelä had shown three puppets, and he had explained what kind of cinematic deaths they had suffered, or were going to suffer – the victim of an air crash, the victim of a train disaster, the victim of a fire on a fairground ghost train. Joentaa wondered why he was the only one to find the whole idea tasteless. He and Larissa, or whatever her name was.

And he wondered whether, for that very reason, his judgement had gone astray and he was developing erroneous theories that led nowhere. Puppets, Kimmo, only puppets. Sundström was quite right.

He looked at the photos with a queasy sensation in his stomach, and couldn't understand now what he had expected them to tell him. Photos clearly classified. A macabre slide show. That was all.

He himself had seen similar pictures in the course of his training. So that he would be prepared, and would acquire the necessary knowledge. Just like Mäkelä, who had put them on file and studied them in order to do his job to the best of his ability.

Photos clearly classified . . . every sub-folder of the main 'CorpsesForDummies' category was labelled with sequences of letters and numbers that Joentaa did not at first understand: *150402NL/AMS*, and *110300US/NY*. When he came upon *201199FIN/TAM* he got the idea. Dates, countries, cities. On 20 November 1999 there had obviously been a train accident in Tampere. Mäkelä had stored four pictures of it in his sub-folder. An unnaturally flat body lying on its back beside a wrecked dining car.

He wondered how Mäkelä had been able to build up this extensive archive. The Internet is full of them, Vaasara had said. Three puppets. Air crash, train crash, funfair accident. Spectacular events. Linked to days, years and locations.

'Here, for you,' said a voice behind him.

Joentaa jumped.

'Sorry,' said his police colleague, handing him a stack of CDs. 'I've copied all those photos in case you need them in Turku.'

'Thanks, that's a great help,' said Joentaa.

His colleague nodded. 'The press conference is about to begin. I'm going down there myself.'

Joentaa switched off the computer, took the CDs and placed them on the table. He probably wouldn't need to look at the photos again. He'd had another outlandish idea.

The puppets would have to help him.

The puppets and the deadly events to which they owed their existence.

41

Irene. And the imps. And the young doctor whose name he now knew: Valtteri Muksanen.

Funny sort of name. Funny sort of day.

The imps stood there facing him, and didn't seem to recognise him any more. They couldn't utter a word, they were inspecting him as if he were an attraction for sightseers and giggling nervously.

A new room. Wintry light came through the windowpanes. From time to time a uniformed police officer put his head round the door, possibly suspecting that the two little girls had explosives hidden about their persons.

The doctor with the funny name, the one he'd been talking to when Irene and the children knocked at the door, withdrew, not without nodding encouragingly at Irene again and shaking hands with the girls.

Kai-Petteri Hämäläinen looked at Irene and his daughters, thinking of Niskanen. He couldn't get the man out of his head. Irene watched the doctor as he closed the door behind him.

'You wouldn't think it to look at that young man, but he's the medical director in charge of this outfit,' said Hämäläinen, and Irene nodded.

'Valtteri Muksanen. Funny sort of name.'

'You think so?' asked Irene.

'Don't you?' he asked back.

She sat down beside him. The children, arms hanging by their sides, inched slightly closer to him.

'He recommends me to stay here a little longer, but he says I've been extremely fortunate, and I may be able to leave hospital within the next few days.'

'Yes,' said Irene.

'Good to see you here,' he said.

Silence.

'Come over here, imps. It's only medicine in that tube.'

The girls went over to the bed and looked at Irene for help.

Irene took his hand and stroked it. He made several faces, and the girls laughed and ventured closer still, finally sitting down cautiously on the bed.

'Have you heard anything from the TV station? Has Tuula called? Or Mertaranta?'

'I disconnected the phone, it was ringing the whole time.'

'Ah.' His mobile. He felt the impulse to reach for it, but he was still supposed to move extremely carefully, and anyway he didn't know where it was. He'd have to ask the doctor about that.

'It's all over the news,' said Irene.

He nodded. And felt a curious satisfaction. All over the news.

'The headline announcement,' said Irene quietly.

He made another face for the children.

'How fragile everything is,' said Irene.

42

Kimmo Joentaa took the train back to Turku. He asked his friendly Helsinki colleague to tell Westerberg and Sundström that he had left.

Sundström would be annoyed, but he had no time to bother with matters of minor importance just now. White buildings, lakes and forests flew past outside the carriage windows. A boy sat beside him bent over a laptop, playing a computer game the point of which Joentaa could not work out. A man in a yellow bird mask reduced the cars he drove to scrap metal and flung himself off high-rise buildings. The man on the screen was smashed to pieces, and the boy looked as if he were about to fall asleep.

'Thrilling stuff,' murmured Joentaa.

The boy cast him a suspicious glance, then concentrated on killing off the yellow man yet again.

Joentaa walked from the station to the police building, thinking about the idea that had occurred to him while he was looking at Harri Mäkelä's neatly stored photographs. An idea that would, presumably, be difficult to put into practice. Difficult or impossible.

Petri Grönholm was out when he arrived, and Tuomas Heinonen was sitting at his desk.

'Kimmo,' he said. 'Back already?'

'Only me. Paavo's still in Helsinki.'

'Ah.'

'I have an idea I'd like to try out . . .'

'What is it?' asked Heinonen.

Joentaa looked at Tuomas Heinonen, and wondered why he shouldn't put what he had been thinking into words, and while he was thinking of that he noticed the changed expression on Heinonen's face. His eyes still looked veiled, he still looked hunted. But something had changed.

'I won,' said Heinonen.

'What?'

'Won it all back. Almost all. There's an international ice hockey tournament on in Germany. The Slovakia versus Canada game.'

'Yes . . .'

'Slovakia won. The idiots who run the betting system didn't realise that Canada was bringing a B team. Funny mistake, not like them to make it.'

Joentaa nodded.

'A three-way combination, two favourites, and Slovakia as an outsider at high odds.'

Joentaa nodded again. He did not understand the way it worked.

'I could tell Paulina everything and put all the money on the table in front of her.'

'I wouldn't do that if I were you.'

'I have plenty of cash with me . . . look.' Heinonen reached for his coat, which was hanging over his chair, and took out some 500-euro notes. 'As much as you could wish for, I'm the king,' he said. 'Sorry I've been such a pain the last few days, and thank you for . . .'

'You must stop,' said Joentaa.

Heinonen stared at him.

'You must stop now, at once.'

'I expect you're right,' said Heinonen.

'If you love Paulina and your children you will stop now,' said Joentaa, hearing the emotion in his voice.

'You're right,' said Heinonen. His own voice sounded toneless and studied.

They faced each other in silence.

'What about this idea you have?' asked Heinonen at last.

Joentaa looked at Heinonen, saw his heated face and the disaster heading his way. He'd have to talk to Paulina.

'Kimmo?'

'Yes?'

'You have an idea.'

'Yes . . . I'm not sure yet. If possible I'd like to check the families of all the people who've died in air crashes or train accidents in the last few years, or of anyone who died in a fire on a fairground ghost train.'

Heinonen nodded, and seemed to be trying to visualise what he had said. 'Ah . . . fire on a ghost train. You mean those puppets in the talk show?'

'Exactly. It would indicate very explicitly what kind of death the puppets were supposed to have died in a film. I think that programme struck a note in a relative mourning a victim who died like that, and then . . .'

'That sounds rather way-out . . . rather specific,' said Heinonen.

'I know, but what's going on at this moment is also rather specific, isn't it?'

Heinonen nodded, but he did not look convinced.

'Anyway, that's what I'm going to do. Never mind what the rest of you say.'

He sat down at his desk, still thinking of Paulina as the computer came on. He would have to talk to her. He just didn't know how. Paulina knew what had been going on, so she must be in a position to stop Tuomas. Who could do it if she couldn't?

He thought of the banknotes in Heinonen's coat pocket. A fortune behind a zip fastener, and presumably Tuomas had brought it with him so that after office hours, or even before then, he could take it to the nearest betting shop.

He shook that thought off and called Päivi Holmquist down in Archives. Her voice sounded pleasantly bright and carefree. 'Of course I can help you,' she said, when he had explained his idea.

'Wonderful. Er . . . how?'

'These days we have very easy and comprehensive access to the newspaper archives,' she said. 'Using the right Search commands, I'm sure I could start by drawing you up a list of the kind of accidents you're after.'

'That's great,' said Joentaa.

'Then we'd have to dig a little deeper to find out the names of the people who died in such accidents. And then, if I understand you correctly, it's a matter of finding the names of their relatives.'

'Yes . . . that's exactly it,' said Joentaa.

'Then I'll start right away,' said Päivi.

'Thank you,' said Joentaa.

He sat there with the phone in his hand, and suddenly felt great reluctance to find the relatives of the dead. To rekindle their grief on the basis of what was probably a wild, hare-brained idea.

'Do you really expect something to come of that?' asked Heinonen, sitting opposite him.

'I don't know.'

'Patrik Laukkanen had debts,' said Heinonen.

Joentaa raised his head and looked enquiringly at him.

'He'd lost money speculating on the stock exchange,' said Heinonen.

'And what does that have to do with the murder of Mäkelä and the attempted murder of Hämäläinen?'

'We haven't got that far yet,' said Heinonen.

Joentaa nodded.

'It was simply an observation,' said Heinonen.

Joentaa stood up abruptly. He wanted to go home. At once. Stand in front of the little tree with Larissa. What business of his were Patrik Laukkanen's debts? He had no right to know about them.

He went down and past the tall, lavishly decorated Christmas tree to the drinks vending machine. He fed in coins and took a bottle of water. When he went back up, Heinonen was coming towards him. With that veiled, hunted look in his eyes.

'I have to go out,' he said.

Kimmo Joentaa nodded.

'Back in ten minutes.'

Joentaa watched Heinonen head out into the driving snow. After walking a few metres he began to run.

43

That afternoon the two policemen who had introduced themselves as Sundström and Westerberg the day before came to see him.

'Hämäläinen,' said Hämäläinen.

'I beg your pardon?' said Sundström.

'Meant to be a joke,' said Hämäläinen.

'I see,' said Sundström, and he did indeed laugh, a short, dry laugh, then pulled up the chair on which Irene had sat that morning. 'How are you?' he asked.

'Fine. In the circumstances. The doctor in charge here, Valtteri Muksanen, thinks I can soon go home.'

'That's what we're here about,' said Sundström. Westerberg was getting another chair from where it stood by the window. There was a vase on the windowsill containing red and yellow flowers. He didn't remember Irene bringing flowers . . . maybe they were part of the décor.

'It's like this . . .' said Sundström.

'Those flowers,' said Hämäläinen.

Sundström followed his gaze. 'Yes?'

'Are they real or plastic?'

Westerberg rose, ponderously, and felt the flower petals. 'Real,' he said.

Hämäläinen nodded.

'We would like you to stay here a while longer,' said Sundström.

Hämäläinen, looking at the flowers, asked, 'Why?'

'And then we'll accommodate you in a safe house for some time, until all this has been cleared up.'

Hämäläinen turned away from the flowers and looked at Sundström.

A safe house . . .

'Sounds rather like a spy film,' he said.

'That's only the usual term for it,' said Sundström.

Hämäläinen nodded.

'You and your family too, if you like,' said Sundström.

A safe house . . .

'You do realise, don't you, that you are in danger while our investigations are still going on?' said Sundström.

A safe house. Surrounded by forest. In a picturesque winter landscape.

'Do you know Niskanen?'

'The cross-country skier?' asked Westerberg.

'I'm sorry, but the answer is no,' said Hämäläinen.

'What?' asked Sundström.

'Thank you for the offer, but I'd rather be at home.'

'That won't be possible,' said Sundström.

'Of course it will be possible.'

'In view of the . . .'

'I'm feeling fine. I have the show to present on New Year's Eve. Our annual retrospective. The show will go out live. We can't just use pre-recorded footage for that one.'

Sundström gaped at him. Westerberg seemed to be thinking of something else entirely.

'That won't be possible,' Sundström repeated.

There was a knock on the door.

'Yes, who is it?' asked Sundström, as if it were his room.

'Er . . . do you know this lady?' asked the uniformed officer posted outside.

It was Tuula. She looked grey-faced. Tearful and somehow older.

'Tuula,' said Hämäläinen, surprising himself by the warmth in his voice.

'Just a moment. We haven't finished yet,' said Sundström.

'Yes, we have. Sit down, Tuula,' said Hämäläinen.

'We have to . . .'

'Later,' said Hämäläinen.

Sundström rose abruptly and muttered something that Hämäläinen couldn't make out. He was already out in the corridor when Westerberg, who had reached the doorway, asked, 'Niskanen the long-distance skier?'

'That's the man,' said Hämäläinen. 'Do you know what . . .?'

'The guy who's breeding sheep these days?' said Westerberg.

'What?'

'Niskanen. He's breeding sheep in Ireland.'

'What?'

'Read it somewhere,' said Westerberg. He nodded to them again and went out.

'What was that about?' asked Tuula.

'Sheep in Ireland. Did you know that?'

'Know what?' asked Tuula.

'You must check it.'

'Check what?'

'Whether Niskanen is really breeding sheep in Ireland. Now, do sit down. We have things to discuss, with the show going out in two days' time.'

44

That evening Päivi Holmquist brought up a list. She stood beside Joentaa while he read it. *September 2003, aircraft, Russia, four victims Finnish, known by name: Sulo (aged 43) and Armi (48) Nieminen, address Rautatietori 32, Helsinki; May 2005, aircraft Vaasa/FIN, light plane, two Finnish victims, both known by name: Matti Jervenpää (29) address Kalevalankatu 45, Vaasa, Kaino Soininen (42) address Täälönkatu 83, Helsinki; January 2006, train crash, Kotka/FIN, one dead, Eija Lundberg (16) . . .*

The list comprised fifteen victims and nine surnames. The letters flickered before Joentaa's eyes. He thanked Päivi Holmquist.

'It will probably be quite easy to find out the names that are still missing. I'll go on with it later today.'

'Yes . . . thanks again.'

'There are still gaps in the list, but accidents of the kind you're after aren't all that common. So if you're looking exclusively for people who died in disasters exactly like that, then you should be able to find the people most affected here.'

Joentaa nodded. He read the names and no longer understood his own idea.

'Of course, there are many unknown factors in the

equation. I began by going back over air and rail accidents from now to ten years ago, but the incident you're looking for could presumably be even further back in the past. Or it could be an accident that didn't get into the media, although that seems to me rather unlikely. Even the crash of that light plane in Vaasa was reported in several newspapers. Another problem is that I began by concentrating on victims who were Finnish citizens, which may be an unreliable criterion.'

Joentaa nodded.

'I did find a fire on a ghost train, but that was over fifteen years ago. Three children died in it. It was at a funfair in Salo.'

'Yes . . .'

'I haven't been able to find out their names yet.'

'No. Thank you, Päivi. I know . . . well, now I don't know any more. My idea seems rather far-fetched. Vaasara was probably right.'

'Vaasara?'

'Yes, Mäkelä the puppet-maker's assistant. He couldn't make out what I was getting at when I talked to him about it.'

Päivi Holmquist did not reply.

'I don't know why I came up with the idea. Somehow or other Larissa – that's a friend of mine – she put it into my mind. Because of the funeral the wrong way round.'

Päivi Holmquist gave him a wry smile and said, 'Kimmo, this is one of those times when it's difficult to understand what you're saying.'

'Sorry. Anyway, thank you for the list.'

'Would you like me to carry on with it?'

'Yes . . . yes, please.'

Päivi Holmquist nodded and smiled at him before going away, and Kimmo Joentaa couldn't take his eyes off the words that she had written down, and behind which, he suspected, an answer might lie.

Name, address, date of birth.

Sanna Joentaa, address . . .

He rang his own number. Waited. Heard the manufacturer's standard wording. Please leave your massage after the tone. He cut the connection, and a moment later the phone rang.

'What do you think you're doing, Kimmo?' asked Sundström.

'I got them to tell you I . . .'

'I couldn't care less what you got them to tell me. I want to know what you're doing. Why did you simply go off?'

'I had an idea that I . . .'

'Such as what?'

'What I was saying to you this morning. I think there's an irrational motive to do with the puppets and the way they were displayed on the talk show.'

Sundström said nothing, and seemed to be waiting for a more detailed explanation.

'It was a funeral the wrong way round.'

'A what?'

'And Hämäläinen. Mäkelä and Patrik were . . .'

'Were what?'

'Were . . . desecrating a grave, if you like. Without meaning to, of course. But I don't know . . . maybe that's a blind alley. I have a note here of names that Päivi found for me, but I doubt whether they mean anything.'

Sundström said nothing for a long time.

'Paavo?'

'Hämäläinen is better. He wants to go home and be back presenting the show in the near future. In fact, on New Year's Eve. And a Happy New Year to you too.'

'That's bad,' said Joentaa.

Sundström laughed mirthlessly. 'Or good. The perfect bait. Always supposing we're dealing with one of those weirdos who seem to populate this country in increasing numbers these days.'

He seemed to be waiting for either contradiction or agreement.

'The Institute of Criminal Technology is still working on the tread of those tyres. There were two witnesses who say they saw a small dark car outside Mäkelä's house. Exact colour unknown. Maybe a Renault Twingo. If we can line up the tyre tread of that car we'll be getting somewhere.'

'Good,' said Joentaa.

'I'll stay here for the time being and concentrate on Hämäläinen's security. I can hardly believe that our comatose friend Westerberg is capable of doing it.'

Joentaa thought of Westerberg, who had been bright as a button on the phone in the middle of the night.

'See you later,' said Sundström.

'See you,' said Joentaa.

He put the phone down on the desk and picked up the piece of paper. His eyes kept going back to one of the names: Raisa Lagerblom (28). Died in August 2005 when a glider crashed. Had lived in Raisio, not far from Turku.

Joentaa didn't know her name, but he knew the place where she lived. On a country road leading to Naantali. The house number was 12.

He had driven along that road on summer days when Sanna and Raisa Lagerblom were still alive.

45

As she walks to the apartment building with Aapeli, the picture comes back to her. Aapeli opens the door, sighing quietly, and says he is a little tired now.

Then they stand facing each other in the stairwell, and he keeps thinking of something else he wants to say. She can't hear it. Aapeli speaks almost soundlessly, trying to hold on to the day that is slipping away from her.

'Rauna's a great girl . . . you might have thought we were a family. Daughter, Mama, Grandpa,' he says and laughs.

She reads what he is saying from his lips.

Has the sky fallen down? asks Rauna, and she can't move. She doesn't feel the pain, and she looks at Rauna and tries to attract her gaze when Rauna, in the dark, closes her eyes, and she thinks: yes, it has fallen down. Yes.

Aapeli has bent his head, and she can see that he is afraid he has said something wrong.

'I'm going to watch the whole Moomin series now,' he says. 'My sons will be surprised when I ask them to lend me the children's DVDs.'

He laughs.

'Yes. Have a nice evening. See you soon,' he says.

'See you soon,' she says, and waits until the door has latched behind him.

Then she goes into her apartment. A red light is blinking. There's a message on her answering machine, the first in a long time. She presses the button, and hears the announcement, followed by a young man's dynamic voice.

'Hello, Mrs Salonen, my name is Olli Latvala. I'm calling about your arrival here tomorrow. The tickets should have reached you by now. I'll meet you at the station at 18.30 hours. Is that all right? I'm afraid I don't have a mobile number for you. Would you call me back tomorrow morning? Have a nice evening, and we'll speak tomorrow. We look forward to seeing you.'

She thinks about words as she goes into the bathroom.

Tomorrow. We look forward to seeing you.

She sits in the hot water, shivering, and Ilmari and Veikko are shadows in her mind.

46

Tuula Palonen sat in front of the flickering screen and read the press release that she had recently composed for a whole series of newspapers, asking them to make changes at short notice to their front pages.

She had decided on the text along with members of the editorial team, but she still couldn't make up her mind whether or not to send it on its way.

Above all, she wasn't sure whether Kai-Petteri had really thought everything through. In the clear light of day, she had gleaned the opposite impression at the hospital. He had seemed different. Very calm, almost high-spirited. Yet weakened. Of course. And somehow strange . . . abstracted. Several times she had felt he was talking in a confused way, not at all like the Hämäläinen she knew.

So he wanted to come back. Only a few days after an attempt on his life. The programme was to go through as planned. No changes to the guest list, no new contributions. Nothing to be included about . . . about what had happened to him. Even though that was the whole point: how could you have a retrospective look at the subjects of the year without including *the* subject of the year? He wanted to come back as if nothing had happened.

No changes to the guest list with one exception, Niskanen. She was to get hold of the cross-country skier Niskanen in Ireland, or wherever he might be, and have him there on the sofa, and if Niskanen refused she could draw on next year's budget until he agreed. She had done her research, and it was a fact: Niskanen the cross-country skier was now breeding sheep in Ireland.

She looked at the press release, and for one last time withstood the impulse to call Kai-Petteri and talk him out of it. Presumably he'd be asleep by now, and Mertaranta was all for transmitting the show anyway.

Her finger rested on the key for a few seconds, and then, aware of doing something momentous, she sent news of Kai-Petteri Hämäläinen's forthcoming resurrection out into the world.

47

When Kimmo Joentaa got home, Larissa was sitting on the steps outside the house in her white coat. He got out of the car, went up to her and guessed at the look in her eyes in the pale light. 'Brr! It's cold here,' he said.

'Not very,' she said.

'How . . . how was your day?' he asked.

She did not reply for a moment, then she laughed.

Laughed at him heartily until, after a while, he joined in.

30 December

48

Kimmo Joentaa went to Turku early, leaving Larissa asleep. He hoped she would arrive at work too late.

He wrote her a note: *Dear Larissa, see you this evening, Kimmo.*

In Sundström's absence, he was in charge of the morning discussion. He listened to Tuomas Heinonen, who looked as if he hadn't had enough sleep, telling him more details of Patrik Laukkanen's private life; he listened to an agitated Nurmela demanding results and the latest findings; he phoned Sundström every hour.

In between times he read the papers, which reported Hämäläinen's recovery and his forthcoming return to the small screen in crude and sometimes curiously martial language, with outsize lettering.

'Who Is Killing the Lords of Death?' ran the *Illansanomat* headline.

'Hämäläinen Defies Madness, Pain and Fate,' said *Etälsuomalainen*. The words *madness, pain* and *fate* were printed in red.

Whatever that might mean.

At midday Kimmo Joentaa had had enough, and he drove to Raisio. Along a familiar road. A short cut, not many people knew about it.

As he drove he thought of Sanna and how she had been sitting beside him in another life, already in her bathing costume because she wanted to jump straight into the water, and ran towards it as soon as he had drawn up in the car park.

A narrow road in the sunlight, yellow lines running along it, surrounded by woods and water. From time to time a house flew past.

Number 12 was a petrol station. Two pumps for drivers who had lost their way. A snow-capped advertising placard sang the virtues of ice cream and pizza.

He got out of the car and walked into the building, wondering what he was doing here. Two young women in identical clothes stood behind the counter. They wore white aprons, pale blue T-shirts, black trousers and peaked caps with the logo of the petrol-station chain. The place was also a small café. A middle-aged woman was standing at one of the games machines. Judging by the steady clinking she had just hit the jackpot, but her expression did not change. A man with a large paunch sat back in his chair at one of the tables, putting a piece of pizza into his mouth.

'Have you filled up?' asked one of the young women.

'Er, no. My name is Joentaa. I'm from the Turku police.' He showed her his ID.

'Oh,' she said.

'Did you know Raisa Lagerblom?' he asked.

She shook her head.

'She lived here,' said Joentaa. 'Or at least, at the time of her death this address was given for her.'

'There are two apartments upstairs on the first floor.'

'But her name means nothing to you?'

'I've only been here two months. When did she die?'

'2005,' said Joentaa.

'There's someone called Lagerblom lives upstairs,' said her young colleague, who was standing in the background.

'There is?'

'Yes. He used to lease the franchise of this place. That was some time ago, but he still lives here.'

'Is his name Lagerblom, then?' asked the other girl.

'Yes, Joakim . . . Joakim Lagerblom, I think.'

'The man whose eyes always pop out of his head when he sees us?' asked her colleague.

'That's him,' said the other girl.

'How do I get to the apartments?' asked Joentaa.

'Out through that door, then turn left and left again behind the building.'

'Thank you,' said Joentaa, stepping into the open air.

'What's it about?' asked one of the women behind his back. He did not answer.

The door to the entrance of the apartments was open. Joentaa went up the stairs and knocked. A white-haired, sunburnt man of around sixty opened the door.

'Mr Lagerblom?' asked Joentaa.

'Yes,' said the man.

'My name is Joentaa. From the Turku police.' He showed his ID again.

'Yes . . .?' said the man, sounding neither alarmed nor interested. At a loss, if anything.

'I'm trying to find out about Raisa Lagerblom,' said Joentaa.

'Raisa,' said the man.

'Yes . . . she died in a glider crash.'

'In the summer of 2005. My daughter,' said the man.

'May I come in?' asked Joentaa.

The man nodded and led the way. The apartment was larger than it seemed from outside. The living-room window looked out on to the road. Further off, the wooden houses of Naantali began, a strip of sandy beach showed, and on the horizon the grey water of the sea merged almost seamlessly with the sky.

'Beautiful,' said Joentaa.

The man looked at him enquiringly.

'A beautiful view of Naantali,' said Joentaa.

The man nodded.

They were standing in the middle of the room, and Joentaa didn't know what to say.

The man spoke first. 'What did you want to know about Raisa? And why?'

'It's difficult to explain. Can you tell me, are there . . . apart from you . . . any other close relatives of your daughter?'

'Why?'

'In the context of a criminal investigation, we're discussing the relatives of people who . . . who died in accidents such as air crashes.'

'But why?'

'I can't explain that to you in detail.'

The man still did not reply, and Joentaa realised that he was conducting an impossible conversation, one that couldn't really get anywhere.

'I'm sorry,' he said.

'It was only her second solo flight,' said the man.

Joentaa nodded.

'It was her great wish. She was . . . a brave girl. She got that from her mother. My wife always said the bravest thing I ever did was to sit out sunbathing in summer and winter alike, and it would make me ill some day.'

Joentaa nodded.

'But she was the one who died. Of cancer. And Raisa died. Because she so much wanted to fly.'

Joentaa nodded. 'I'm sorry I . . .'

'We ran the fuel station here. My wife and daughter looked after the café.'

Joentaa nodded. He got to his feet, shook hands with the man and said goodbye. He was sweating as he came out into the cold.

He went back into the shop. The two young women behind the counter were leafing through a magazine and giggling. The woman at the games machine was still standing there, while monotonous, staccato, recurrent tunes came from the machine.

'Excuse me,' said Joentaa. 'Does anyone else work here with you? In particular, is there anyone who's worked here for several years?'

'Josefina,' said one of the girls.

'Yes?'

'Josefina bakes the pizzas here. I think she's been doing it all her life.'

The other girl went on giggling.

'They're delicious, too.'

'Where is she?'

'Back there in the kitchen. I'll show you.'

Joentaa followed the young woman. Like the apartment above, the premises behind the shop and café were larger than he had expected. Golden-brown pizzas were baking in two ovens. Josefina, wearing kitchen gloves and with a white plastic cap on her head, was peeling tomatoes.

'This man wants to talk to you,' said the young woman from the cash desk. 'He's from the police.'

'Kimmo Joentaa,' he introduced himself, offering his hand.

'Police?' she asked.

'Yes, I . . .'

'Last time the police came here was when Raisa died. In a glider crash.'

'I know, that's why I . . .'

'They had to investigate. They said every accident of that kind had to be investigated.'

'That's right. I'd like to ask you something,' said Joentaa. Then he dried up, because he didn't know how to put the question.

'Yes?' The old woman was looking at him expectantly.

'Do you think it's possible that there might be a member of her family who . . . who maybe has never been able to come to terms with Raisa's death? Who could be going about . . . feeling angry over it?'

'Angry?'

'It's not easy to explain.'

'Raisa's mother is dead. She'd been sick with cancer for a long time, and after Raisa's death she died too.'

Joentaa nodded.

'Of course, Joakim has never got over it. How could you get over a thing like that?'

'I know. Forgive me, I didn't put it very clearly . . .'

'But angry? I've never known Joakim seem angry. Angry with what?'

Joentaa shook his head. 'I don't know. I'm sorry.'

He shook hands with both women and left. A blind alley, he thought. An investigation leading nowhere.

He thought of Sanna. Sanna standing in the sunlight at the water's edge, looking as if she were waiting for something.

He drove back towards Turku along the narrow grey road beside the water.

49

Paavo Sundström followed the editor Tuula Palonen through a labyrinth of glass corridors. She had her mobile to her ear, and she was tearing someone off a strip. When the conversation ended she hissed like a cat, making Sundström jump.

'All okay so far?' he enquired.

'Apparently we can't get Niskanen here.'

'The cross-country skier?' he asked.

She did not reply, and was already talking to someone else on her phone. 'Kai wants Niskanen, dammit. It must be possible to get the man away from his sheep for a couple of hours . . . I don't care about that, the important thing is to get him to agree, by this evening at the latest . . . Because that's when the press release goes out to the guests, you fool, that's why! So you want to see the studio, right?'

It took Sundström a few seconds to realise that this last remark was meant for him, not the fool at the other end of the line.

'Yes, exactly. That would be kind.'

'Why do you want to see it?'

Yes, why, he wondered, why indeed?

'We'd like to position security guards at sensitive points. We need an overall view of the studio,' he said.

'Ah,' said Tuula Palonen, who seemed to be giving him only half her attention.

'That's why it's important for me to see the studio and the entrance area for the audience,' said Sundström.

'Bodyguards for Kai,' said Tuula Palonen, seeming thoughtful.

'Yes, until our investigations are . . .'

'Do you think we could get that into the show?'

'Er . . .'

'Only in passing. Maybe a short interview with one of the police officers?'

'No. I'm sorry, but no.'

'Kai probably wouldn't like it anyway,' she said. Her mobile played a symphony, and she began talking about Niskanen again.

They entered a large, dark room, with a front wall consisting entirely of a huge glass window that had a view into a brightly lit studio. To one side stood mixing desks, just below the ceiling there were large flat screens showing various programmes. One displayed the show now being recorded in the studio beyond the glass window.

It was fitted out like a law court. A judge in his robes, a defendant with stooped shoulders, a girl in the middle who was presumably playing the part of a witness. To right and left were the audience, all the seats full. He cautiously approached.

'Don't worry, they can't see us,' said a man whom he saw only now. He was sitting in a swivel chair, leaning back and looking alternately at what was going on in the studio and on the screens.

'They can't?' asked Sundström.

'No, it's the same glass you use yourselves. When you're interrogating suspects.'

Sundström nodded vaguely.

'You are one of the police officers, aren't you?'

'Yes,' said Sundström.

'Then you'll know all about it. We can see them in there, but they can't see us.'

'I understand,' said Sundström. I understand, he thought. The imaginary judge is examining the imaginary defendant. The audience is examining them both. The man in the swivel chair is examining everyone. 'Ah,' he said, and Tuula Palonen shouted to her colleague on the other end of her phone and said she was going to call Kai now and tell him Niskanen had died.

'Figuratively speaking,' she said as she caught Sundström's eye. She tapped a number into her mobile, waited, and took a deep breath. Hämäläinen didn't seem to be answering his phone.

The voice of the judge raising an objection came tinnily over some loudspeakers. The girl witness spoke quietly, in a trembling voice. The audience looked spellbound, as if they were concentrating hard.

'That's the studio we use,' said Tuula Palonen, bringing Sundström out of his thoughts and back to earth.

'Yes,' he said.

'It will be on a similar layout. Kai's desk will be where the judge is sitting, and as seen from here the guests will be to his right. The audience will be where the audience for this show is sitting now.'

'I see.'

'Just in case that could be important to you in any way.'

'Yes, thank you. Where does the audience come in?'

'Over there. The door on the right leads straight into the entrance hall. The audience will come through the main entrance and will then be escorted through the hall and the cafeteria to the studio.'

'I see. We'll have to check out the audience.'

'What?'

'We'll have to check them out,' said Sundström. 'Frisk them for weapons.'

'That's . . . er, interesting,' said Tuula Palonen.

'There won't be any great fuss. How many people does the studio hold?'

'Yes, interesting,' repeated Tuula Palonen. 'We'll have to shoot a little footage of that. We can't just leave the subject alone. Right at the beginning,' she said.

'That's okay,' said Sundström. 'How large an audience will the studio hold?'

'About two hundred and fifty. Many of them prominent people. Tickets go to the sponsors. And invited guests. The tickets for this retrospective are sold out at least six months in advance. Which means you really don't have to worry.'

Sundström nodded. Good, he thought, one thing less to worry about. He would have to get the guests checked out, all the same.

'Is Kai really in danger?' asked Tuula Palonen.

Sundström looked at her and wondered how anyone could ask such a stupid question. 'Not if we're prepared for all contingencies,' he said.

The judge's tinny voice was saying something about a last chance and a period on probation. Tuula Palonen's mobile played a symphony.

'It'll be a great programme with Kai-Petteri tomorrow,' said the man in the swivel chair, yawning.

50

In the afternoon she sits in the lawyer's office. The secretary brings black coffee, and the little old man sits behind the dark brown desk dominating the room and says their chances are slim.

'So there's no news?' she says.

'No. I'm sorry.'

She nods.

'The boss of the firm that did the renovation still can't be found.'

She nods again.

'Proceedings against municipal employees are about to be withdrawn.'

She nods.

'There's still the possibility of claiming compensation for pain and suffering caused,' he says.

She nods.

'It's a . . . a question of tactics and choosing the right moment.'

She nods.

'I know that's not what you want.'

She looks at him, and remembers the days when the lawyer was younger and more nervous, first more timid and then more confident. Days when Veikko wasn't alive yet, and before she had met Ilmari. The snow has melted, the flowers are beginning to come out. She sees spring beyond the window, lies on her bed and has left the door of her room open just a crack so that she can hear what they're saying. The lawyer and her parents. The lawyer tries to talk calmly, her parents shout at each other. The lawyer advises them to think it all over, and then think it all over again, and her father laughs and says the lawyer has chosen the wrong career, he obviously doesn't understand what he's here for.

A few weeks later she moves to the apartment in Paimio with her mother, and she sees her father three more times after that, on birthdays. On the third occasion he forgets to bring a present and says he will give her one later, but he never does, because on his way home to Helsinki he collides with a motorbike. The newspaper cuttings are kept in a shoebox in a cupboard in their apartment. Her mother does not cry at the funeral. The motorbike rider is only slightly injured, and the lawyer says, 'We're not giving up.'

She nods.

'Believe me, I'm not giving up. It matters to me. I'm in constant contact with your co-plaintiffs.'

She nods.

A few months back she went to see him because he was the only lawyer she knew, and because, long ago, he was the only person who tried to make it more difficult for her parents to separate. He didn't recognise her, and sat quietly behind his desk while she told him what had happened.

'We're not giving up, we'll keep in touch with the other plaintiffs, and when the time comes we'll be well prepared,' he says.

'Good,' she says.

'Yes . . .' he says.

She reaches for her bag, opens it, and takes out the tin of biscuits she baked herself.

'Oh,' he says as she hands him the tin.

'Home-made,' she says. 'With maple syrup.'

'Well, thank you very much.'

'Because Christmas isn't so far behind us,' she says.

51

There was an updated list from Päivi Holmquist on his desk when he got back. Eleven new names. In all twenty. *This should be complete so far as plane crashes and rail accidents are concerned*, wrote Päivi, *and in addition there's the ghost-train accident in Salo*.

He looked at the list, read the names. Thought of Joakim Lagerblom, and Josefina, and conversations that couldn't be conducted.

He called the editorial office for Hämäläinen's show and got Tuula Palonen on the line. She said she was short of time and didn't understand the question he was asking her.

'It's about the puppets shown on the talk show,' he repeated.

'Yes?'

'The audience was told exactly what kinds of deaths the attitudes of the figures were based on. Do you understand?'

'Not entirely.'

'The discussion set out to show how the puppet-maker,

that's Mäkelä, modelled the puppets on precise kinds of death, and something was said in that context about the deaths the puppets were to illustrate on film. Death in an air crash, in a rail accident, in a fire on a ghost train.'

'Yes . . . yes, I remember.'

'What I'd like to know now is this: did you get any reactions? Letters or some such communications from viewers criticising the show?'

'Presumably, but nothing out of the ordinary. We get letters and emails after every programme, criticism and praise. Much more praise than anything else, incidentally.'

'What I mean is anything immediately striking, maybe a text message with a threatening undertone, a text attacking one or several of the participants personally.'

'No, definitely not.'

'Or something relating directly to real air crashes, rail accidents, or a fire on a ghost train that actually happened . . . people who maybe lived through such an experience and . . . and thought the tone and nature of the conversation was too close to the bone, if you see what I mean?'

Tuula Palonen thought for a while.

'Yes, I do see what you mean,' she said. 'But no, I don't think we had anything like that. Unusual reactions of that kind are few and far between, and I always look at them myself.'

'I see.'

'But I'll ask again,' she said.

'Thank you.'

Joentaa rang off and once again looked at Päivi Holmquist's list. She had also found out the names of the three children who lost their lives in the ghost-train fire. Seven, nine and twelve years old. In September 1993.

He stared at the names and came to a decision. He copied the list, spent two hours on the phone, and at the discussion held at 16.00 hours confronted Heinonen and Grönholm with a change of direction within the inquiry.

Grönholm, frowning, looked at Päivi Holmquist's note, and Heinonen asked if Joentaa had agreed all this with Sundström.

'More or less,' said Joentaa.

Heinonen nodded.

'Eleven of these people lived in South Finland, and we'll look at those. I've delegated the others to our colleagues in the cities concerned. They were very cooperative.'

'A countrywide investigation,' said Grönholm. 'Everyone wanting to contribute the crucial piece of evidence.'

'It's a question of doing the research to discover whether relatives of those victims can be found anywhere near our case – people who reacted particularly strongly to the accidental death or were traumatised for a very long time. And finding the one whose grief broke out in irrational aggression.'

'Sounds pretty speculative,' said Grönholm.

'I know,' said Joentaa. 'I've allotted the names. Between us, we should be able to take a look at all of them by tomorrow afternoon.'

'Hm,' said Grönholm.

'Who Is Killing the Lords of Death?' said Tuomas Heinonen.

'What?' asked Grönholm.

'Today's headline in the *Illansanomat*.'

'Ah,' said Grönholm.

'Maybe Kimmo's idea isn't so outlandish after all,' said Heinonen.

'Kimmo's ideas are always outlandish,' said Grönholm, smiling.

52

She leaves the lawyer's office and glides over the snow as if on rails.

She is sitting opposite a man, and there is a small table between them. The man is tapping alternately at the keyboard of a small computer and the keypad of his mobile. From time to time he briefly raises his head and seems to look right through her as if through a pane of glass.

She looks at him, and the steady drumming sound of his fingers makes its way into her and forms a pleasant, harmonious contrast to her present sense of hovering in the air. The conductor comes along to stamp tickets. Now and then children run past, laughing, now in one direction, now in another.

'Slowly, slowly,' murmurs the man, without taking his eyes off the keyboard.

At Helsinki station a young man, who has been waiting to meet her, comes towards her smiling. A cheerful, genuine smile. He has a firm handshake. 'Welcome. I'm Olli Latvala. We're very glad you agreed to come,' he says.

She nods. Agreed. An interesting word. She thinks about words so often now that she finds it difficult to speak them out loud.

'To be honest, I'm relieved that you're here. Somehow we could never get hold of each other on the phone,' says Olli Latvala.

She nods.

'It's often like that in our outfit,' says Olli Latvala. 'All arranged at the last minute. But it works in the end.'

The last minute, she thinks.

'Very good to see you,' says Olli Latvala. 'Let me carry that.' He takes her overnight bag and walks briskly ahead.

She remembers the first call. A few months ago now. A late summer day. Shimmering heat. The ringing of the phone crystallises in the silence, and as she goes to pick it up she is wondering who it can be. No one has called her for some time now.

The woman's voice sounds strange and soft and insistent all at once. She introduces herself as Tuula Palonen and talks for some minutes about the moment when the sky fell in, about Ilmari and Veikko, without mentioning their names and without understanding.

'You don't understand,' she tells Tuula Palonen in the end, then she says nothing for several seconds.

'Then help me to understand,' says Tuula Palonen finally. 'Help me and everyone else to understand. That's why we're inviting you. Because who can understand it if not you?'

When Tuula Palonen calls again two days later she agrees, and Tuula Palonen is glad and asks her a series of questions about the day when the sky fell in and what it was like for her, and while she answers she feels as if she is taking an examination. In the end Tuula Palonen says she is sorry that it isn't possible for her to offer a fee.

Fee, she thinks. Thinking about words. The young man puts her little travelling bag in the boot of the car and holds the car door open for her.

'You're spending the night at the Sokos. A good hotel.'

She nods.

That call was in summer.

The card of thanks and the invitation came in the autumn. Now it is winter.

'Maybe you'll run into Bon Jovi in the hotel,' says Olli Latvala. 'He's touring Scandinavia at the moment; we were lucky enough to get him on the show at short notice. You know who Bon Jovi is?'

She nods, and the young man steers the car into a red, yellow and black sea of lights.

'I'd like to discuss the course of the show with you tomorrow morning. After breakfast, if that's all right. I could come to the hotel.'

She nods.

'A car will come for you at 17.00 hours.'

'Yes,' she says.

'About your husband and son . . . I'm very, very sorry about them,' he says.

She turns her eyes away from the street and looks at him.

'I think it's impressive that you . . . you're willing to talk about it,' he says.

Talk about it, she thinks.

Who can understand it if she can't?

The hotel lobby is full of golden light. A pageboy takes her bag, and the young man tells the lady at reception, 'Salme Salonen. The reservation is with the block booking for the *Hämäläinen* talk show.'

'Welcome, Mrs Salonen,' says the hotel receptionist, smiling, and Olli Latvala presses her hand firmly, for a long time, before hurrying through the broad swing doors and out into the night.

'Shall I lead the way?' asks the pageboy.

She nods, and follows him to the lifts.

53

Grönholm was looking down at the list when he left the room, and Heinonen was fanning himself with his copy and seemed relaxed. He's won, thought Joentaa. Presumably at good odds. He must speak to Paulina.

He called Sundström in Helsinki. Sundström seemed to be in high spirits, told him to do as he liked, and laughed his good-old-Paavo-Sundström laugh, the one that sounded menacing and infectious at the same time.

At least Sundström's on the way to improving, thought Joentaa as he rang off.

He spent the rest of the day working through the names he had given himself to investigate. Besides Raisa Lagerblom they included a married couple from Salo whose daughter had died in the fire on the ghost train. Erkki and Mathilda Koivikko. Looking at the date, he thought it was too long ago. 1993. Plenty of time to grasp the fact, come to terms with it, forget or suppress it. He had had an event closer to the present in mind when the idea first came to him.

All the same, he went to Salo, because a comment in Päivi's research notes had seemed important to him.

In the big market square of Salo, where there had been a funfair with a ghost train in the autumn of 1993, people sat shivering on benches, watching the skaters on the river falling down and getting up again.

Erkki and Mathilda Koivikko lived in a red house no more than a hundred metres from the market place. Their name was on the letterbox: Koivikko. It was not clear from Päivi

Holmquist's notes whether they had already been living here in 1993. Probably. He stood indecisively outside the house for a little while, imagining Erkki and Mathilda Koivikko seeing the burning ghost train through their own windows.

He turned away, walked across the market place and over the bridge. The Somero bank was on the ground floor of a large, new-looking shopping centre. Coloured placards of happy people promised high rates of interest and a secure, sheltered life. A young woman behind a reception desk gave him an encouraging smile as he came in.

'My name is Joentaa, I'm from the Turku police,' he said. 'I'd like to speak to Erkki Koivikko.'

He showed her his ID, and she studied it for a while. She seemed about to say something else, but then refrained.

'Is he here?' asked Joentaa.

'Yes, of course. This way.'

She went ahead, through a door in the back part of the bank, past men and women on the phone or staring at screens. Erkki Koivikko, unlike most of the employees here, had an office of his own. The woman knocked and waited for a reply, which came a few seconds later, the speaker's voice muted by the door. She opened it.

A man of powerful appearance sat behind a pale brown desk. He wore a dark suit and a strikingly colourful tie, and was deep in a phone conversation. He went on talking for a little while before turning to the woman, who was waiting in the doorway beside Joentaa. 'What is it?' he asked.

'This gentleman is from the police,' said the woman.

Koivikko sat there motionless.

'I won't take much of your time,' said Kimmo.

'Right,' said Koivikko. 'Yes, thank you, Sonja. We'll do this on our own.'

The woman nodded and left. Joentaa went in and closed the door.

'Police,' said Koivikko.

'Nothing that need disturb you,' said Joentaa. He went closer and handed his police ID to Koivikko. He had deliberately not called in advance to say he was coming. He was pestering a man who had presumably been given news of his daughter's death fifteen years ago by a police officer. He felt a pang in his stomach and watched for Koivikko's reaction, waiting to hear what he would say.

'Forgive my . . . slight surprise. It's not every day that a policeman turns up in my office.'

'It's about your daughter Maini,' said Joentaa.

Koivikko did not reply. A powerful man, sitting there looking relaxed, surprised but otherwise in perfect control of himself.

'I know that she died in an accident fifteen years ago,' said Joentaa.

Koivikko nodded.

'At the time you did something that occupied the minds of my colleagues here in Salo for a while.'

'You're talking in riddles, but I think I know what you mean,' said Koivikko.

'You threatened the man running the funfair that day. He was suspected of contributing to causing the fire through negligence.'

Koivikko nodded.

'You offered him violence during a confrontation after the trial.'

Koivikko nodded.

'The man was found not guilty.'

'I still think he was guilty,' said Koivikko. 'It wasn't done on purpose, of course. Negligence, as you put it. An idiot. One idiot too many. And I needed to blame someone anyway, so the court's decision carried no weight with me. I knew he was guilty, I didn't need any evidence.'

Joentaa nodded.

'Not back then,' said Koivikko. 'It's a long time ago.'

A long time ago, thought Joentaa.

'I gave the man a black eye. It swelled up in seconds, it really did. He got off with a black eye. Unlike my daughter.'

A long time ago, thought Joentaa. Koivikko sat there unchanged, focused but calm.

'I was questioned about the incident at the time. It didn't come to charges or a court case. The man who had killed my daughter was kind enough not to take it to court.'

'I know,' said Joentaa.

'However, here I am today, working at my profession. I expect my colleagues out there are already gossiping. Koivikko . . . wasn't there something, back in the past? That terrible case. And now here's a policeman in his office again. How did you know where to find me, by the way?'

'It's part of our job,' said Joentaa, and thought of Patrik Laukkanen, who was dead and whose life was laid out in detail, in impersonally bureaucratic language, on his desk.

'I'd be interested to know why you are here,' said Koivikko.

Joentaa nodded. He forced himself to hold the man's gaze and asked, 'Do you know the *Hämäläinen* talk show?'

Koivikko still sat there looking just the same, with his eyes narrowed. 'Who doesn't?' he asked.

'Did you see the programme when the puppets were used as models for bodies?'

'You surely don't think . . .'

Joentaa waited.

'You surely don't think I . . . you don't think Hämäläinen's show of dead bodies interests me personally?'

'Did you see that programme?'

Koivikko looked at Joentaa. He seemed to be concentrating, and almost imperceptibly shook his head. 'Interesting,' he murmured.

'Did you?'

'This'll make you laugh; yes, I did. With my wife. We like that talk show. Well, we did like it.'

'Not any more?'

'We watch only occasionally,' said Koivikko. 'We didn't like the way it put those puppets on display.'

'Exactly what didn't you like?' asked Joentaa, and after a couple of seconds Koivikko began smiling to himself.

'When the trailer said there would be bodies specially made for films in it, my wife said at once that she didn't like the idea,' he said. 'But I thought it was an interesting topic. Then, when they talked about a fire on a ghost train and the camera moved to a puppet modelling a dead body, my wife began crying, and I went into the bathroom and threw up.'

He said no more for a while.

'Then I went back and watched the rest of it. In principle, a fascinating subject. I soon got over my first reaction. My wife had already gone to bed, and next morning she said she thought it was tasteless and she wasn't going to watch the *Hämäläinen* show any more.'

Joentaa nodded.

'Although, incidentally, she does still watch it now and then. Has done for some time. Is that what you wanted to know?' asked Koivikko.

'Yes. Thank you.'

'I don't know exactly what you suspect, but I think there's one thing you should know.'

'Yes?'

'Our daughter's death is fifteen years in the past. And the charred plastic figure on the stretcher in that TV show was male.'

Joentaa nodded.

'Do you understand me?'

'Yes. Thank you very much.' He got up, and offered Koivikko his hand. Koivikko shook it.

'Good luck,' said Joentaa, removing his hand from Koivikko's.

Then he quickly walked down the corridor and out into the fresh air, feeling a little better when he was surrounded by the biting cold.

54

Kai-Petteri Hämäläinen left the hospital under cover of darkness, through a side entrance.

The young doctor with the peculiar name had shaken hands with him, keeping hold of his hand for a long time, and asked him once again to take it easy in the coming days and weeks. The nurses and patients had stared at him as he went down the long corridor towards the lifts. Now, flanked by two police officers, one of them tall and the other very tall, he and an anxious-looking Tuula Palonen were walking through the cold air to a limousine. The police officers wore long coats; their faces were expressionless. Tuula peered to left and right, and seemed relieved when they were in the car and the very tall man threaded his way into the evening traffic.

'It worked,' said Tuula. 'No one saw you.'

Hämäläinen nodded, and thought of the conversation he had had that afternoon, a discussion over the phone with Tuula and Raafael Mertaranta, the TV station's controller, who had congratulated him on his imminent discharge from hospital as if it were a major achievement.

He had been sitting on his bed, with one of the nurses

watering his flowers, and Tuula and Mertaranta had agreed to pick a good moment to smuggle him past the waiting cameras and back into everyday life unseen, so that his reappearance on the screen would be all the more effective and make a lasting impression. On New Year's Eve. Back to health, in cheerful mood, to present a retrospective look at the past year to viewers.

Phoenix from the ashes, he thought, and the car, driven by a silent giant, rode smoothly through a clear winter night. They left the city behind them, and he closed his eyes for a while.

When they came to a halt, the officer on the passenger seat spoke for the first time. 'We're here.'

Hämäläinen looked out of the window in search of his house. The big garden, the terrace surrounded by tall fir trees, the swimming pool with its plastic cover, the warm, muted lighting behind the windows. Irene. The twins. 'We're where?' he asked.

'Your home,' said the very tall officer who had been driving.

He looked out of both side windows again.

'We're going to approach from some way off, making for the back of the house,' said the other man. 'Come along.'

He got out.

His eyes adjusted to the darkness. They were standing on the outskirts of a wood rather rocky in places.

'Haven't you ever walked home through this wood?' asked the very tall man, and Hämäläinen shook his head.

'The path is quite steep, but it's a nice walk,' said the not so tall man.

Hämäläinen nodded and gritted his teeth as the others walked easily ahead of him. Obviously no one seemed to remember that he had been the victim of an attempted murder only two days ago.

'Are you all right?' asked Tuula, as the façade of the house emerged from the darkness some way off.

'Fine,' said Hämäläinen, and the very tall police officer opened the little gate that was always kept locked.

'I didn't even know we had a key to this gate,' said Hämäläinen.

'It was hanging on a board with the other keys,' said the tall man.

'I see.'

'Your wife gave it to us,' said the very tall man.

Hämäläinen nodded. They were standing in the far corner of the large garden. Beyond the white fir trees were the windows, behind the windows there was light. Irene, he thought. He had spoken to her on the phone at midday, feeling that she was a long way off.

'We'll go over to the terrace,' said the very tall man. He hunched his shoulders as he walked. Tuula followed, and the other police officer came behind Hämäläinen. He suddenly took Hämäläinen's arm and held it for a few seconds. But there was nothing in sight; it was only wind rippling the plastic tarpaulin that covered the pool.

The very tall officer had reached a window in the façade and tapped the glass. Irene's silhouette appeared behind the pane. A door opened.

'Welcome home,' said the tall officer, with a gesture inviting him into his own house.

55

Kimmo Joentaa sat at his office desk in the neon lighting for a long time, studying the notes made by Heinonen and Grönholm on their research, reading the newspaper reports that Päivi had left in neat piles ready for him. Each of the disasters, to a greater or lesser extent, had provided material for columns in the press, many of them mainly objective, some lurid. Columns well or badly written.

A local paper in Savonlinna had dwelt for weeks on the subject of a young family who died when a passenger plane crashed over Russia. Pictures of the young father, the young mother, even a picture of the still unbaptised baby, pixelated to obscure the face. An interview with the parish clergyman. One with the husband's sister. Another with his colleagues at work. All the articles were by the same journalist. Joentaa made a note of his name.

Finally the front page of the newspaper published a picture of the house where the family had lived. In the foreground stood a smiling, middle-aged man who had bought the house to live there in future. The man had been interviewed. He was asked if he didn't feel it was uncomfortable to be living in that house, knowing about the tragedy, and he had said no, adding that he was a widower himself and used to tragedies.

Kimmo Joentaa looked at the picture of the smiling man for a little longer, then he put the report down and picked up the next one.

He made notes, drew up lists, arranged the relatives of the dead in order, rummaged around in other people's grief, and brought nothing to light but names. Names like the name of Erkki Koivikko, father of a daughter, a bank manager. There was something Koivikko had said that he couldn't get out of his head. Fifteen years ago. And it hadn't been his daughter on the stretcher, but . . .

He closed his eyes and tried to concentrate on what Koivikko had said, but it was no use. He looked at the names on the white paper a little longer, then put the list back with the newspaper reports on the rest of the files that Päivi

Holmquist had brought up, and switched off the light. He drove home.

On the way he thought of Erkki Koivikko getting out of his chair, going to the bathroom and throwing up in the washbasin. A strong man who looked as if he was in control of himself. He had said that on the stretcher in the TV show . . . no, he'd lost it.

He thought of the smiling man who had bought the empty house.

A widower.

Used to tragedies.

He felt as if he were floating over the road; now and then his eyes closed for a second or so. Fresh snow had fallen. Once he was on the woodland track the tyres spun, and he had to turn the wheel to avoid ending up in the ditch. He switched the engine off and went the last hundred metres on foot, as so often at this time of year. He thought of Sanna, who had liked that. When they had first found out that it was often impossible to drive right up to the house in snowy winters, he had stomped through the snow in a bad temper, and Sanna had laughed.

There was a light on in the kitchen; he saw the silhouette of a naked woman behind the windowpane. He stood outside the window for a while, watching as she made the lasagne he had promised her several days before.

Then he moved away from the window, took the few steps to the front door and opened it. The warmth came to meet him, and Larissa called, 'There you are at last. Supper's nearly ready.'

He stood in the doorway.

'You look pale,' she said.

He nodded.

'Midnight feast,' she said, taking the bubbling dish of lasagne out of the oven.

'Looks delicious.'

'It tastes delicious too,' said Larissa. Or whatever her name was.

'Nice that you're here.'

She took two plates out of the cupboard, cutlery out of the drawer, and asked, 'Why?'

Kimmo Joentaa looked at her.

'Why is it nice that I'm here?'

'I don't know,' said Joentaa.

They ate in silence.

After they had finished, she undressed him, got on top of him, and moved in what seemed a practised, rhythmic way until he came.

She went to shower.

'Twenty-five,' she said when she came back.

Kimmo looked at her.

'I'm twenty-five years old. Grew up in a conventional household. My father raped me over a long period, and my mother never noticed, so I moved out when I was sixteen.'

'I see,' said Joentaa.

'Actually that was all lies.'

Joentaa nodded.

'I'll tell you another tomorrow, if you like,' she said.

56

That night, on the news, she sees the smiling man. A photograph of him. He has left hospital, no one saw him leave, but he is said to be getting better.

She sits on the hotel bed, which is soft, with smooth sheets.

She takes an apple and a peach from a white bowl and begins to eat them while she watches a woman with a microphone standing outside the dark house where the smiling man lives. What the woman is saying dies away, and what happened is a tingling on the surface of her skin.

The empty hall.

The questioning look.

The sky made of glass.

Rauna. Veikko. Ilmari.

She feels Rauna's skin against her cheek, and sees Ilmari apparently about to say something. A little way off, but she can't hear him. She tries to catch his eye, but both his eyes are closed. One leg is missing. 'Has the sky fallen down?' asks Rauna, and she thinks: one leg is missing. Ilmari has put his arm round Veikko, whose body is lying flat on the floor at an unnatural angle to his head. One leg is missing, she thinks, and Veikko is asleep, and only a minute ago everything was still all right.

A rent in the sky. Then another.

Rauna is dancing. Ilmari skids on the ice. Veikko laughs.

Who would understand it if she didn't?

She is lying on snow, her hand is trembling as she reaches out for Rauna. Sirens and flashing blue lights. Frantic voices. Soothing voices. She nods. Nods and nods and nods, and does not let go of Rauna's hand.

'These two must belong together,' says a voice.

Ilmari's body is raised and lowered.

Veikko's body is raised and lowered.

Her body is raised and carried away. The voices retreat.

Rauna is hovering beside her, and asks, 'Has the sky fallen down?'

The clatter of an engine. 'Ready for take-off,' says one of the voices above her. 'Turku hospital. Land on the lawn outside the main entrance, you're expected.'

'Right,' says another voice.

A door is closed. She shuts her eyes.

'And now, back to the studio,' says the woman with the microphone.

Only a minute ago, she thinks.

'It's going to be all right,' says a voice.

Only a minute ago.

'Everything okay,' says the voice.

Only a moment has passed.

57

Kai-Petteri Hämäläinen looked up at the ceiling and the light and shadows on it. Irene lay beside him. She seemed to be fast asleep.

The tall man and the very tall man spent the night in the guest bedroom. One of them was always awake while the other settled down on the couch that offered normal people a place to sleep, but was much too small for these two. The very tall man had laughed briefly when he first lay down to try it out.

The imps were lying in their sky-blue world on the top storey, either sleeping or talking in whispers about the funny men. Probably they were giggling quietly, because just after the police officers' arrival the very tall man had suddenly thawed out and played hide and seek with the girls. He had hidden in the wardrobe, under the couch, finally even in the shower. But he took his shoes off first so as not to make the tiles dirty. The imps had enjoyed it and laughed and laughed, and Kai-Petteri Hämäläinen had made a few faces for the two of them before they staggered off to bed in their pink nighties, worn out but happy and no longer worried.

What a strange evening. What a strange few days. He felt under the covers for the places that hurt on his back and his stomach. There would be a scar, the young medical director of the hospital had said, smiling.

Irene moaned and turned over on her other side. He held his breath. He didn't want to wake her up, he wanted to be alone.

The tall man or the very tall man, one or other of them, was probably going round the house. Hämäläinen imagined him standing by the wall of glass, peering out into the dark and concentrating, with his eyes narrowed.

He looked at the light and shadow, and thought about the moment when the tall man had asked him in. A guest in his own house. Irene's silence. The children's uncertain smiles. A kindly personal bodyguard thinking up amusing games to soothe his daughters' anxiety.

He thought of the studio. The burgundy carpet with his desk on it. The spotlights, the curved rows of seating for the audience. The cameras. Questions. Answers. Explaining the world and drinking coffee, or the other way around. A white morning. A stab in the back, and Irene falls silent. And the children play hide and seek with a man they don't know. And Niskanen has refused to come, giving no reasons. At the last attempt he cut the connection before the editorial assistant on the line could even introduce himself by name. Tuula had tried one last time, with the same lack of success, and had then refused to try for the very, very last time. Of course it had been one of the biggest subjects of the last year, which was why, as originally planned, they were going to include a film clip anyway. In which Niskanen claimed to be waiting for the result of the B test.

Tuula had given him a rundown on the sequence of events.

It was now lying on the living-room table. He felt that he would like to look through it. He knew most of it already. The programme was fixed, the little yellow Post-It notes with the questions he was going to ask were in the office, carefully arranged. The presenter's text was on the teleprompter.

He slowly sat up and left the bedroom on tiptoe. The house lay in darkness; downstairs a single light flickered. The television set. He went down the stairs. The very tall man was perched on the arm of an armchair watching the *Hämäläinen* show.

Hämäläinen quietly went up to him.

'Kind of funny,' said the very tall man, turning towards him. 'There you are on TV. And here you are in this room at the same time.'

'Did you hear me coming?' asked Hämäläinen.

The very tall man nodded.

'I was keeping very quiet,' said Hämäläinen.

'All a question of practice,' said the very tall man. 'I didn't know they put the show out this late.'

'They always show repeats at 1.30,' said Hämäläinen.

'Ah,' said the very tall man.

Hämäläinen saw himself on the screen, his lips moving fast but inaudibly. The Hämäläinen on screen looked relaxed and much amused, and beside him stood the forensic pathologist whose name he couldn't remember.

'What's this one . . .?' he murmured.

'What did you say?' asked the very tall man.

'Oh, it's the programme with the puppets,' said Hämäläinen. The very tall man followed his gaze and said nothing. Of course, thought Hämäläinen. A day before his return home they had transmitted the programme with Mäkelä and the forensic pathologist again. It all seemed to be somehow connected with that programme. Tuula hadn't discussed it with him beforehand, why should she? The obvious show to resurrect. The forensic pathologist laughed. Mäkelä laughed. The very tall man asked, 'Shall I turn the sound up?'

'No, no,' said Hämäläinen.

He went to the table where the schedule for the show lay ready. He had only glanced briefly at it before going to bed. He sat down and began to read. The ski-jumping team's gold medals, the flood of the century in and around Joensuu. That rock band's surprise European hit. The conservative MP's sex and drugs orgy. He read until the letters and numbers with which Tuula allotted minutes and seconds to each subject blurred before his eyes. He looked up. His eyes were burning. The final credits were coming up on screen. Keep watching the show. See you tomorrow.

The very tall man switched off the TV set. 'You should try to get some sleep,' he said.

Hämäläinen nodded.

The very tall man left the room, and Hämäläinen watched the blank screen for a long time without thinking of anything in particular.

31 December

58

Kimmo Joentaa slept late, and felt heavy as lead when he woke up.

Larissa had left a note on the living-room table. *Happy New Year, dear Kimmo, see you soon.*

He put the note carefully back on the table. Outside, early fireworks were going off with muffled bangs.

He showered, dressed, made a cup of tea and tried to hold on to the idea that had been there at the moment when he woke.

An idea connected to Erkki Koivikko and what he had said. *Our daughter's death is fifteen years in the past. And the charred plastic figure on the stretcher in that TV show was male.*

He drove to the office. The last day of the year was beginning with a radiant blue sky, like the day before. Fluffy new snow lay in the sunlight. Petri Grönholm was sitting at his desk, and said that Tuomas Heinonen had phoned in to say he would be off sick.

'What?' said Joentaa.

'Sick. Sounded like a heavy cold.'

'Shit,' muttered Joentaa.

'I delegated all the stuff Tuomas was supposed to be working on today,' said Petri Grönholm.

'Hm? Yes . . . yes, good.' He stood there indecisively. He must call Tuomas. Or Paulina. Or both of them. He went down to the cafeteria and sat there for a while beside the big Christmas tree that would be cleared away within the next few days. He saw the reception area, and the place where

Larissa had been standing on Christmas Eve. Everything was different today. There were three of his colleagues in the reception area, the corridors were full of a steady buzz of voices, and there was no Larissa. A plate of biscuits still stood on the table. Star-shaped biscuits. Joentaa helped himself to one and tasted maple syrup. He phoned, thinking what to say to Tuomas, but it was Paulina who answered.

'Hello . . . Paulina, it's Kimmo here.'

'Kimmo, good of you to call. Tuomas is . . . is sick.'

'Yes, Petri told me already. Is there . . . can . . .?'

'A bad cold,' said Paulina. 'He's not feeling at all good.'

'No,' said Joentaa. 'Paulina, listen . . . I know about it, you don't have to . . .'

'Know about what?' said Paulina, her voice suddenly sharp.

'Tuomas has told me about his . . . his gambling addiction. I thought you knew about that . . .'

'Tuomas has a bad cold,' said Paulina.

'Yes. Can I have a word with him?'

'He's not feeling at all well.'

'I really would like to speak to him. I'd like to speak to you both, I think you two will have to do something . . .'

Paulina was silent for a moment, then uttered a shrill laugh. Joentaa was thinking that he had no idea. He didn't know what was happening to Tuomas and Paulina, and he wouldn't be able to help them.

Suddenly Tuomas was on the line. 'Kimmo?'

'Hi. I only wanted to ask how you are. Whether everything's . . . well, all right.'

'Sure,' said Heinonen.

Joentaa did not reply.

'I have this cold. I'll have to stay off work today.'

'Tuomas . . . have you lost again?'

'A cold. I can't come in to work.'

'No.'

'See you soon, Kimmo.'

'I'd like to help you. I think you need to do something fast to get the better of this thing.'

'Sure,' said Heinonen.

'Think of Paulina. And the children,' said Joentaa.

'I will,' said Heinonen. Since the beginning of their conversation he had been speaking in one and the same tone of voice. Quiet and monotonous.

'I wish I could say something to help you,' said Joentaa.

'See you tomorrow,' said Heinonen.

'Tuomas?'

Heinonen had ended the call.

Joentaa went back to the office and thought he would really have to talk to Paulina. Get her to keep the money safe. All there was of it. Once Tuomas had no money left to fall back on he wouldn't be able to go on gambling. It was as simple as that.

Grönholm was brooding over the files when he came back into the office. He looked up when he saw Joentaa. 'I don't think this is going to get us any further,' he said.

Joentaa went to his desk, took the stack of Päivi Holmquist's printouts, and rearranged them. 'The event isn't long ago.'

'What event?' asked Grönholm.

'We're going to concentrate entirely on the most recent incidents now. Probably something that happened in the course of this year,' said Joentaa.

'We've already done that. At least, I've worked my way from the more recent cases back to the older ones.'

'Yes, but now let's concentrate exclusively on incidents of quite recent date,' said Joentaa.

'Why?' asked Grönholm.

'I don't know,' said Joentaa.

'Now that', said Grönholm, 'is a real Kimmo-Joentaa kind of answer.'

Joentaa sat down and read Päivi's list. Only three of the cases she had researched were less than two years ago. Two dead in the crash of a light plane in Tampere, four Finnish victims when a passenger plane came down over Estonia, one dead in a rail accident near Paimio. He looked at the names and dates and thought that they didn't add up to anything.

'I really don't know that we're on the right track here,' said Grönholm.

Joentaa nodded, and thought of Tuomas Heinonen, and the old woman who had baked pizzas, and the giggling cashiers in the fuel station, and the road leading to the water, and then of what Erkki Koivikko had said.

It's fifteen years in the past.

And the figure on the stretcher in the TV show . . .

Unrecognisable, Vaasara had said. Certainly unrecognisable. True to life but unrecognisable. Cloths being raised and lowered again. Men laughing.

On the stretcher in the TV show, Koivikko had said. He had gone to the bathroom to throw up, and then he watched the end of the programme.

Joentaa abruptly sat up, and Grönholm raised his eyes enquiringly. 'All right?'

'Maybe it wasn't seen on TV at all,' said Joentaa.

'What?' asked Grönholm.

'It must have been immediate.'

'Oh?'

'Immediate. No TV screen in between,' said Joentaa.

'Oh,' said Grönholm again.

Joentaa picked up the phone and called the number of *Hämäläinen*'s editor Tuula Palonen. No one answered. He tried again, also unsuccessfully. 'I don't believe it, there must be someone there,' said Joentaa, and tried again a few seconds later.

'What's up?' asked Grönholm.

The phone rang and rang and no one picked it up.

'I want to ask if they still have material from that programme in the archives. They always show the audience as well.'

'What programme?' asked Grönholm. 'What audience?'

He looked for the list, updated daily, of all names and contact details of importance for the investigation. But there was no mobile number given for Tuula Palonen.

'Damn it, I don't believe this.'

'What is it, Kimmo?' asked Grönholm.

'She has five mobiles, one for each ear,' said Joentaa.

'No one has more than two ears, Kimmo.'

'What?'

'Two. No one has more than two ears,' said Grönholm.

He called Sundström's mobile, and got an answer at once.

'What is it, Kimmo?' asked Sundström. Judging by the background noise he was in his car.

'I've been trying to reach Tuula Palonen or one of her colleagues in the editorial office of the *Hämäläinen* show, but no one there is answering the phone.'

'I'm not surprised. They're all busy with this evening's programme. All sorts of personalities are coming, They're all twiddling knobs. There's news. I'm on my way to see Vaasara, Mäkelä's assistant and partner.'

'Yes . . .?'

'He tried to kill himself.'

Joentaa said nothing. He thought of the weary, monotonous voice on the phone the night when he had called Vaasara.

'An amateurish effort. He's doing fine now,' said Sundström.

'Oh,' said Joentaa.

'Cut his wrists like a woman, then got scared and called the emergency doctor.'

He thought of Leena and the baby, Kalle. Of Patrik Laukkanen, who had told Hämäläinen about Kalle, a proud father even before the baby was born.

'With the best will in the world I can't help you to get hold of Tuula Palonen just now,' said Sundström.

'But I need something from her. Please would you tell her that . . .'

'I won't be seeing her until this afternoon.'

'That's too late. Do you have her mobile number?'

'No.'

'I don't believe this, dammit. I'll try calling the TV station again. Maybe I can get them to rustle up someone from that editorial department.'

'What's all this about, then?'

'I don't know yet. I'll be in touch later.'

'Kimmo . . .'

Joentaa ended the call and immediately rang the TV station's switchboard. One of the doormen answered and said he'd connect him. Joentaa waited in a queue, hearing classical music. Violins and piano. Out of the corner of his eye he saw Kari Niemi come into the office and talk to Grönholm.

The music while he waited never seemed to end, and Grönholm stared at Niemi as if there was something he couldn't believe.

Joentaa put the phone to one side.

'Anything new, Kari?' he asked.

Niemi nodded. 'We've separated the contaminated tracks from the usable ones as far as possible. The boys who found Patrik left their own footprints. Trainers, around size 37. But we were able to distinguish a third tread from the footprints of those two.'

'Yes?'

'Trainers again,' said Niemi. 'Size 38.'

'Ah,' said Joentaa.

'It was damn difficult, because the treads are almost identical, but if we're right then the murderer was wearing size 38 shoes.'

Joentaa nodded.

'The angle of entry of the stab wounds indicates a murderer of normal size, but that shoe size makes us think of a young person or . . .'

'Or a woman?' said Grönholm.

'Although according to Salomon's analysis, the wounds were delivered with considerable force,' said Niemi.

Joentaa nodded. Unmitigated, uncontrolled rage. Going hand in hand with concentration and patience.

A shadow, Hämäläinen had said.

A voice spoke quietly on the telephone lying on the desk. Joentaa picked it up. 'Hello?' he asked.

'I'm sorry, I can't reach anyone in the editorial department at the moment,' said the doorman.

'Do you have a mobile number for Tuula Palonen?' asked Joentaa.

'Wait a minute.'

The violins came in again.

Then the doorman was back on the line. 'No,' he said.

'No?'

'No, sorry.'

'Thank you,' said Joentaa, and he called Sundström's mobile again.

'Kimmo?'

'Some news. Kari is here,' he said.

'Yes?'

'The tread of those trainers. Size 38.'

'What?'

'38.'

'That's a child's size.'

'Not necessarily.'

A shadow, thought Joentaa. He closed his eyes and thought he could see a picture. Hämäläinen lying in the silence of an empty hall, feeling no fear. No flight impulse in Patrik

Laukkanen. Mäkelä went over to a car in the middle of the night and asked if he could help.

'I'm coming to Helsinki,' said Joentaa. 'I'll be off at once. We need all the photos the TV station has of the talk show on which Patrik and Mäkelä appeared. All the camera angles. I hope they're still available.'

'Hm. And why?' asked Sundström.

'I think the woman we're looking for was in the audience.'

59

Covering the picture with a white cloth. A man is lying under the cloth. The man has one leg. The leg is a stump. The breakfast buffet has an enormous number of dishes.

'Enjoying your breakfast?' asks Olli Latvala.

She nods.

'May I sit down?' asks Olli Latvala.

'Yes, of course,' she says.

'I'm a little early because we're running slightly behind time, and I have to go to the station soon to pick up Kapanen. The actor who played Jaws in the latest Bond film.'

'Oh,' she says.

Ilmari liked those films. She watched some too, to please him. A perfect world, she always used to think. A simple world, and Ilmari was angry because his enthusiasm amused her. He'd have been interested by the idea of a Finn in the part of the baddie.

'That looks good. I could do with a little something myself.

I think I'll slink unobtrusively up to that buffet,' says Olli Latvala.

She watches him.

Somewhere outside her field of vision people are laughing. They are with her, beside her, above her, below her, but she can't see them. She only hears their laughter. She tries to laugh with them.

The cloth is lowered and then lifted again. Now she can see the face. The look of the closed eyes.

Olli Latvala comes back and explains the course of the day's events to her, while he eats scrambled eggs and bacon.

'You're fifth in our running order,' he says. 'Pencilled in for 21.15 hours, but that could change at short notice.'

She nods.

'We'll do it like this: I'll collect you here at the hotel at 17.00 hours and accompany you until the curtain goes up, so to speak.'

'Thank you,' she says.

'It's only when the show actually begins that I must stay out of sight,' he says. 'But you'll be in the best of hands with Kai-Petteri Hämäläinen.'

She nods.

'He's really great, particularly in conversation with people who . . .' He stops, and seems to be searching for the right words. 'Particularly in conversation with people who have had a bad experience.'

'Yes,' she says.

'We're all delighted that he can appear on today's programme. I'm sure you know about . . . what happened to him.'

'Of course,' she says.

Olli Latvala drains his coffee cup and stands up. 'I'm always rather jittery on days like this, forgive me. I'll be off to the station now. You don't keep actors waiting, especially not when they have the privilege of going for James Bond's jugular. We'll meet at five this afternoon, then?'

She nods.

'See you later,' says Olli Latvala, smiling, before he strides across the lobby.

60

Late in the afternoon Tuula arrived, bringing Raafael Mertaranta in person.

Kai-Petteri Hämäläinen was standing in the kitchen as Tuula steered the car on to his property. He saw Tuula and Mertaranta climb out, watched them coming towards the house in a flurry of flashlights. Several journalists held microphones over the fence and shouted requests for a short interview.

Hämäläinen went to open the door.

'Good heavens,' said Raafael Mertaranta.

'Fantastic,' said Tuula, hugging him with a broad smile, before Mertaranta shook his hand fervently and for a long time. The tall man, the very tall man, Irene and the girls were standing in the background.

'Irene, good to see you,' said Mertaranta. He went towards her, bent down and sketched a kiss on her hand. 'Hello, you two,' he said to the girls.

'Hello, Raafael,' said Irene. 'Hello, Tuula.'

The two women exchanged a brief and distant embrace. The two police officers withdrew quietly into the back part of the house, and Mertaranta asked for coffee as strong as possible.

'I'll make coffee for us all,' said Irene, going into the kitchen.

'Your . . . bodyguards?' asked Mertaranta.

'What? Oh, yes. So to speak. Come on in,' said Hämäläinen, leading the way into the living room. 'Imps, you can go and play anywhere you like.'

The girls ran upstairs. Tuula sat down on the sofa, and Mertaranta dropped into an armchair with a contented sigh. Hämäläinen sat on the second sofa, so that they formed a triangle. In the kitchen, the coffee machine gurgled and hissed.

'Let me say something,' said Mertaranta after a few seconds of silence. 'Let me just say first how enormously glad I am that you're here, that we can all be together here today. And that I'm proud, really proud, and I mean it when I say that you are the flagship of our TV station.'

'Thank you,' said Hämäläinen. He waited for his usual warm reaction, but it didn't seem to be setting in. It was not unusual for Mertaranta to make such remarks; one of the most pressing duties of the head of a station was to take good care of its star, support him at bad times, and be the first to congratulate him at the moment of triumph. Kai-Petteri Hämäläinen knew that, he had learnt to take it for granted, and he had enjoyed it. But today the good feeling somehow wouldn't materialise.

'Thank you,' he said again, and Irene brought in a white tray on which stood white cups and a white coffee pot with steam rising from it.

They drank coffee. Put their cups down. Then Tuula began explaining the strategy that she and Mertaranta had worked out.

'Well, here's how we'll do it. After this you drive to the TV station with the two policemen. And please don't look down your nose at me if I say you ought to be smiling.'

'Smiling,' said Hämäläinen, without looking down his nose.

'Yes, smiling. Giving the impression that everything's all right. And of course you won't say anything, just get in the car. You'll keep your mouth shut until the show begins.'

'Giving the impression that everything's all right . . .'

'And I have just the right opening line for you,' said Tuula.

'What would I do without you?' said Hämäläinen.

Irene cleared her throat and asked if anyone would like more coffee.

'Yes, please,' said Mertaranta.

'It may be rather a strain, I know, to get through it, but we all agree that we . . . that we want to make as much of an effect as possible,' said Tuula.

'Of course,' said Hämäläinen.

'What you're doing today is great, and extraordinary, and we want it to come over like that,' said Tuula. 'Right?'

No one raised any objections.

'Well then, you will get in the car and be driven to the station, where you get out, still acting the same way – smiling, saying nothing – and then you withdraw and the two of us will go over the final schedule for the programme again, and the list of questions. We'll do without your few words with the guests before the show. Olli Latvala and Margot Lind are briefing them.'

Hämäläinen nodded. 'Sounds good,' he said.

Tuula leaned back in relief.

'Wonderful coffee, Irene,' said Raafael Mertaranta.

61

The sharp outline of the glass tower thrust up against the pale blue sky. Kimmo Joentaa entered the building through the broad swing doors. One of the doormen greeted him and tried to call Tuula Palonen, but she was not in her office. He tried again and reached one of her colleagues. After a short conversation the doorman ended the call and said, 'He's just coming. You can wait in the cafeteria.'

'Thank you,' said Joentaa. He went through another door into the large hall. The place where Hämäläinen had been stabbed was still secured by a barrier of yellow tape, and looked a little like something in an exhibition, or an artist's installation with some indefinable meaning. He went past it, on to the cafeteria, and sat down at an empty table.

Soon a young man came towards him with quick, purposeful footsteps. 'Olli Latvala,' he said. 'You must be the gentleman from the police?'

'Yes. Kimmo Joentaa.'

'I don't think we've met before.'

'No.'

'I've been busy for the last few days with plans for the annual retrospective. That's why I'm also pretty busy at the moment. You want to speak to Tuula Palonen?'

'Yes. Although maybe you could help me just as well,' said Joentaa.

'Sure, if I can.'

'It's about the show with Harri Mäkelä and Patrik Laukkanen, the forensic pathologist.'

'Yes?'

'I'd like to see any recorded material available. I'm particularly interested in the audience.'

'The audience?'

'Yes, there's always a camera turned on the audience, isn't there? To catch their reactions.'

'Ah . . . yes, of course.'

'Is that material available? Will it be in the archives somewhere?'

'Er . . . you may laugh, but I have no idea. I'm responsible for preparations for the show and assessment of it afterwards.

In between, the programme itself is in other hands. I'd have to ask the director, or the cutter responsible.'

'That would be kind of you. It's rather urgent. And one more question: are the names of the audience for a given show on record?'

'Er . . .'

'I mean, are there lists of their names?'

'Well, no. Unless we've specially asked someone to come. In that case we have the records because we send the tickets for the show by post. But anyone can turn up spontaneously and ask if there's still space in the studio.'

'Good. I'd very much like to see any such lists.'

'I understand. I tell you what, you have a cup or two of coffee here while I try to dig up any material.'

'Fine,' said Joentaa.

'You're welcome. I'll be back in quarter of an hour,' said Olli Latvala, walking purposefully past the yellow tape towards the lifts, and Joentaa sank back into his chair.

The waitress came and wiped his table with a cloth. 'Can I get you something?' she asked.

'Er . . . tea,' said Joentaa. 'Peppermint tea. No . . . camomile tea, please.'

62

A sunny winter's day. Like the days back then.

It's a long time ago. An age has passed, and the next age is beginning, and like the one just past it will last only a moment.

'Everything's all right,' says the voice.

'Has the sky fallen down?'

'It will be all right,' says the voice.

'Yes,' she says.

Through the window she can see the sea, and a café where she sat with Ilmari and Veikko. Whenever they were in Helsinki they went to this café. Veikko wants ice cream even though it is winter; Ilmari eats cheesecake. Veikko wants ice cream and cries when he gets hot chocolate instead. She glances at the counter and the ice-cream cornets, and Ilmari looks at her sternly. Veikko has hot chocolate, Ilmari has cheesecake. She drinks tea, and gives Veikko the little round biscuit beside her cup.

The sea is frozen over.

The sky is so blue that it hurts your eyes.

Rauna dances and twirls, and Veikko laughs, and Rauna twirls faster and faster, and Veikko laughs louder and louder.

Ilmari skids.

'Have you hurt yourself?' she cries.

Ilmari waves the idea away, and acts as if nothing at all has happened. Something like that always embarrasses him. He gets up. Veikko laughs, Rauna laughs, the sky falls down.

Ilmari ducks, and she tries to meet his eyes, but she can't find him any more, and Olli Latvala will be fetching her. Soon. After an eternity. At 17.00 hours.

63

A quarter of an hour later Olli Latvala came back, and after another ten minutes Kimmo Joentaa was sitting up in a glass room close to the sky.

'Not bad, eh? Only the boss, Raafael Mertaranta, is a floor higher than this,' said Olli Latvala.

Joentaa nodded.

'I'm afraid I can't stay, but Tuulikki will show you everything. She knows this technical stuff much better than I do anyway.'

The handshake of the slender young woman standing beside Latvala was perfunctory, and there was no reading the expression on her face. 'Hello,' she said.

'Hello,' said Joentaa.

'You're lucky, we've found it for you. We even managed to rustle up the full version of the show, I mean before cutting, and some of the tapes of material cut later,' said Latvala.

'Aha . . .' said Joentaa.

'I still have to look for the lists of names and addresses. But it will be best if you look at all this first with Tuulikki. Good luck.'

'Thanks,' said Joentaa, but Olli Latvala was already in the corridor and out of earshot.

'Uncut version?' asked Tuulikki.

'Hm? Er . . . is there a tape showing only the audience?'

She looked at him as if he were an extraterrestrial. 'Only the audience?' She sounded put out.

'Yes, that would be just what I'm looking for.'

'You'd better look at the uncut version first while I find the stuff from the hand-held camera.'

'Er . . . fine.'

'The hand-held camera is used to film the audience,' she explained.

Joentaa nodded. She pressed several buttons, then there was music, and on the screen against the glass wall high up here in the sky, with a few winter clouds, Kai-Petteri Hämäläinen greeted his guests.

64

The low-built blue house looked deserted, thick snow lay in the drive leading up to it, the letterbox was crammed. An ambulance stood by the roadside, and a young woman doctor opened the front door to let Sundström in.

Nuutti Vaasara was sitting on the living-room sofa with his forearms bandaged, and greeted him in an exhausted voice. Sundström thought of Hämäläinen and wondered instinctively why, these days, he was always having to grapple with people who survived instead of being dead.

'How are you, Mr Vaasara?' he asked.

'All right, I think. In the circumstances.' He glanced at the doctor; she smiled and nodded agreement. A paramedic busy packing a bag was kneeling on the floor beside Vaasara.

'Yes, he is,' said the doctor. 'Doing fine. Just at the right moment . . .' She turned to Vaasara. 'Just at the right moment you made the sensible decision to call us.'

Vaasara nodded.

'Would it be all right for me to ask you a few questions here and now?' asked Sundström.

'Of course,' said Vaasara.

'We're on our way,' said the doctor. 'Don't forget about that appointment tomorrow, Mr Vaasara.'

Vaasara nodded. 'Thank you.'

'Goodbye and good luck,' said the doctor,

'Yes, good luck,' murmured the paramedic.

Vaasara nodded.

Then they were alone, and Sundström sat down and looked

at Nuutti Vaasara, slumped on the sofa, and felt a vague queasiness at the thought of all he knew about him. Nuutti Vaasara, born 25 June 1971, grew up in Hanko with a mother who was none too bright and a father inclined, in certain situations, to outbreaks of violent rage. Left school after year eleven, moved out of the parental home, then disappeared for two years claiming he wanted to see the world, which had his few remaining friends and relatives still wondering, twenty years later, how he could have done this without any money. In March 1990 Vaasara had met Harri Mäkelä at a university that he had no right to be attending at all. Since then the two of them had lived and worked together. As a couple. Hard as Sundström tried to be liberal and open-minded, every time he thought of men doing it with men it still turned his stomach. Naked and up to . . . well, whatever they did get up to. His own Lutheran Christian inclinations, dammit.

Did Vaasara guess that his homosexuality was worth a passing note in the files? Even the rainbow media had allowed a bold surmise or so relating to this aspect of the case, but presumably Nuutti Vaasara didn't read the papers, and he certainly had no idea that in the broad, wide-ranging probing that called itself an investigation he was high up on the list of suspects.

He just sat there looking at the wall, and somewhere beyond it into a strange world, his bandaged arms in his lap.

Sundström cleared his throat, looked at the tall, thin man, and Vaasara raised his eyes.

'Do you take shoe size 38, Mr Vaasara?' asked Sundström.

Vaasara did not reply for a long time.

'No,' he said at last, without a sign of annoyance, mockery, or even amusement in his voice.

65

Raafael Mertaranta blew her a kiss before he got into the lift and went up to the next floor.

Tuula Palonen turned away and went into the cafeteria. She felt a brief pang as she passed the area marked off by tape, the rectangle of smooth floor on which Kai-Petteri had lain fighting for his life. The thought was unreal.

She chose avocado soup, risotto, and a pink dessert garnished with raspberries, which looked suspiciously creamy but delicious. With her meal she drank a glass of water and black coffee.

She sat at a table over to one side, ate fast, and was so deep in thought about the course of the next few hours that she hardly noticed the taste of the food.

Finally she drew the raspberry cream and her coffee towards her, and took the schedule and a red pen out of her briefcase. She began reading, taking a spoonful of raspberry cream and a sip of coffee now and then, and ticked items that had already been dealt with.

At one point she stopped for a moment and thought about that police officer, Joentaa. She'd call him and tell him there had been no unusual reactions to the interview with Mäkelä and the forensic pathologist. No threatening letters or anything of that kind. Of course not. There'd been many appreciative letters and emails about the information given in the programme, and the writers had expressed thanks, but that probably wasn't what Joentaa was looking for. In fact, she wondered exactly what he *was* looking for, and thought of the mysterious questions he had asked about the puppets and imaginary causes of death.

She looked at the schedule, the warm-up sequence and the presentations, and her glance fell again on the fifth main subject of tonight's programme.

She thought of Harri Mäkelä. Of the cheerful and well-irrigated evening after the recording. Mäkelä had downed beer after beer and talked his head off. About a plane crash that wasn't a plane crash. She remembered that she hadn't really understood what he had been trying to say. But maybe that taciturn policeman could make something of it.

She made a mental note to call him as soon as she had a free moment, and took a last spoonful from her dish of rasp-berry cream. She drained her coffee, went through the hall, past the rectangle marked off by police tape and over to the lifts, then up to the twelfth floor.

Margot Lind was sitting in the open-plan office of the *Hämäläinen* talk show, telephoning. 'Olli's looking for you,' she said as she put the receiver down. 'And one of those policemen called. Or rather it was someone from reception, to say he hadn't been able to connect the policeman with us, and the policeman would like someone to call back.'

'Oh yes?' said Tuula Palonen.

'Just a moment. I wrote the name down. Yes, Joentaa, from Turku.'

Joentaa, thought Tuula Palonen, that pain in the neck. At that moment Olli Latvala came into the office, cheerful and confident as ever and said, 'There was a policeman looking for you. Man called Joentaa.'

Margot Lind giggled. 'Persistent, isn't he?'

'How do you mean?' asked Latvala.

'Okay, I'll call him,' said Tuula Palonen. 'Give me the number, Margot.'

'There's no need, he's here. Sitting up there with one of the cutters watching some archival material.'

'Oh,' said Tuula Palonen. 'What kind of archival material?'

'The uncut version of the show with Mäkelä and that forensic pathologist. And anything else we could find from that edition. Footage from the hand-held camera, for instance.'

'Oh,' said Tuula Palonen.

'Mainly he wanted to see pictures of the audience,' said Latvala.

'Right,' said Tuula Palonen. 'I'll go and see him right away.'

'No need for that either. If I understood him correctly I've already been able to find him everything he wanted,' said Latvala.

'Oh, good. All the better,' said Tuula Palonen.

'If you have time I'd like to discuss a couple of ideas about the set for today's show,' said Olli Latvala.

'Go ahead,' she said, and Latvala sat down beside her. She thought again of Harri Mäkelä, who had sent them that impossible puppet. It was no good, they'd had to reject it on the very day of the show, but Mäkelä had provided a substitute all the same. And in the evening, after his tenth beer and fourth chaser of schnapps, he had said there'd been a little misunderstanding. Maybe she ought to go up one floor and see what Joentaa was doing. Archival material. Pictures of the audience.

'Er . . . Tuula, are you with me?' asked Olli Latvala.

'What? Yes, of course.'

'Well . . . did you hear what I said?'

'Begin again at the beginning,' she said.

'Right, the idea is for Kai-Petteri to move from the sofa to the other group of seats depending on the subject,' said Latvala. 'And I'd definitely have the ski-jumpers sitting on the sofa, particularly as they're bringing their skis . . .'

'What?' asked Tuula Palonen distractedly.

'Their skis.'

'They're bringing their skis into the studio?'

'Yes, it's something to do with their sponsor's contract. Kai-Petteri is supposed to be asking several questions about the composition of the skis, and skis for ski-jumping are very long, so the group of seats with the desk wouldn't be so suitable, if you see what I mean.'

'Yes, of course,' said Tuula Palonen.

'The problem is that we've also planned to use the sofa for the next item in the show, so the effect would be static, and the directing team doesn't like my suggestion of deliberately bringing the ski-jumpers into the picture with the hand-held camera.'

'I see,' said Tuula Palonen.

'So have a word with them, will you?'

'I will,' said Tuula Palonen.

66

The tall man sat at the wheel, the very tall man on the back seat with him, and the sunny winter day began to move towards afternoon twilight. The tall man sat upright saying nothing, the very tall man sat upright saying nothing. You would never have known that the very tall man had been playing hide and seek with the twins the evening before, like a child himself. A quick-change artist, thought Hämäläinen, and he thought of the evening ahead, and the Spanish girl-friend he'd once had in a life long ago.

To this day he found a certain consolation in assuming

that she had left him because of the Finnish winter and not for other, more personal reasons. Once, when the Spanish girl came to see him, she had walked through Customs wearing a summer jacket, and when they were waiting for the bus in the cold and the dark she had asked whether the sun always set so early in Finland. Only in winter, Hämäläinen had told her, and a week later she had flown home, never to return.

'Dark outside,' said Hämäläinen, and the very tall man looked enquiringly at him.

'When you think that the sun was still shining only fifteen minutes ago, I mean,' said Hämäläinen.

67

She goes swimming. The words over the entrance say 'Wellness Oasis', and in front of it stands a man in the hotel uniform who asks for her room number. She takes the key out of her bathrobe pocket and gives him the number.

'Welcome,' says the man, and he begins to tell her about the various saunas, steam baths and massages from which she can choose.

'I just want to swim,' she says.

'You're welcome,' says the man, showing her to the pool. The water splashes softly and lies calm in the dim light.

'Thank you,' she says, and the man withdraws.

She takes off her bathrobe and carefully puts it down on one of the loungers. Then she stands under the shower for a few minutes. She hears a loud splash; someone has jumped into the water. She comes out of the shower, goes towards the pool over the cool, smooth tiles. A man is just getting out of the water, and stops when he sees her. He seems to be intrigued, maybe because she is naked. She hasn't brought a bathing suit with her, she hadn't thought that she might be able to swim at the hotel.

'Hi there,' says the man in English.

She would like to explain about the bathing suit to him, but it's a long time since she spoke any English, and the words elude her.

'Hi,' is all she says.

'See you later,' says the man, walking away, and she lets herself slip into the water.

She dives down and wraps herself in its cold, heavy blueness like a blanket, until life forces her back up to the surface.

68

'All I needed today was someone like you,' said Tuulikki.

'Hm?' Joentaa turned his eyes away from the screen.

'Never mind,' said Tuulikki.

'Could you please wind it back a few minutes again? To the place where the camera begins tracking over the audience.'

'Right,' said Tuulikki.

Joentaa focused on the pictures flying backwards and said, after a while, 'Stop. I think this is where it begins.'

Tuulikki let the tape run on.

'That's it,' said Joentaa, leaning forward.

The audience was in sight on screen, sitting side by side

in rows, concentrating as they listened to Patrik Laukkanen, who was not in the picture but whose voice filled the studio. Joentaa thought of Leena Jauhiainen and baby Kalle, and looked at the audience, all of its members, curiously, reacting as one to what Patrik Laukkanen was saying. Collective laughter, collective gravity. Patrik Laukkanen made what he was saying sound interesting and informative. Then Mäkelä was asked to come up on stage. The hand-held camera lingered on the applauding audience.

Joentaa leaned even further forward, because the conversation about the puppets was now beginning on the stage, out of sight. Hämäläinen was asking questions in an easy, cheerful tone, and Mäkelä said, 'A corpse burnt to death in a fire isn't necessarily what it seems.'

Now and then Patrik Laukkanen made a comment, and the hand-held camera moved over the spectators grimacing or laughing or listening spellbound. The mood changed from moment to moment.

'The legs are at an angle,' said Mäkelä, 'the arms outstretched.'

'Forensic science can draw conclusions from that,' said Patrik Laukkanen. 'For instance, it makes it possible to work out which part of the body began to burn first and where the fire spread to.'

Hämäläinen asked a question, and Laukkanen said, 'The internal organs are usually well preserved in victims of fire, that's characteristic.'

Hämäläinen moved on to the next puppet. Some of the spectators looked away, others stared at the stage, even more fascinated.

'How cute,' said Mäkelä.

Hämäläinen laughed.

'I mean that charming cloth you've draped over the hips,' said Mäkelä. 'It wasn't there when I made the puppet.'

There was a short silence.

Hämäläinen injected a serious tone into his voice, presumably to smooth over the brief moment of embarrassment.

'So here we have the victim of a plane crash,' said Hämäläinen.

Another short silence, and Mäkelä cleared his throat. Joentaa noticed that only incidentally, because he was concentrating on the faces of the audience. Horrified, amused, repelled, interested. They were no longer reacting in unison, yet their cohesion was still maintained. The spectators could choose from a range of possible reactions, but none of them reacted out of character.

Except for Erkki Koivikko, who had been sitting on his living-room sofa. Who got to his feet, went to the bathroom and threw up.

Joentaa narrowed his eyes, and Mäkelä made another joke about the cloth covering the corpse's genitals.

The audience laughed, reacting in unison again. The handheld camera lingered on the spectators as a whole for a few seconds, before moving over the crowd and beginning to study individual faces again.

'Stop,' said Joentaa.

Infuriatingly slowly, Tuulikki leaned forward and pressed a button.

'Back,' said Joentaa.

Tuulikki wound the tape back.

'Stop,' said Joentaa again.

He looked at the frozen picture.

Nine people sitting close together, beside each other or one behind another. Eight of them were laughing. Four heartily and uninhibitedly. Two teenagers and two young men. An older woman was laughing in a rather forced way, an elegantly dressed middle-aged man was laughing absently as if his mind were on something else. The woman beside him was laughing hysterically, and a white-haired man was chuckling with tears in his eyes.

Joentaa leaned back. He focused on the slender, tall woman in the middle of the picture. She was wearing a plain dark dress. He sat there motionless for several minutes.

'Are we going on with this?' asked Tuulikki.

Joentaa heard her voice only vaguely.

'Hello?' said Tuulikki.

'Sorry,' said Joentaa.

'Because I have to go down to the studio soon. There's a meeting about camera angles before the show begins. And we've been sitting here for ever.'

'Yes,' said Joentaa.

For ever, he thought. The word echoed through his mind. 'What do you see there?'

'What do I see?' asked Tuulikki.

'Yes.'

'I see people in the audience falling about laughing at Kai-Petteri. Or at that puppet-maker guy . . . Mäkelä. Probably at both of them.'

'Yes,' said Joentaa.

He looked at the woman sitting upright in the middle of the screen. A frozen smile in a frozen picture. 'Could you please let it run on very slowly?' he asked.

'Sure,' said Tuulikki.

The picture moved on in gentle slow motion. Joentaa felt pain behind his eyes, and Tuulikki said, 'That woman in the middle doesn't seem to be having as much fun as the others.'

Joentaa nodded.

'Oh, my goodness,' said Tuulikki.

The door behind them was opened, but neither Joentaa nor Tuulikki could take their eyes off the screen.

'She looks like living death,' said Tuulikki.

'I hope you don't mean me,' said Tuula Palonen, laughing.

69

Marko Westerberg listened to the acid comments with his usual composure. Anyway, most of the company seemed more amused than anything by the safety precautions, and Westerberg himself was among those who were amused.

He had always thought well of Paavo Sundström, but he was at a loss to understand what had come over the man now. Sundström had seen to the setting up of a security zone at the entrance area. It was more reminiscent of the departure gate in an airport than the way into a TV studio.

The visitors to the show, slowly coming in and including prominent figures of all kinds, frowned now and then, and made themselves look as if they found the whole thing funny, and his officers tried hard to do their job with suitably straight faces, while cameras were turned on them from all angles, recording the whole procedure, contrary to the original agreement. Presumably to go on about it at length in the show itself, letting everyone know what a big star Hämäläinen was.

Westerberg buried his hands in the pockets of his jacket, brought out again specially for this occasion, and watched for a while as the rows of seats slowly but steadily filled up. Once past the airport security gate, members of the audience were handed drinks and small snacks, Karelian rice cakes spread with fish roe.

His mobile rang. It was Sundström.

'All clear there with you?' he asked.

'Yes. Apart from the fact that they're recording the whole thing here from every angle,' Westerberg answered.

'That was only to be expected. Never mind,' said Sundström. 'Is Hämäläinen there yet?'

'Not so far. But according to my information he'll be arriving shortly.'

'Good. I'm on my way now. See you soon.'

'See you,' said Westerberg, slipping the mobile back into his side pocket.

One of the good-looking young women editors, Margot Lind if he remembered rightly, came up to him, her eyes shining. 'Can't we persuade you to give us a little interview? Simply to . . . to do justice to these special circumstances.'

'Sorry,' he said. 'And please make sure that the faces of the police officers being recorded on film here don't go out on the show. That was clearly agreed.'

She nodded, and was going to ask something else, but then she turned to the blitz of flashing lights illuminating the darkness beyond the glass panes. 'That'll be Kai-Petteri now,' she said.

Westerberg followed her gaze. They were turned to the entrance hall. Hämäläinen came through the broad swing doors and, flanked by the two personal bodyguards assigned to him, walked purposefully to the lifts.

The three of them got in, the doors closed, and outside the lights went on flashing for several minutes, until word got around that the subject wanted by the photographers for their pictures was not there any more.

70

'A m I . . . er, disturbing you?' asked Tuula Palonen. The two of them did not respond. Tuulikki and the policeman Joentaa were staring in silence at the screen, on which Tuula Palonen could see nothing very startling.

She came closer. The audience. The footage taken with the hand-held camera. Laughing people. 'Anything special?' When neither Joentaa nor Tuulikki reacted she added, 'I have to go down now. They've already started letting people in. And Kai-Petteri will be here any moment.'

Joentaa said nothing. Nor did Tuulikki.

'You were looking for me?' Tuula Palonen asked Joentaa.

'I have what I wanted,' said Joentaa.

'We didn't get any letters that might interest you,' said Tuula Palonen, just to make Joentaa take his eyes off the screen at last, and turn to her.

'What did you say?' he asked.

'You wanted me to find out whether there were any reactions to that programme, letters or emails attacking Kai-Petteri or the other participants.'

'Yes,' Joentaa agreed.

'No, there weren't,' said Tuula Palonen.

'Thank you,' said Joentaa. He didn't even seem to have heard her.

'But one thing did occur to me. It might interest you,' she said.

'Yes?' asked Joentaa.

'The causes of death were important to you in some way, weren't they?'

At last Joentaa looked at her.

'I mean you wanted to know whether we'd had any correspondence about the . . . the kinds of death. The causes of death of the . . . the puppets.'

Joentaa nodded.

'Like I said, we had no correspondence of that kind, but there was a . . . a complication on the day of the programme, and I only remembered it today.'

'Yes?' Joentaa was paying attention now.

'Mäkelä supplied three puppets; we'd discussed it all and agreed on certain puppets that would give as wide as possible an idea of the work of a puppet-maker producing models of dead bodies like that . . .'

'Yes,' said Joentaa.

'The problem was that among the puppets Mäkelä delivered there was one we couldn't use. The victim of a plane crash, as agreed, but it was a little girl.'

'Yes,' said Joentaa.

'We couldn't possibly show a little girl on the programme,' said Tuula Palonen. 'Do you see what I mean?'

'Not entirely,' said Joentaa.

'We can't put a dead little girl on show. We put the puppet aside and asked Mäkelä for a substitute. We wanted three puppets, but not that little girl. Then it was all rather hectic, Mäkelä sent us one of a man, and we thought that puppet too was the victim of an air crash. But in fact it had been made for a film about the collapse of that indoor skating rink in Turku.'

Joentaa nodded, but he didn't understand. He felt dizzy. A little girl. A plane crash.

A man. An ice rink.

'I'm not entirely with you,' he said.

'After the show we went to have a drink, Mäkelä, the forensic pathologist, Margot Lind and I.'

'Yes,' said Joentaa.

'And after a while Mäkelä began talking at length about his puppets. He said it had been annoying for him during the show when Kai-Petteri described one of his puppets as the victim of a plane crash, when really his puppet had . . . died another kind of death. He said he hadn't liked to contradict Kai-Petteri at the time, and in the end it made no difference, because sometimes there were no characteristic features to show whether someone had . . . had fallen to his death or whether his death had fallen on him.'

Joentaa nodded. It was a few seconds before he understood the comparison.

'He put it something like that. The way the bodies look is sometimes the same, never mind whether they died in an air crash or in the collapse of a building. As in the case of that ice rink.'

Ice rink, thought Joentaa.

'Do you understand?'

'No,' said Joentaa.

Ice rink, he thought. Turku.

'Well, the puppet delivered to us just before the show had been made for a documentary. The accident at that Turku skating rink when the roof collapsed. It made headlines early this year.'

Joentaa nodded. Mäkelä's archives. CorpsesForDummies. He stood up and reached for his rucksack. The CD that his friendly colleague in Helsinki had burnt for him was lying in its side compartment.

'I don't suppose it's important,' said Tuula, 'but I wanted to tell you because you were interested in that . . . that aspect of it.'

'Thank you,' said Joentaa. He looked around him. 'I'd like to play a CD. Can I use that computer?' He pointed to the one standing on a desk to one side.

'Of course,' said Tuulikki. She took the CD and put it into the computer drive.

Tuula Palonen's mobile played a symphony.

'Yes? Oh, good. Wonderful. I'll be with you right away.'

'There are only photographs on it,' said Tuulikki.

Joentaa sat down beside her at the desk.

Ice rink. Turku, he thought. The accident had dominated the news. At the beginning of the year. For several days he had investigated the scene until the vague original suspicion of intentional murder had been ruled out. It was an accident. A tragic accident.

He thought of the cheerful widower who had moved into an empty house. Who was used to tragedies.

'I have to go down. Kai-Petteri has arrived,' said Tuula Palonen. 'See you later.'

'Yes,' said Joentaa.

'Do you want any particular folder opened?' asked Tuulikki.

'Why is a dead man better than a dead girl?' asked Joentaa.

'What?' replied Tuulikki.

'Never mind. CorpsesForDummies, please.'

'What?'

'That's the name of the folder I want to look at.'

'Ah, got it.'

The name of the file ran: *170208/FIN/TUR*.

17 February 2008. Skating rink, Finland. Turku.

Tuulikki pressed a key, and thumbnail views of all the photographs came up on the screen.

'Do you want to look at them all?'

'Yes, please,' said Joentaa, and Tuulikki pressed another button.

Flickering pictures.

A macabre slide show, thought Joentaa, nothing more.

'Edifying stuff,' said Tuulikki.

A winter evening lit up in bright colours. Black and yellow. Firefighters in red. Paramedics in white. A mixture of colours in the dark, blurring before his eyes.

'Oh,' said Tuulikki.

Falling to your death, having your death fall on you. Used to tragedy. Would you like to stay with her? the doctor had asked. At the hospital, in the minutes after Sanna's death.

'Did you see that?' asked Tuulikki.

'What?' he said.

'I'd like another look at that photo. Just a moment.' Tuulikki pressed buttons, and then they were sitting side by side in silence again in front of a frozen picture.

'Look at that, the dead man in the middle next to the firefighter, under the rubble.'

She pointed to the screen, gently touching the picture of the dead man with her forefinger.

'It reminds me of one of the puppets in the programme. He's lying in just the same way. They look identical. And he has only one leg. As if he'd been the model for the puppet.'

How cute, thought Joentaa.

'If it weren't for the closed eyes and injuries everywhere, I'd say they were the very image of each other,' said Tuulikki.

'Yes,' said Joentaa.

'It's eerie,' said Tuulikki.

'I have to find out who he is,' said Joentaa.

Tuulikki leaned forward and touched the screen again. Very lightly and carefully. She showed him what he had just seen. 'I think that . . . that bundle lying in front of the larger body is . . . it looks almost like a . . .'

'A child,' said Joentaa.

71

When Olli Latvala entered the hotel lobby the woman was already sitting on one of the sofas. She did not seem to notice all the comings and goings around her. She was looking straight ahead into nothing.

Olli Latvala slowed down. He was a little anxious. He wondered if she would be up to appearing on the show, and thought of what had happened to her. It was unimaginable. He had no idea what this woman must be feeling, and he asked himself whether Kai-Petteri would succeed in getting through to her.

The questions that he and Tuula had put together were good questions. They built up from each other, and there was plenty of scope for dealing with anything unforeseen. What was important today was the fact that the show was going out live. No one was better than Kai-Petteri at dealing with the unforeseen, no one could break the ice better.

Break the ice, he thought. To lose her husband and her son, to see it happen. Severely injured herself. And to this day no one knew exactly why the roof of that skating rink had fallen in.

He thought it had been the right decision to fetch her from the hotel himself and not leave it to one of the drivers. He had a feeling that she needed special attention, and had . . . well, deserved it.

He quickened his pace again and injected a certain amount of volume and confidence into his voice as he said, still some distance away, 'Hello, here I am. It's nearly time now.'

The woman took her eyes off the driving snow outside the panes and looked at him.

'Shall we go?' asked Olli Latvala.

The woman stood up.

'There's a good deal of traffic, and it's snowing. But I know a way of my own to the TV station,' said Olli Latvala. He smiled at her.

The woman nodded and followed him into the open air. His car was parked directly opposite the gilded main entrance to the hotel, in a No Parking zone. The hotel doormen flanking the entrance nodded at them, and Latvala said, 'Good, no parking ticket, I'm in luck. Sometimes it takes our helpful friends only a minute to write one of those out for you.'

He let the woman into the passenger's side, got in himself, and moved the car out into the evening traffic. Fireworks were going off sporadically in the sky; they drove past a rear-end collision. One of the cars had slipped into the roadside gutter, the other had a slightly dented bonnet.

'I don't think it's anything serious,' said Olli Latvala, and the woman nodded.

'How are you doing?' asked Olli Latvala. 'Do you like the hotel?'

'Yes,' said the woman.

'Did you come across Bon Jovi?'

'Yes,' she said.

He turned his eyes away from the road. 'You did?'

'Yes, in the swimming pool.'

'Seriously?'

'Yes.'

'I don't believe it,' said Latvala.

'At least, that's who he looked like. And he was speaking English,' she said.

'Must have been him,' said Latvala.

'Maybe he was surprised because I was swimming naked. I hadn't brought a swimsuit with me.'

Olli Latvala laughed and turned his eyes back to the road ahead. He felt relieved, without being able to say why.

Maybe because now he was sure that this woman was still taking part in real life, even if only by meeting a rock star in the swimming pool.

72

He sat beside Tuulikki looking at the picture of two bodies under rubble.

Tuulikki phoned a colleague and asked him to stand in for her at the meeting with the cameramen, and Joentaa called Grönholm's mobile.

'The collapse of the ice rink in Turku, early this year,' he said.

'Yes, what about it?' asked Grönholm.

'I'm sure you remember it.'

'Of course.'

'We need the names of the dead. A complete list. We could be looking for a father and son.'

'Father and son?'

'We have a photo here. The body of a man, a child with him. They could be father and son. At the moment it's only a theory, but they're lying . . . well, as if closely entwined. Anyway, we need those names. Ask Päivi Holmquist to help you with the research.'

'Sure. Then is it . . . why is the ice rink suddenly part of the case?'

'I'll explain it all later. We need to move fast now, we're near the solution.'

'Right, I'll get to work.'

'Thanks. Call me as soon as you have something.'

'I'll get in touch,' said Grönholm.

'Do that,' said Joentaa, and ended the call. Tuulikki got up and went to the screen with the still of the laughing people still flickering on it. And the picture of the woman in the middle who wasn't laughing with the rest of them. Tuulikki began pressing keys and adjusting controls, and Joentaa called Sundström's number.

'Hello? Kimmo?'

'Where are you at the moment?' asked Joentaa.

'In the TV station. Entrance hall, at the security check. I've just arrived.'

'Then please come straight up to floor thirty-six.'

Sundström said nothing for a few seconds. Then he asked, 'What do you mean?'

'I'm here in the TV building too, on the thirty-sixth floor, in the office of one of the cutters, her name's Tuulikki.'

'Tuulikki?'

'And tell Westerberg.'

'He's right here with me.'

'Then both of you come up. We have something here that you ought to see.'

'Yes . . . right. We'll be with you,' said Sundström.

'See you,' said Joentaa, breaking the connection again.

He looked at the two dead bodies lying in a sea of rubble and snow, against the background of a dark, starlit winter night.

Behind his back, Mäkelä said, 'How cute.'

Tuulikki had changed the tape. 'Identical,' she said in a toneless voice.

Hämäläinen laughed. Laughed at Mäkelä's comment. The audience joined in.

Joentaa turned to Tuulikki, and on the screen saw the puppet lying on a stretcher in the warm illumination of the spotlight.

The dead don't have faces, Vaasara had said.

He thought of the moment that never ended, and the winter behind the panes of the glass tower was indistinguishable from last winter, when the roof of a skating rink in Turku had collapsed.

73

Kai-Petteri Hämäläinen was looking at Tuula as she carefully arranged the yellow Post-It notes in order, side by side or above each other. From time to time she rearranged them, or removed a note because the point mentioned on it wasn't needed now. Kapanen, who had inflicted a gunshot wound on James Bond, had agreed to come only on condition that he wasn't asked any questions about the soap opera in which he had begun his career.

The politician who had dominated the headlines for several weeks on end, after snorting cocaine during a grand reception in Sweden, asked them not to touch on that subject, although it was the only reason why he had been invited to appear on the show in the first place.

Several other Post-It notes found their way into the wastepaper basket, and Tuula said, 'Makes no difference. Of course we'll have to ask him about it, but you'll make it arise naturally from the situation.'

Arise naturally from the situation, thought Hämäläinen. 'Of course,' he said.

'He'll know it's coming, he can't be that stupid. He probably only wants to make sure you won't be too hard on him.'

'Yes, probably,' said Hämäläinen.

'I'll let him know just before the show begins, say we came to the editorial conclusion that the subject had to be mentioned, but at the same time I'll indicate that there's nothing for him to worry about.'

'Right,' said Hämäläinen.

Tuula laughed. 'As if there was still anything to be hushed up. The man doesn't seem to realise that it was the only reason for his popularity.'

'Sometimes people don't understand things,' said Hämäläinen. He stared at the yellow notes, and after a while sensed Tuula's eyes resting on him.

'Good to have you back,' she said.

'Yes,' he said.

He thought of the imps looking at him as if he were a stranger.

He thought of Irene's hesitant touch, and the trembling in her voice that only he could hear.

He thought of the girlfriend of the gunman who ran amok, the girl who had said she could have helped him, she was sure she could.

He thought of a night under neon lighting in hospital.

'Good luck,' said Tuula.

He nodded.

'After the show we'll slip off and celebrate your return.'

'Let's do that.'

'Sound check in five minutes?' asked Tuula.

He nodded.

He could feel the make-up on his face.

He sat there for a few more minutes, then he got to his feet, and as he went along the corridor towards the babble of voices growing steadily louder, he thought of the very tall man who had hidden in the shower and made the children laugh until, for a while, they had forgotten everything that frightened them.

74

The woman passes a soft brush over her face and says she really ought to do something about that, and she doesn't understand what the woman means.

'Your lips. They're so rough, you ought to do something about it.'

'Yes?' she says.

'I can't deal with that here and now. It's more of a long-term project.'

'Yes,' she says.

'I can only cover it up a bit,' says the woman, going over her lips with the brush. 'That's better. I can't do any more. More colour, Ukko.'

Ukko, a small, youthful-looking man, brings up a tray presumably holding the colours.

She closes her eyes and feels the fibres of the brush on her cheeks again. Stroking, tickling.

'We can make a reasonable job of this,' says the woman. 'You're the very fair-skinned type. I can't get rid of that, I can only mitigate the effect a bit.'

She nods.

Get rid of it, she thinks, mitigate the effect. She thinks about words, and behind her back Olli Latvala asks, 'Everything okay here?'

'Nearly through now,' says the woman. 'I can't do much about the lips, but I've covered up the sore places.'

'Good,' says Olli Latvala.

Then she walks down a corridor beside Olli Latvala to a large room. There are trays of open sandwiches and fruit on tables along the wall.

'Help yourself,' says Olli Latvala. 'Would you like something to drink?'

'I don't think so,' she says. 'I'm not thirsty.'

'By the way, you mustn't take my colleague in make-up too seriously. Your lips are perfectly all right.'

Music comes through loudspeakers.

'Here we go,' says Olli Latvala. 'But we have a little time yet. You'd better make yourself comfortable, and I'll come and fetch you at the right moment. Then, like I said, I'll go just up to the stage with you, not beyond that. Okay?'

She nods.

'I'll be back. By the way, the white baguettes with eel and chopped egg are particularly delicious. I can recommend them highly,' says Olli Latvala. 'And if Bon Jovi happens to burst in here, mind you don't confuse him any more! He has to sing today.'

He smiles.

She likes his smile.

Then he goes away, leaving her alone in the big room.

75

Paavo Sundström and Marko Westerberg were out of breath when they entered the room.

Outside, the snow had turned to driving sleet, and frozen pictures were flickering on the screens.

A puppet on a stretcher in a TV studio.

And two bodies, a man and a child, under rubble in the snow. The man had only one leg. His eyes were closed.

Sundström and Westerberg looked at the pictures for a long time, went back and forth between the flat screen and the computer monitor, and finally Sundström asked, 'What is it?'

'The photo is from the collapse of the skating rink in Turku. You remember, early this year, in February.'

'Of course.'

'The dead man in the photograph looks very like that puppet. They're practically identical,' said Joentaa.

'Yes,' said Sundström, looking at the puppet on the flat screen on the wall. 'I see what you mean.'

'The woman we're looking for saw someone she was mourning lying on that stretcher. Not a puppet, she saw a man she knew. Mäkelä did justice to his own claim.'

'Meaning?' asked Westerberg.

'He wanted to create a perfect imitation of reality. And he did. As the woman saw it, there was no difference. While the others were amused, she saw a real person lying on the stretcher, just as she'd seen him at the moment of his death, and . . . maybe she was in the skating rink herself, and survived the accident.'

Sundström nodded without taking his eyes off the screen.

'I also think she didn't see the show on TV, I think she saw it here. She was in the studio audience.'

'What?' said Sundström.

'Can we run the other tape again?' he asked.

Tuulikki nodded. She swapped the tapes, and wound the one now in the machine back to the place where eight people were laughing and one was not.

'I think that's the woman we want. The woman in the middle,' said Joentaa.

Sundström did not reply. He focused on the picture, his eyes narrowed.

'That's terrible,' said Westerberg in the background.

Sundström nodded. 'I see what you mean. All the same, she could simply be a woman who found the whole thing rather less amusing than the rest of them.'

'That may well be so,' said Joentaa.

'That woman looks . . . she looks dreadful,' said Westerberg.

'I've asked Petri to get together with Päivi Holmquist and dig up all the data about victims of the accident at the ice rink,' said Kimmo Joentaa. 'That ought to be the quickest way. There's also a list of the people in the audience at the chat show, but it's incomplete, and because there were no numbered tickets it will be difficult to identify the woman that way in a hurry. And as you rightly say, we can't be sure about the woman in the audience.'

Sundström nodded.

'Petri will ring back soon and then we'll know more.'

'Yes,' said Sundström.

Tuulikki had risen to her feet and was leaning over the computer monitor. 'Who takes photographs like that?' she asked.

Joentaa, Sundström and Westerberg followed her gaze.

The child was lying turned away from the camera, as if to hug the man, and one of the man's hands rested on the child's unnaturally flat body. In the light the camera had cast on it the picture looked as if the photographer had been fascinated by the scene.

'Who takes photographs like that?' Tuulikki asked again.

76

All eyes were on him. The cameras were turned on him. His legs were rather weak. He felt a smile on his face and sweat on his forehead. The button in his ear was working. The assistant stood a few metres away, both hands holding up the card showing his cues. The first presentation was waiting in the teleprompter. He had forgotten just what Tuula had written for him. He stood there at the centre of the world, searching for words.

'Welcome,' he said. 'I'm very glad to be here this evening. And very glad that you . . . that you are here with me.'

He turned to the bright red group of seats including the sofa where he was to welcome the first guest. It looked comfortable.

Whatever Tuula had written for him had been different. Probably better.

He sensed the camera on his back. He sat down. The full text of the presentation came up on the teleprompter. The cues were on the large piece of cardboard that the assistant was holding up.

'A year is ending, a new year is beginning. We are here together to look back. We will try to discover what was important in the year just gone. Good enough or sad enough to accompany us into the New Year. The things that stand out from everyday life, creating memories that will stay with us. Things that we cannot forget, or do not want to forget, or ought not to forget.'

He felt dizziness behind his forehead, and an impulse to wipe the sweat away from his hair.

'I would like to say hello to my wife, who is usually in front of the television when I am on it. My most important and best critic. In fact, my only critic.'

The audience laughed, and he laughed with them. The sweat on his body felt good.

'And I'd like to say hello to my daughters. Hi, you two. See you after the show. Too bad if you can't stay awake until midnight, because I have any amount of fireworks waiting.'

More laughter from the audience. He felt their glances without being able to see the people. All he saw was the radiance of the spotlights.

He had a feeling that he weighed less and less all the time, and he looked at the text of the first presentation on the teleprompter for a little while before he began to speak again.

'And not least, of course, I would like to welcome my first guest. A man who felt the full force of happy chance in the year just past. This lucky person can boast of achieving the age of seventy-four, and he won the biggest jackpot in the history of the Finnish lottery. Welcome, Elvi Laaksola!'

Applause burst out, and a white-haired man came towards him, looking unsure of himself rather than lucky.

77

A dead man in the snow, a puppet on a stretcher, a woman in the audience, and on the fourth screen Hämäläinen was talking to a winner who said he had been a loser all his life.

'And now it's too late,' he said. 'What am I supposed to do with all that money now? I don't feel like travelling, and I can't drive a car because of my eyes.'

Hämäläinen smoothed over the situation with a joke.

The audience laughed.

The white-haired man remained waspish, and seemed unwilling to be disabused of the idea that winning the jackpot was an unreasonable imposition, the last thing he needed in his old age.

'Very funny,' said Sundström. 'That's how I'd like to be when I get old.'

'Seriously?' asked Tuulikki.

'It was a joke,' said Sundström.

The monotonous ring tone of Joentaa's mobile sounded. He took it out of his trouser pocket. 'Petri?' he said.

'Hi, Kimmo. Well, we already have something,' said Grönholm.

'Yes?'

'When the roof of the skating rink collapsed, twenty-four people lost their lives. We have their names.'

'Good.'

'Can I fax them to you? Or if you can lay hands on a computer I'll send you the list in an email.'

'Do that. As soon as you can, please.'

'Right,' said Grönholm. 'You'll see that several of the victims had the same surnames. We haven't gone through them yet to find two who might be father and son. We're going to do that now.'

'Fine,' said Joentaa.

'I'll ring back as soon as I have news.'

'One more thing: does the list include the names of injured victims who survived?'

'Er, no.'

'We need to know about them too.'

'That could take more time. As far as I remember, there were quite a lot of them, and it'll be a good deal more difficult to get a full list of those names.'

'Try, please. And as soon as you find the name of a survivor that matches any of the victims let us know. We may be looking for a man and boy who died, and a woman who was among the survivors.'

'Okay, we'll get to work on it. More later,' said Grönholm, breaking the connection.

Joentaa turned to Tuulikki. 'Can you reach Olli Latvala?'

'I can try, but I'm afraid it's not likely. He's looking after the guests, and we have an enormous programme today.'

Joentaa nodded. 'He said there were names of at least some of the audience, and if they wrote ordering tickets those were sent by post. I'd like a list of any names.'

Tuulikki nodded. She tried ringing Olli Latvala, but after a while she shook her head. 'No good. He has ears for nothing but his headset right now, and the people taking part in this evening's show.'

Joentaa nodded. 'Never mind. I have to call up an email. Is that computer connected to the Internet?'

'Yes, of course,' said Tuulikki.

Joentaa sat down in front of the monitor and minimised the photograph from Mäkelä's CorpsesForDummies archive folder.

'What was Petri able to tell us?' asked Sundström.

'They have the names of the dead. He's sending a list.'

'Maybe I'm rather slow on the uptake,' said Westerberg, who had also come over to the computer, 'but I don't quite see the connection.'

Joentaa opened the email that Grönholm had sent him; it contained no text, only an attached Word document.

'The list must contain the names of the man and the boy you can see on that photograph.'

'Ah,' said Westerberg.

Joentaa opened the attachment. Another list, he thought. First name, surname. No dates of birth yet. Mertaranta and Päivi Holmquist were working on that, because the age of the victims was important. They all leaned towards the screen and read:

Leo Aalto
Seppo Aalto
Markku Aalto
Petra Bäckström
Sulevi Jääskeläinen
Eva Johansson
Ronja Koivistio
Ella Kuusisto
Lara Kuusisto
Pentti Laakso
Kielo Laakso
Viola Lagerbäck
Sipi Lindström
Raija Lindström
Ilmari Mattila
Veikko Mattila
Kaino Nieminen
Tuomas Nieminen
Arsi Peltola
Urho Peltola
Tuomas Peltonen
Akseli Pesonen
Tapio Pesonen
Laura Virtanen

Joentaa felt that at any moment he might come upon a name he knew. Someone he had met at some point and lost sight of, only to find him again on this list years later. But the names remained strange. Strange black characters on virtual white paper, on a monitor in a strange room. In alphabetical order.

'Was Petri able to give us anything else?'

'They're still working on it, trying to make out which are the relevant names. I told him to look for a man and a boy, possibly father and son. He'll be in touch as soon as they have anything new,' said Joentaa.

Sundström nodded.

On one of the big screens on the glass wall, Hämäläinen was saying goodbye to the gloomy jackpot winner, and the white-haired man left the stage leaning on a stick.

78

The white-haired man disappeared in the beam of the spotlights as if dissolving into mist, and the ski-jumpers who had just come on stage to resounding applause waved to the audience without changing expression. They looked rather comical in blue jeans and brightly coloured shirts, with their gold medals round their necks and their skis over their shoulders. Like children.

Although one of them was in fact only sixteen, and sportsmen never had to grow up anyway, because they were not forbidden to play games or weaned off them; on the contrary, playing games was how they earned their money.

He thought of Niskanen. Waiting for the result of the B test. Hoping against hope, flying in the face of logic, obsessed by an urge to tell lies upon lies, one after another, until he believed them himself. And when at last that urge had worn itself out you could always go to Ireland to breed sheep, cutting off the connection when your past was on the line.

The ski-jumpers sat down on the comfortable sofas, and Hämäläinen lost his train of thought. The show was going well. The best thing about it was that he hardly had to pay attention. It just flowed on. He thought of the gunman's girlfriend, and felt a slight pang, he couldn't say just where. The pain wandered through his body, and he asked a question about the composition of skis for ski-jumping. Read it out from one of the yellow notes.

One of the ski-jumpers answered, and he thought how clean everything was. So red and gold and dark blue and orange. So precisely adjusted, not a speck of dust in sight. The smooth parquet floor, the handsome desk at which he would sit later. Leaning a little way forward, not too far. Summoning up a smile, then wrinkling his brow. Then the smile again.

The next question was about the fall in the penultimate round. When everything had suddenly been balanced on a knife-edge, and they no longer had a clear lead but were trailing slightly. The ski-jumpers laughed. They had come to terms with that past episode. The star among the victors explained how he had engineered the team's triumph. A record jump in the last round, holding his attitude elegantly in the air over a distance that appeared physically impossible.

Hämäläinen remembered. The microphone he had used for questioning the expert at the time, early in the year, during the live showing of the Finnish victory had been yellow, just like the notes in front of him now. Driving snow. The ski jump a monster, spewing out skiers like vermin. A flight of two hundred and forty metres through the air. Not bad for a human being.

Hämäläinen had asked an expert how far this could go, would they be able to travel a kilometre or more through the air on skis some day, might that become a new and inexpensive mode of travel, and the expert had laughed, and the last man in the opposing team, previously in the lead, paid the price of nervous stress, failing in his flight like a bird whose wings had dropped off.

He thought of Niskanen, leaned forward and smiled. The questions left his lips, and he heard his own voice sounding like a stranger's.

One of the ski-jumpers held up his medal to the camera, another made a joke in doubtful taste, then the four athletes went towards the mist, which swallowed them up, and Hämäläinen announced the summer hit by the rock band that the imps had liked.

They'd probably be singing along at home, and Irene would join in, but only humming the tune, because she didn't know the words.

79

She knows the song coming over the loudspeaker. It went gliding past her in a summer that she had seen disappear through a pane of glass.

80

'We have something,' said Grönholm.
'Yes?' asked Joentaa.

'Got that list there?'

'Yes, it's here.'

'Right, looks as if there was only one little boy among the dead. The names you probably want are Ilmari and Veikko Mattila.'

Kimmo read the two names.

'Father and son,' said Grönholm. 'The father was thirty-five, the son five, registered address in Turku, Asematie 19.'

Name, address, date of birth.

'However, so far we haven't found anyone of that name among the injured. The name of Ilmari Mattila is still in the phone book, no one else is listed there.'

Kimmo and Sanna Joentaa, he thought. And a number at which Sanna Joentaa could no longer be reached. In autumn a woman had rung trying to sell Sanna a magazine subscription.

'Have you called the number?' asked Joentaa.

'Er, no.'

'Let me have it.'

'Just a moment.'

Joentaa heard paper rustle, then Grönholm was back, dictating the number to him.

'Thanks,' said Joentaa, 'I'll call you back.'

'Do we have something?' asked Sundström.

'A number,' said Joentaa.

He rang it.

This is Veikko speaking. I'm not here. Papa isn't here. Mama isn't here either. See you later. Byeee.

A child's voice.

'Well?' asked Westerberg.

And now the message for serious enquiries. A woman's voice, slightly self-conscious, because she had felt it awkward to be sending a message out into nowhere. The child was laughing in the background. The woman gave the full names of the people mentioned by Veikko only as Papa and Mama, and promised to call back as soon as possible.

Then the sound of the signal.

'Well?' asked Sundström.

Joentaa thought for a moment, then he typed the woman's name into Google and looked for pictures. He recognised her at once, although she was a good deal younger in the photograph. She was wearing a fancy dress costume and standing at the wheel of a ship, with the sea and Naantali beach behind her.

'Who's that?' asked Sundström.

'Little My,' said Westerberg. 'Or at least, she's dressed up as Little My.'

Joentaa maximised the picture, which was illustrating a local newspaper article. It was about the beginning of a long-forgotten summer and the introduction of new attractions to Moomin World, like the ship. The woman in the photo was laughing heartily and seemed to be turning the ship's wheel in a direction of her own choice.

'But that . . . that's the woman who was sitting in the audience, isn't it?' said Tuulikki.

Joentaa nodded. He glanced at the screen on which the Finnish boy band were singing their summer hit. The catchy music seemed to be coming at them from several loudspeakers.

His mobile rang.

'We have something,' said Grönholm. 'Ilmari Mattila was married, but his wife kept her maiden name.'

'I know,' said Joentaa.

'You do?' asked Grönholm.

'Who is that woman?' asked Sundström.

The applause was dying down. Hämäläinen's voice came over the loudspeakers.

'Salme Salonen,' said Joentaa.

'Salme Salonen,' said Hämäläinen.

'What?' asked Sundström.

'Salme Salonen,' Joentaa repeated.

'Welcome to our next guest, and I am particularly glad to have her here today . . . Salme Salonen,' said Hämäläinen.

81

He was sitting at the desk in the beam of the spotlights. The wood of the desk was exquisite and clean. He felt the smooth paper of the note in his hands. The contrast was too great. He would have to discuss it with Tuula. First the summer hit, now this. Tuula liked such extreme contrasts.

The woman was coming out of the mist towards him, to a background of applause. She had long red hair, held herself very upright, and seemed to be gliding as if on rails. She sat down opposite him and put her handbag on the empty chair beside her.

The firefighter who had been one of the first on the scene of the accident would have to put the bag somewhere else when he came on stage in a little while, because he was to join the conversation and sit beside the woman. Hämäläinen decided how to deal with that little complication smoothly.

'It's a wonderful step that you have taken,' he began. 'I think I can speak for all of us here, and for all viewers who are watching on their screens at home, when I say it is a step that we deeply respect without being at all able to imagine how . . .'

The woman smiled at him.

He returned the smile.

Later he wouldn't be able to explain that moment, he could describe only what he felt, and even that only a few times.

Before the intent gaze of his hearers, which was otherwise hard to interpret, he would explain that he had been unprepared for that moment of understanding, that he had never seen the woman before, and didn't know what impulse had set it off. That he had looked into her eyes.

And he had felt it was a perfect moment, a moment of pain and of beauty.

82

The lawyer ate one of Salme Salonen's biscuits, and had just been offering them to his guests. He thought she ought to have told him about this.

She certainly ought to have told him she was going to appear on television to talk about the accident, about her husband and her son.

The biscuit was really very good. Fireworks were going off out in the garden, laughing children were whirling sparklers about, and his guests, most of them other lawyers and their wives, were all talking about cases that had turned out well and other cases that had turned out just as well, and something strange was happening on the screen.

His wife Kirsti was clearing the table, taking out the plates and the leftover food, and after a while she stopped and asked, through the buzz of voices, 'Have we lost the sound, or are they simply sitting there saying nothing?'

83

On the screen Kai-Petteri Hämäläinen and Salme Salonen were sitting opposite each other, and Sundström, Westerberg and their colleagues were deep in phone conversations which were notable for the fact that no one understood anyone else.

'Get her!' cried Sundström several times, but his colleague at the other end of the line didn't take his meaning.

'The woman on stage seems to be the person we're after,' said Westerberg, and his own officer too had questions to ask.

'What do you mean, what woman? There's only one woman on stage,' said Westerberg.

'Did we post anyone near the stage?' asked Sundström. 'What do you mean, you don't know . . .?'

'No. No, of course the guests weren't searched for weapons, only the audience,' shouted Westerberg.

Joentaa sat beside Tuulikki and heard the voices of the other two as if in the distance. He didn't understand why they were so upset. Their agitation was in stark contrast to the silence emanating from the TV screen.

There was a pause.

Hämäläinen sat there motionless.

The woman sat there motionless.

They were looking at each other, and seemed to have said everything even before the first word was spoken.

84

Kai-Petteri Hämäläinen looked at the woman, at the mist caught in the spotlights behind her, and beyond that at the silhouettes of the people watching and listening while the two of them said nothing.

Instructions came through to him from time to time by way of his earpiece. The director's rather hoarse but loud voice asking what the hell was going on. Hello? Hello, Kai-Petteri. Can you hear me?

He looked down and let his eyes move over the questions that he wasn't going to ask. Questions resting on the dark, smooth wood, spellbound there in cues and transitions between subjects on yellow Post-It notes. Mrs Salonen, you yourself were a victim of the accident in Turku on 17 February this year. Do you have a clear memory of what happened? How do you live with it? How long were you in hospital? How are you today?

How much time had passed? He had no idea.

Tuula was gesticulating in the mist, waving her arms in an uncoordinated way; it was impossible to work out what her signals meant.

The woman on the other side of the desk was gazing past him into the far distance. She looked neither happy nor sad. He had never seen a more neutral face. He did not know this woman.

Perhaps it was her dress. The shadow of a dress that he had seen.

Perhaps it was the silence in her face.

The very tall man appeared, emerging from the mist. He looked relaxed, and smiled encouragingly both at Hämäläinen and at the woman. He picked up her handbag and sat down on the chair which was really meant for the firefighter. Lightly, barely perceptibly he placed his hand on the woman's left arm. The woman didn't seem to notice it.

'Do you have any children yourself?' Hämäläinen heard himself asking him.

The very tall man shook his head. 'Unfortunately not,' he said.

Hämäläinen nodded. Advertising break, said the voice in his ear, adding that the show would go on in three minutes and fifty-eight seconds' time.

85

His son Sami and Meredith, the daughter of a woman colleague of his, were rolling about on the floor in front of him, and he wondered vaguely why the daughter of two Finns was called Meredith, and when and in what circumstances you had to trace a sexual component in this kind of childish playfulness.

He had read something on the subject only recently, an interesting article in a psychological journal, but he couldn't remember the exact content of the article now, probably because what was happening on the TV screen was distracting his thoughts.

Now came the advertising break. A beautiful melody provided the background music for a car company's inane advertising spot.

'What was that about?' asked Seppo.

He turned to him and the other guests who were still sitting at the table, dipping their fondue skewers into the hot oil.

'Sorry,' he said. 'That . . . that was a patient of mine.'

'A patient of yours? On the *Hämäläinen* show?' asked Seppo.

'Er, yes.'

'The lady who was sitting there just now?' asked Sami, who was lying on the floor sweating and taking advantage of a moment when Meredith left him alone.

He nodded.

'No, don't! Stop! Stop it!' cried Sami, because Meredith had begun tickling him again.

'How did she acquit herself?' asked Seppo.

'Hm?'

'Your patient,' said Seppo.

'Oh. I . . . I don't really know,' he said.

'Leave the box on, will you?' said another guest. 'Kapanen's going to be on next. The actor. I'd be interested to see him.'

He nodded, and decided to call Salme Salonen first thing in the morning.

Then he stood up and went back to the table.

86

The interview, which was still described as an interview over the next few days even though the two participants had not exchanged a single word, lasted two minutes thirty-four seconds. The following advertising break occupied four minutes.

While the ads were running on screen, the very tall man led Salme Salonen off the stage. Hämäläinen watched them go, and thought they looked like a couple, leaning close together, the woman seeming to place her head trustingly on the man's shoulder.

Hämäläinen felt very calm, calmer than he had felt for a long time, and Tuula came on stage and asked what the matter was.

He shook his head and said, 'Nothing.'

'Nothing?'

'That's right, nothing.'

'What . . . what was the matter with that woman?'

'Nothing,' said Hämäläinen.

'What's that supposed to mean, Kai?'

'Everything's fine,' said Hämäläinen. 'Who's on next?'

'What?' asked Tuula.

Hämäläinen studied his notes. 'The firefighter. And then Kapanen,' he said. 'Send them on.'

'Kai, we have to . . .'

'I've seen the Bond film. Kapanen was excellent,' said Hämäläinen.

A girl assistant materialised out of the mist and mopped the sweat off his face with a cloth.

'Kai, we can't just . . .' said Tuula.

'Yes, we can. You'd better get off the stage now, we'll be on screen again in a moment,' said Hämäläinen, looking down at the questions he was going to ask Kapanen. One after another. He wouldn't leave out any of them.

Tuula watched him for a little while longer. He could feel her watching, but he kept his head bent over the questions, and Tuula, weak at the knees, disappeared into the dazzling light. The voice in his ear was counting down the seconds.

87

Salme Salonen was taken to the police station on the outskirts of Helsinki for questioning. At no time did she offer any resistance. No knife was found in her handbag, only a photograph presumably of her husband and her son against a wintry background in Stockholm.

She sat perfectly still on a chair in a grey room while Sundström questioned her. Westerberg and Joentaa stood on the other side of the glass pane of the interview room, and Salme Salonen willingly gave answers. She spoke slowly, her voice sounded calm, soft, clear and abstracted. She seemed to be thinking very carefully before formulating a sentence. Yes, her name was Salme Salonen. She was twenty-eight years old. Born on 24 March 1980. Yes, she lived in Turku, Asematie 19. She had been married to Ilmari Mattila, she had had a son. Veikko Mattila. She was a widow.

Name, address, date of birth, thought Joentaa, and Sundström's own voice sounded clear and gentle and curiously abstracted. A burden seemed to be weighing down on the woman as she sat very upright at the table, and a burden seemed to have fallen from Sundström's shoulders.

'Profession?' asked Sundström.

Until 17 February of this year Salme Salonen had worked as a clerical assistant in the accounts department of a company that manufactured children's toys. She had survived the collapse of a skating rink in Turku late on the afternoon of that day, but with severe injuries. She had suffered several broken bones and trauma to the skull and brain, and she spent three and a half months in hospital.

Along with others affected, she was involved in a legal dispute with a firm that had constructed the roof of the skating rink nineteen years ago, and had renovated it a few weeks before it collapsed. The head of the firm had left the country and could not be traced. Presentation of the evidence for the causes of the accident was not yet complete.

She talked about a woman called Rauna.

'Rauna?' asked Sundström.

'My friend,' said Salme Salonen. 'She was lying beside me when the sky fell down.'

Sundström said nothing.

'She can skate very well. She is dancing on the ice. Veikko is laughing, and Ilmari slips. Ilmari is not a good skater, but it doesn't bother him. Then the sky falls down, and Rauna is lying beside me. We look at each other.'

'Have you known this Rauna long?' asked Sundström.

'No, we meet for the first time that day. She asks me if the sky has fallen down, and visits me in my room in the hospital. While she is getting better. All she has is a broken arm. I would like to adopt her.'

'Adopt her?' asked Sundström.

'Because her parents are dead.'

'Her . . .?'

'Rauna is nearly six. Her parents were at the skating rink too. Rauna is living in the Children's Home on the Klosterberg. She would like it if we could live together, but they have to do tests first.'

'What . . . what do they have to test?' asks Sundström.

'The authorities are testing to see whether it's possible. And a psychologist is testing too. To see if I'm legally competent.'

Sundström said nothing again.

'That's what they call it. Funny sort of phrase,' she said. 'I often think about words.'

The woman smiled slightly, and Joentaa thought that smile was for Rauna.

'Why did you go to see the Hämäläinen talk show on 8 November this year?' asked Sundström.

'Because I was invited,' she said.

'Invited . . . who by?'

'By him. There was a photograph in the letter too, with a signature.'

'An autographed card?' asked Sundström.

'Yes. And the ticket. I had agreed to be on the show on New Year's Eve . . . that's today . . . and talk about Ilmari and Veikko and that day at the skating rink, so I was invited to be in the audience at an earlier show. As a present because they . . . they couldn't pay me a fee.'

Sundström stared at the woman.

'I was surprised, too. About the fee. I didn't want a fee, I just wanted to talk about Ilmari and Veikko, and Rauna and her parents, and explain that everything had to be done to put it right again.'

'I see. You told us, when we arrested you, that you didn't want your lawyer present at this interrogation,' said Sundström.

She nodded. 'He'd have had to come rather a long way. He lives in Turku. And he's not as young as he used to be.'

'I see,' said Sundström. 'You are accused of the murders of the forensic pathologist Patrik Laukkanen and the puppet-maker Harri Mäkelä,' he added.

'I don't know their names. But that's right. You are right.'

'Right about what?' asked Sundström.

'I did it. What you say.'

'You attacked and killed the forensic pathologist Patrik Laukkanen and the puppet-maker Harri Mäkelä with a knife,' said Sundström. 'And you stabbed Kai-Petteri Hämäläinen.'

The woman nodded.

'Louder, please,' said Sundström.

There was a long silence.

Sundström sat down and lowered his gaze to the softly humming tape recorder.

The change in the woman's body language took place very slowly, almost imperceptibly. Something seemed to be happening under her skin. She began to stroke her arms, very lightly at first, then pressing harder and harder, scratching them as if she had been bitten by an insect.

Sundström did not look up until, with abrupt movements, the woman began tearing at her hair.

'Can I . . .?' he began, but whatever he had been going to say next was drowned out by the long scream that the woman uttered. It seemed to come for her inmost depths.

She had closed her eyes.

She screamed and screamed and screamed.

Call Larissa, thought Joentaa.

'Dear God,' said Sundström.

The screaming died away, and the woman slumped where she sat. She looked at Sundström, who was sitting opposite her, transfixed.

'A desert in my head,' she said.

'What?' asked Sundström.

'It didn't help,' she said.

'What didn't help?' asked Sundström.

'I can't remember. I know it happened, but I can't remember.'

Sundström seemed to be waiting for her to go on.

'Did you see the photo?' she asked.

'The photo in your handbag?' asked Sundström.

'Yes.'

Sundström nodded.

She seemed about to say something else, but then she

didn't, and Sundström said no more either. After a few minutes he switched off the recorder.

88

The show went on. Hämäläinen felt that he weighed very little. Which must be to do with the way he was hovering above the floor. He was surprised that his guests didn't seem to notice.

He spoke earnestly to the firefighter who had brought the dead out of the skating rink. He chatted to the relaxed Kapanen. He announced Bon Jovi and, after his appearance and mention of the dates of his tour, he even got some cheerful remarks about the Finnish winter out of him.

It was all flowing by. The audience listened and laughed. The woman and the silence might never have been there. He didn't understand it. The show ended with a firework display based on some clever pyrotechnics, and everyone stood on stage and waved, and Hämäläinen waved too.

Then, as if gliding on rails, he went to his dressing room and drank what, according to the label on the bottle, was freshly pressed grapefruit juice, and Tuula and Olli Latvala were yakking away at him, and he raised one hand and said, 'Quiet.'

They stopped talking.

'Absolute silence, please,' he said.

After a while Tuula said that the woman had been taken away by the police, she still didn't understand why.

Did he know what had happened? She said the editorial team working on the teletext and Internet versions, who had

been processing the incident directly afterwards, had spoken only of a woman overcome by grief and a sympathetic presenter who hadn't wanted to press her for answers.

Hämäläinen felt that slight pang again; within a few seconds he felt it in different parts of his body. 'Oh yes?' he said.

'I think that's how the studio audience took it,' said Olli Latvala.

'Interesting,' said Hämäläinen.

'But the woman was taken away. And I know they suspect some connection with the accident, the roof of the skating rink that fell in . . .' said Tuula. 'Do you know the woman?'

'No,' said Hämäläinen.

'You must have been annoyed when she didn't say anything. You both just sat there for minutes on end in silence. Why didn't *you* say something?'

'I couldn't think of anything to say,' said Hämäläinen.

'Could she have been the person who stabbed you?'

'Of course,' said Hämäläinen.

'Of course?' asked Tuula.

'Of course she was the one who stabbed me.'

'Then you recognised her?'

'No. How could I recognise someone I'd never seen?'

'Kai, I don't understand any of this.'

'Nor do I,' said Hämäläinen.

'Can they quote you on that? That she was the woman who . . . attacked you. Or at least that's what you suspect.'

'On the news . . .' said Hämäläinen.

'Well, yes, I'm asking because Lundberg has spoken to me about it,' said Olli Latvala. 'He's editing the news today, and they haven't been able to get any statement out of the police. At the moment no one knows exactly what really happened.'

'Ah,' said Hämäläinen.

'They want to know if they could do an interview with you,' said Olli Latvala.

'An interview,' said Hämäläinen. Suddenly he couldn't help laughing.

'I'm only passing on what Lundberg said to me,' said Latvala.

'Don't worry, Olli,' said Hämäläinen. 'It's not your fault, really.' He paused for a moment, and chuckled to himself again.

Go home, he thought. Let off a firework display. A proper one. Light up the dark sky. Irene smiling. The imps gazing at the fireworks wide-eyed.

He wiped the smile off his face, and for some moments felt full of dwindling, fleeting strength as he said, 'I'm afraid the answer is no. I'm fed up with interviews for this year.'

89

Kimmo Joentaa and Paavo Sundström spent the night in Helsinki again. In the same hotel. It was after two in the morning when they checked in.

The interrogation of Salme Salonen had been resumed and interrupted again several times. She had answered most of the questions that Sundström and occasionally Westerberg asked her with a simple 'Yes'.

Kimmo Joentaa had stood on the other side of the window looking at the woman, and the longer she agreed, the more often she nodded, the less he had understood.

Salme Salonen had talked about a picture she had seen, but when Sundström asked her she couldn't describe it in any detail.

'It doesn't do any good,' she had said.

'Why don't you leave me to be the judge of what will and will not be any good in this case?'

She had nodded, but said nothing.

She's at peace, thought Joentaa. She has come to a standstill.

She said, several times, 'It didn't help.'

Sundström had asked no more questions, presumably because he didn't think he would get any further explanation of that remark.

'When the third man was lying on the floor I didn't feel angry any more,' she had said.

Sundström had nodded.

'I don't know what it is now. Anger, I mean.'

Sundström had nodded again.

Westerberg had gone home, and Sundström and Joentaa had taken a taxi to the hotel.

The woman who had opened the computer terminal for Joentaa a few days ago, when he wanted to watch the DVD of the chat show in the middle of the night, was at the reception desk. She gave them their keys and seemed about to say something. They had already turned away when the woman began to speak. 'Sorry I wasn't very friendly a few days ago.'

Joentaa turned round. 'No problem,' he said.

'I saw you on TV,' she said. 'Both of you. I didn't know . . .'

On TV, thought Joentaa.

'Taking that woman away. Is she . . . is she guilty?'

Guilty, thought Joentaa.

They took the lift up to the fourth floor and went along a red and orange corridor.

Sundström was listening to his mobile. 'Nurmela,' he said. 'Congratulating us.' He switched off the mobile and said goodnight to Kimmo.

Joentaa went into his room. He spent a long time standing

in the dark, thinking of the picture that Salme Salonen saw and couldn't describe.

Beyond the glass of the window, late rockets shot skywards now and then. As they went off they glittered in all colours of the rainbow.

1 January

90

Aapeli Raantamo was woken by the footsteps. And the tables or chairs being pushed back and forth. It was still dark outside. The clock said 4.30.

He had spent New Year's Eve alone. Had made himself tomato soup, pasta with a cream sauce and curried prawns. When the time came he had watched the firework display. The couple who had recently moved into the apartment right at the top of the building had been giving a party, and he had stood outside in the cold, knees shaking, among a crowd of young people, and some of them had hugged him and wished him a Happy New Year.

He had returned their good wishes, and he looked out for Salme, but she wasn't there, and there had been no lights on in her apartment. He had asked the couple from the top floor about her as they watched the fireworks, closely entwined. They didn't know where Salme was either.

But now she seemed to be back. Chairs were being moved about in her apartment, and he heard footsteps and voices. He sat up and concentrated on the noises. Men's voices, lowered, but easily audible. And now steps in the stairwell too. Several men.

He got up, put on his coat and his slippers, and opened the door. The stairwell was brightly lit. One man jostled him as he came out.

'Sorry,' murmured the man, and hurried on downstairs. Aapeli Raantamo went up. The door to Salme's apartment was open. He approached it cautiously. When he reached the

door, a tall, broad-shouldered man came towards him and said, 'There's nothing to see here.'

'Excuse me, please,' said Aapeli. 'Who . . . who are you?'

The man seemed about to reply brusquely, but then he stopped and said, 'You live here?'

'Yes, down below. One floor under Salme.'

The man nodded. 'My name is Grönholm. Police, Criminal Investigation Department. What's yours?'

'Aapeli . . . Aapeli Raantamo. Where . . . where is Salme, then? Is everything all right?'

'Weren't you watching TV?'

'Why . . . why do you ask?'

'Never mind. I have things to do here. I'll look in on you later.'

'Oh, yes, I was,' said Aapeli.

'You were what?'

'Yes, I was watching TV. Yesterday evening.'

'Then you must have recognised Mrs Salonen.'

'I was watching an old film. With Cary Grant,' said Aapeli.

'Oh,' said Grönholm.

'What's happened to Salme?'

The man said nothing for a while. 'I'll look in later. Get a little more sleep, all right?'

Aapeli nodded, and the man turned away and went back into the apartment. Salme's apartment. But Salme wasn't there.

Aapeli slowly went downstairs. Something bad, he thought. Something bad has happened. His hands were shaking as he turned on the TV. The teletext.

The first headline ran: *Murderess on the sofa with Hämäläinen.* Underneath, it said: *Assumed murderess Salme S. arrested during chat show.* A line lower down, in green lettering: *Chronology of events.* Under that the sports reports. Ski-jumping. A Finn had won the qualifying round in Garmisch-Partenkirchen. Aapeli

looked at the lines of text. He read and read and didn't understand anything. He felt the strength drain out of his body.

He sat on his bed and could not take his eyes off the text on the screen. Up in Salme's apartment, there were footsteps and men's muted voices. After a while he looked away and saw the card leaning against the candleholder. Salme's Christmas card.

He stood up and went over to the table, picked up the card and opened it. Ilmari and Veikko in Stockholm. Salme must have taken it herself. His hands began trembling again, so badly this time that the card dropped from his fingers.

He sat down on a chair and looked at the card lying on the floor, while outside the darkness gave way to dawn.

91

A friendly nurse put new bandages on his wrists. She carefully wound the strips of white muslin from his hands up to his elbows.

'Thank you,' he said.

'You're welcome,' she replied.

In the waiting room the news had been running on a TV screen. He'd had to look almost vertically up to see it.

The photograph had shown Salme S. with red hair, wearing a strange costume. A newsreader mentioned that the picture had been taken several years ago. As yet little was known about the background, said the objective voice. The investigating authorities were holding a press conference at 14.00 hours, which would be transmitted live.

'Just a moment . . .' said Nuutti Vaasara.

'Yes?' asked the nurse.

'Could you make them a little looser? Because I . . . I probably ought to work today.'

'Work? But this is New Year's Day. I thought only people like us worked today. What do you do?'

'I'm a puppet-maker.'

'Oh,' she said. 'Marionettes?'

'Something like that.'

'My little daughter loves puppet plays. We had a puppet theatre recently in our parish hall. Classical stuff. Punch and Judy, Little Red Riding Hood and the wolf.'

Vaasara nodded.

'Do you really have to work today? You ought to take it easy for a while.'

'I know. It's just that I'm under pressure of time.' Because Harri is dead, he was going to add, but then he bit back the words.

'Let me have a look,' she said, and began loosening the bandages round the palms of his hands and freeing his fingers. 'Better?' she asked after a few minutes.

'Yes, thank you,' he said. He stretched his fingers and clenched them into a fist. 'Yes, that should be all right.'

She smiled. 'Take care. And all the best,' she said, and he thanked her again before he left. Photographs of the forensic pathologist and Harri were flickering on the TV screen as he crossed the entrance area. He stopped to watch for a little while. The photos disappeared, the announcer came on. Then there was a landscape of palm trees with dead bodies. They were carefully lined up in front of the wreck of a crashed plane. The bodies were covered with something shiny, but some of their arms were sticking out.

Nuutti Vaasara turned away from the pictures on the screen and went home. The low-built blue house looked strange

with the snow piled high. Newspapers, letters and advertising brochures lay scattered around outside the door. He opened it and went in, making his way straight through the dividing door and down the passage to the studio.

The clown puppet which had startled that policeman Joentaa so much was leaning up against the wall. The policeman had probably been upset because the clown was holding the model of a dead man. Vaasara stood there for a while undecided, then he took the puppet out of the arms of the clown and laid it against the opposite wall, in a corner where it was hardly visible.

A middle-aged woman lay on the workbench. A drowned body. The puppet on which Harri had been working in the days before his death. The job was urgent, because the deadline for shooting that scene in the film was only two weeks away. The production company had called, and Vaasara had promised to deliver the puppet in time.

He went up to the workbench and stood motionless there too for a while. He felt reluctance, awe, a joy that he couldn't explain, and a fear that had been with him for days.

He closed his eyes and took several deep breaths. Then he bent over the lump of material in front of him and, carefully and with concentration, began completing Harri Mäkelä's last puppet.

92

Kimmo Joentaa drove back to Turku about midday to help Grönholm. Sundström stayed in Helsinki to appear at the press conference with Westerberg and a representative of

the state prosecutor's office. Heinonen had reported himself off sick for another day.

When he reached the outskirts of Turku, Joentaa bypassed the city centre and made for the Klosterberg. He knew the Children's Home. Sanna had pointed its lemon-yellow building out to him, years ago, when they had been going for a winter walk on a sunny day like this.

He had only a vague recollection of the conversation, but Sanna had wondered whether it was sensible to have children of your own when there were so many growing up with no parents. He had only nodded, and tried to look interested, because at the time he had not felt any connection with the subject, whether the children in question were his or someone else's.

He walked uphill and saw the children racing past him on their toboggans. When he entered the brightly lit front hall, a young woman asked him his business. He showed his ID and asked to see whoever ran the Home.

'Pellervo Halonen,' said the woman. 'Come with me and we'll see if he's here.'

They found Pellervo Halonen in a large room where children were playing and looking at books. The young woman fetched him out of a conversation, and Halonen quickly came towards him. His handshake was firm, and the expression on his face reminded Joentaa of the eternal confidence of the face of Niemi, head of the scene-of-crime team.

'Good afternoon,' said Pellervo Halonen, leading him into the corridor out of earshot of the children. They faced each other, and the confidence drained away from Pellervo Halonen's face as he said, 'I know why you're here. Salme Salonen.'

Joentaa nodded.

'I wish it hadn't happened,' said Halonen.

Joentaa nodded again.

They said nothing for a while.

'She talks about a little girl living here,' said Joentaa at last. 'A child who lost her parents in . . . in the accident at the skating rink. Rauna.'

'Yes,' said Halonen.

'Mrs Salonen said she wanted to adopt Rauna.'

'Yes, she did,' said Halonen. 'But permission wasn't forthcoming. Mrs Salonen was considered too . . . too unstable. She hasn't worked since the accident. I had a feeling that Mrs Salonen mattered a lot to Rauna, that's why I was always glad when she came to see her. They went through the whole thing together – the accident, I mean.'

'I know,' said Joentaa. 'Mrs Salonen . . . described it.'

Halonen nodded.

'Has Rauna heard anything about what's happened?'

'No,' said Halonen. 'And she won't in the immediate future. Of course she will ask where Mrs Salonen is. She came to visit Rauna here at least once a week.'

Joentaa nodded. 'I hope you'll be able to help Rauna and . . . and find the right way to explain to her.'

'So do I,' said Halonen.

'I don't want to speak to her now – there wouldn't be much point in that,' said Joentaa. 'I simply wanted to form a picture in my mind.'

Halonen nodded, and seemed relieved. 'I'm glad you see it like that. Incidentally, she has a visitor at this moment. Over there, doing a jigsaw puzzle, that's Rauna.'

Joentaa followed his eyes, and saw the little girl, kneeling on a chair, elbows on the table as she contemplated the pieces of the jigsaw. There was an elderly man sitting beside her, and now and then Rauna laughed when he said something. Joentaa could hear their voices, muted by distance.

'A neighbour of Salme Salonen's,' said Halonen. 'Aapeli Raantamo. I had a long talk to him, and thought it all through,

but he insisted that he wanted to see Rauna. And she was pleased. They went on an outing together a few days ago, he and Rauna and . . . and Mrs Salonen.'

Joentaa nodded, and looked at the girl and the old man. He seemed to be extremely sad and extremely happy at the same time.

'Done it!' cried Rauna, and Aapeli clapped his hands. Then she said something that Aapeli didn't appear to understand, and Rauna's explanation came over loud and clear. 'The lions, of course, silly! The other lions. And I'll steer the ship, not that man with the long beard.'

Aapeli laughed, and Rauna held an invisible but impressively large ship's wheel in her hands as she spoke.

93

That evening Kimmo Joentaa sat in an empty house and watched the children out on the lake, playing ice hockey in the pale moonlight.

Joentaa sat back and let himself be lulled by the game. By the children's shouting, the dull thud of the hockey sticks colliding, and he thought, vaguely, that the goalies had a tough job. You could hardly even see the puck.

The game seemed to be endless. After a while Joentaa began keeping track of the score. It was an evenly balanced match, although he had realised that only late in the day, so he didn't know whether one team already had a clear lead or not.

The game never flowed smoothly; there were constant discussions, and now and then players sat down on the ice

at the rim of the playing area, presumably sent to the sin bin for two minutes, and Joentaa wondered where the referee making these decisions and timing the penalty period was. He couldn't see anyone. Goals were being scored all the time.

Finally one side was jubilant, its team members hugging one another, and the other side collapsed, exhausted. The game was over.

A few minutes later they all came off the ice together, shouting greetings to each other before running off home in different directions. Joentaa recognised Roope, the boy from one of the houses nearby, and the goalie, who was wearing an unsuitable cycle helmet, came up to the window where he was standing. The goalie knocked at the glazed door to the terrace, and as he opened the door Joentaa thought he must be suffering from some kind of delusion.

'We won,' said Larissa. She took off her skates, threw the helmet down on an armchair, and ran her hands through her hair. 'Twenty–eighteen. Great game.'

'Oh . . .' said Joentaa.

'I'm sweating like a pig. I'll go and shower.'

'Yes,' said Joentaa.

She pulled her sweater off over her head, 'Everything okay with you?'

'Yes,' said Joentaa.

'Great. Be with you in a moment.'

She took off her trousers, and was halfway to the bathroom when Joentaa said, 'But eighteen goals against you – that's a lot.'

'It's winning that counts,' she said without turning round.

'Only joking,' he said. 'Hang on a moment.'

'What is it?' she said. 'I need to shower.'

'If you'd told me you were an ice-hockey goalie, I'd have thought that was guaranteed to be a lie,' said Joentaa.

She studied him for a long time.

Then she turned away and went into the bathroom.

Joentaa heard the rushing and pattering of the shower.

When she came back, he was lying stark naked on the sofa, arms reaching out to her ostentatiously, with a silly grin on his face.

She seemed baffled, and frowned. 'Er . . . Kimmo,' she said.

He laughed at her confused expression for several minutes before joy finally overcame him, and he began to shed tears.

Jan Costin Wagner was born in 1972 in Langen/Hesse near Frankfurt. After studying German language, literature and history at Frankfurt University, he went on to work as a journalist and freelance writer. He divides his time between Germany and Finland (the home country of his wife). His previous crime novels featuring Detective Kimmo Joentaa are *Ice Moon* (2006) and *Silence* (2010). *Silence* won the 2008 German Crime Prize.